DEAD UNTIL DAWN

Paul Cave

2QT Limited (Publishing)

First Edition 2013
2QT Limited (Publishing)
Lancaster
www.2qt.co.uk

Cover design Hilary Pitt
Images sourced by iStockphoto.com

Printed in Great Britain by Lightning Source UK Ltd

A CIP catalogue record for this book is available
from the British Library
ISBN 978-1-908098-87-0

For Ellis and Sarah.
Love you both.

Contents

PART I - Poles Apart
Chapter One - Mexico   9
Chapter Two - Alaska   15
Chapter Three - Chamela - West Mexico   22
Chapter Four - Fairbanks - Alaska   26
Chapter Five - Chamela - West Mexico   30
Chapter Six - Fairbanks - Alaska   37
Chapter Seven - Chamela - West Mexico   46
Chapter Eight - Fairbanks - Alaska   56
Chapter Nine - Chamela - West Mexico   61
Chapter Ten - West Mexico   68
Chapter Eleven - Fairbanks - Alaska   74
Chapter Twelve - Chicago - Illinois   79
Chapter Thirteen - Chicago – Illinois   84
Chapter Fourteen - Mexico   89
Chapter Fifteen - Flight 263A from Chicago   96

PART II - Fairbanks
Chapter Sixteen - Fairbanks International Airport   101
Chapter Seventeen - Airport Runway   105
Chapter Eighteen - Police Department   109
Chapter Nineteen - Fairbanks – The Outskirts   115
Chapter Twenty - Alpine Lodge Fairbanks   119
Chapter Twenty-One - Sawmill   123
Chapter Twenty-Two - Police Precinct   127
Chapter Twenty-Three - City Morgue   129
Chapter Twenty-Four - Alpine Lodge Fairbanks   134
Chapter Twenty-Five - City Morgue   137
Chapter Twenty-Six - Richardson Highway   142
Chapter Twenty-Seven - Alpine Lodge Fairbanks   146
Chapter Twenty-Eight - Richardson Highway   153
Chapter Twenty-Nine - Fairbanks Correctional Facility 157

Chapter Thirty - The Mall   162
Chapter Thirty-One - Police Precinct   167
Chapter Thirty-Two - The Alaska House Art Museum 172
Chapter Thirty-Three - Police Precinct   177
Chapter Thirty-Four - Police Precinct   182

PART III - Dead Until Dawn
Chapter Thirty-Five - Police Precinct   191
Chapter Thirty-Six - Denali Park Train Station   196
Chapter Thirty-Seven - Richardson Highway   201
Chapter Thirty-Eight - Denali Park Train Station   206
Chapter Thirty-Nine - Iniakuk Lake   212
Chapter Forty - Police Precinct   216
Chapter Forty-One - Train Tracks   222
Chapter Forty-Two - Police Precinct   227
Chapter Forty-Three - Denali Park Train Station   231
Chapter Forty-Four - Snowplow   234
Chapter Forty-Five - Fairbanks Elementary School   239
Chapter Forty-Six - Snowplow   245
Chapter Forty-Seven - Denali Park Train Station   250
Other titles by Paul Cave   257

PART I

Poles Apart

Chapter One

Mexico

The night sky held nothing but an inky blackness. No stars, no moon, no clouds, nothing. Had someone thrown a blanket over the small town the resultant darkness would not have been so totally complete, or so it seemed. Waves broke against the nearby shore, a rumble of distant thunder, which grew in amplitude, only to break and then peter out disappointingly. Yellow, murky streetlights did not possess sufficient power to reach the few hundred yards to shore. Instead, they fell short, leaving shadows to fill in where they failed.

In stark contrast to the surrounding gloom the town buzzed with energy and life. Markets that would have been exuberant in the daytime were now decorated to the point of the magnificent. Colours exploded in kaleidoscopic brightness, banners fluttered in the night breeze like multicoloured-winged bats, fireworks lit the black canvas of sky, momentarily burning holes there, with explosions of red, green, white-phosphorous, and a dizzying rainbow of other colours.

Music played out from radios that were all tuned to the same frequency. And the strings of violins and guitarron, punctuated occasionally by the sharp blast of trumpets, bathed the townsfolk in a layer of song and delight.

Considering he was almost a head taller than most, Josh

Sawyer walked among the revellers mostly unnoticed. He wore simple shorts and T-shirt; the breeze that blew in from the coast was cool and gentle, and a pleasant relief from the heat. His feet kicked up dust as he went.

The town of Chamela, West Mexico, was the last place one would expect to find this young fugitive. Not necessarily due to Josh himself, but rather, his cohort. Almost as tall as Josh, his companion walked at his side, the gentle wind blowing dark wisps of hair about her face.

Josh reached up to brush them aside. "You sure this is a good idea?"

Her face broke into a mischievous smile. "Don't worry, Josh. I'll be back before you know it."

He stopped. Turned to face his companion. His heart fluttered for a moment, like it always did, and always would do, when his eyes fell upon her beautiful face.

"I don't like this. Not one bit," he said, his face was serious and he looked worried.

Anna Privalova just laughed. "Relax. Nothing's going to happen. I promise."

She pushed herself onto her tiptoes and kissed him on his furrowed brow.

Josh sighed in resignation. "Promise?"

Anna grinned in a flash of bright enamel. "Promise."

Josh groaned in discomfort.

Anna's bright-white smile simply widened. "You worry too much."

Josh nodded in subconscious agreement. "You promised things would remain boring – at least for a little while." It was a statement. Not a question.

An explosion of white light burst silently behind him. Anna's brown eyes absorbed the light for a moment before they turned suddenly white themselves. Feral. The resultant boom of the firework sounded, which masked the guttural laugh that followed. Anna laughed again, squeezed Josh's hands, and then slipped away, into the night, instantly absorbed by the multitude of people.

Josh stood alone for a moment. Then he turned away from the gathering, unwilling to put faces to the happy voices he could hear, not wanting to remember any individual, someone young or old, yet more importantly, unable to stand the thought that some of those faces would never again smile, laugh, or even exist, once morning had come.

With what felt like the weight of the entire ocean crashing against his back, Josh walked away from the festivities. Alone in the knowledge that the woman he loved, the woman he had willingly brought here, would soon extinguish the life force of some of those that lived here.

***

The night held Anna in its eternal embrace. She moved swiftly, her feet pressing silently into sand, and closed in on the only distinguishable light source available. Like a large firefly, the light ahead bobbed about, swinging first one way, and then the next, giving Anna a single direction to follow.

She looked eastwards, beyond the lights of the nearby town, way out over surrounding mountain-tops, and smiled unrepentantly. The night was her ally. It would be awhile yet before the sun broke above those peaks. This gave her plenty of time.

The gloom held fast, allowing Anna to reach the outer radius of the light unseen. Had the town's lighting been extended past its furthest rim, then the sandy beach and swell of ocean would have been easily distinguishable. It seemed like darkness was the intended design of this place.

Clever, she thought to herself. The lack of illumination was not from a planning oversight, the town's committee would not have overlooked such a thing. There would be no case for incompetence or otherwise. This was what the town wanted, what it required to remain a town, the very thing in which it had been built upon, a festering darkness within the hearts of its people. People that lived here, who harboured a secret, which if ever exposed would totally destroy the flimsy and transparent façade that resided here.

The sudden flash of fire erupted high in the sky. Anna dropped to the sand as the firework burnt magnificently for a moment, and then waited for the rainfall of blinking fire to fade out. Climbing to her feet, she circled quietly around the group of people that clung close to the single light source. A boat bobbed its way to shore, the light guiding it away from treacherous rocks and the invisible pull of undersea currents.

Anna squinted to gather more detail about the boat. Unspectacular in its appearance, she wondered if she'd made a mistake, and that the little boat was nothing more innocuous than a simple lost fishing vessel, brought back to safety by worried and concerned townsfolk. It was only when the clunk of metal – well-oiled and well-maintained metal – sliding into place, did she fully understand that something far more malignant was underway.

***

The pit of Josh's stomach felt as if it had been filled with ocean brine. Nausea threatened to stop him in his tracks. He paused for a moment, bent slightly to fill his lungs. The tang of the nearby sea, which carried with it the stench of marine life and salt, did nothing to quell this feeling of sickness.

Finally gathering his senses, he pushed on, making his way back towards the small hotel that both he and Anna had shared these past two nights. Days actually. Neither of them had spent any time in the close confinements of the sparsely furnished hotel room once dusk had fallen.

They were here on business, not pleasure. Although, as Josh thought about what Anna was about to do, he couldn't dismiss the notion that a certain amount of pleasure on her behalf would be granted. It was what she did. What she had to do to survive that had brought them here.

Forced to flee from the US authorities, they had crossed the Mexican border in the dead of night. Surprisingly they had encountered little, if any, resistance. It was Josh's summation that the wire-tipped fences and armed patrols were predominately for keeping illegal immigrants out of the states of Texas and Arizona, and not for sealing US citizens in.

Still, they'd had to remain vigilant, they had fled from both the FBI, and a legacy that would forever hold them bound. Josh could still remember vividly the first time he had met the beautiful and mysterious woman, Anna, who he now undeniably loved.

The sound of footsteps pulled Josh away from his thoughts. An impenetrable blackness filled the spaces between the tightly formed buildings. Most of these dwellings were simple adobe homes. A combination of clay-based soil, straw and water, held the buildings erect, which were topped by the traditional red slant of terracotta tiles. The hotel in which they stayed was the main building here, it stood out over the entire town and had a unique colonial design.

A grumble of irritated voices grew louder.

Josh looked towards the Jeep parked close by. A layer of thick dust covered it. The off-road 4x4 looked little more than an extension to the night. He had parked it here earlier, confident that the shadows would keep it well hidden.

He had a moment of indecision – should he bolt for the Jeep, or stand his ground and see what the night had to offer him? Yet chance resolved to dictate when a shadowy figure broke from cover, directly beside the 4x4.

The guy looked taller than Josh, unusual in this western part of Mexico, which leant itself towards the shorter and dark skinned South American natives. This guy looked to be every bit the European descendent, as did Josh. Tall, almost equal to Josh's 6 foot height, but stocky, unlike the athletic and defined frame that Josh possessed. This newcomer's arms practically burst from his short shirt-sleeves, and his neck looked to be thicker, by half, than the shaven-head that sat perched above.

The guy's eyes were tight, unreadable slits. Had they not been, Josh imagined that they would have been incapable of holding anything but contempt within them anyway.

"Leaving in a hurry?" the guy asked. A Slavic slur twisted itself around the guy's words.

Before Josh had time to respond, the noisy chatter of voices, coming from the neighbouring shadows, revealed themselves.

Now, here stood the native-looking Mexicans that one would have expected. Dark-skinned, short, squat, mean-eyed, and, a trait that was particularly relevant to this town, all three were armed to the teeth.

For a brief second Josh was reminded of the year earlier, a time when innocence had been abandoned, when, like now, he'd been confronted by another group of mean spirited individuals. Only difference being, back then in Chicago his would-be assailants were only looking to empty his pockets. Here and now though, they were more interested in spilling his guts.

Josh looked beyond the armed assemblage, towards the terracotta roofing, in the hope of seeing a familiar silhouette. Was Anna stalking them silently, ready to dispatch this enemy and save him in the process? Like the first night they had met. A moment of hope clung desperately to his senses, but then, the whip-crack of gunfire sounded, somewhere off towards the beach, and Josh's moment of optimism was forever lost.

Chapter Two

Alaska

The starched, white shirt collar itched like hell. Beads of sweat rolled down from the nape of the neck, adding to the irritation. Not only that, it was stiflingly hot − the small fan atop the desk doing little to cool the room; if anything, it just inflamed the immediate area with its constant grinding of over-heated bearings.

Special Agent Sebastian Fernandez took a handkerchief from his breast pocket and then used it to dab sweat from his brow. The agent stood, sick now of the insistent grating coming from the fan. He moved over to the office window. And then looked out wistfully.

The meagre amount of daylight threw a bleached cover over the city of Fairbanks, a city that boasted a population of little more than thirty-five thousand. From his vantage point here on Cushman Street, looking out from this tiny corner office, Fernandez could clearly make out the church-like façade of The Alaska House Art Museum. He'd visited the museum not long after arriving here, and had been instantly impressed by its commitment to preserving the artwork and culture of the native Alaskan Indian.

At just five eight, the agent stood ever so slightly taller than a native Alaskan Indian. Slim in build, barely 155lbs, he looked almost boyish in his tailored suit. Although the tone of his skin was similar to that of Alaskan heritage, his eyes were large ovals, hazel in colour, which contained a hint, if not a constant, look of cynicism about them.

Special Agent Sebastian Fernandez was not a man to take people at face value. Indeed, in his line of work, it was imperative that one could look beyond the outer layer of a human being, and instead look deeper into the elemental spirit.

The agent caught his reflection within the glass window pane. He ran his hand over his hair in an attempt to flatten his normally neat side-parting. Then, turning his attention back outside, he scanned along the quiet streets of Fairbanks. Not much in the way of pedestrians. Early evening, coupled with the meagre amount of sunlight available, was probably the reasons for the lack of human traffic.

This, the winter solstice, shortened the day – sunlight to be precise – to just 3 hours and 43 minutes at its height. Which, considering, that left exactly 20 hours and 17 minutes of darkness, didn't give the residents of Fairbanks much scope to do daily activities. Some things just demanded daylight to achieve, survival for one thing.

Sub Arctic temperatures could freeze a person solid within hours. And Fairbanks was at best the epicentre of all things frozen. Eight inches of snow had fallen in the short time since Fernandez had arrived here, and would remain here for months to come after he had left. Situated within the base of the Tanana Valley, the city was not unaccustomed to temperatures of well below -30°C.

Most tried to do their daily chores prior to nightfall, and before thermometers plummeted beyond the blue.

Yet there was something else out there that forced the residents to hurry between daylight hours.

For a city that spent an inordinate amount of time swathed in night, there were few homicides per annum, 8.5 to be exact.

How a person could only be half murdered was beyond Fernandez's understanding. But what did he know? He wasn't a goddamn statistician.

What he did know was simple:

More people = More opportunity to do bad things.

So, for a city of just over thirty-five thousand, the probability of being murdered was relatively low. Domestic crime, bar brawls, neighbourly disputes, were high for such a small city, but considering the weight of oppressiveness that most carried, it wasn't a disproportional amount, nothing like Detroit for example.

Until, that was, 28 days ago. Then the murder rate suddenly soared. In under a month three women had been murdered. Again, Fernandez didn't fully know the percentages, but knew that it was an alarming statistic to inexplicably increase.

And this is why **FBI Agent Fernandez** found himself in this frozen wasteland in the State of Alaska.

No one had been arrested for any of the crimes. Not yet. There didn't appear to be anything that tied the victims together. Two blondes, and one of undetermined colour. Principally because the latest victim had been found headless.

Other than the fact that they were all female, the agent could not determine any link. One victim had been married, actually separated at forty-two years of age, but the estranged husband was doing an 18 month stretch in the Fairbanks Correctional Facility for domestic rape – hence 'estranged'. The other blonde had been single, in her early-to-mid twenties. She had house-shared with three other girls. All the housemates checked out. No previous convictions or priors outstanding, nor had they any reasonable motive for doing such a thing.

The last victim added another layer to the puzzle. Headless. The neck area had been hacked away with tremendous force, beheading the poor victim in one or two ferocious attempts. The body had been discovered deep in the woods that surrounded Fairbanks by sheer chance. A deer hunter, lost from the main group of enthusiasts, had stumbled upon the grisly findings. His cries for help had echoed eerily across the woodlands, finally drawing his party of huntsmen to both himself and the victim.

The agent pressed his forehead to the window, in an attempt to cool his brow. He felt the subzero temperatures radiate through the glass. A happier moment from his childhood flashed to mind. He used the memory to help draw his attention away from the macabre crime photos of the headless victim that were laid out behind him.

As a child he had grown up on a small working-class estate situated in Yorkshire − England. His parents had arrived in England as immigrants, shipped in from India, now that the UK borders had opened up to welcome its fellow commonwealth citizens.

Both his parents had taken up jobs within the then prospering steel industry. Sebastian had followed shortly, then his younger brother, Ricardo. Summers in England were hot at times, the Gulf Stream bringing warmer weather with it, and it was one such memory that filled the agent's mind with lighter thoughts.

They'd been playing outside, in a time when children roamed the streets, without being supervised constantly, and were considered to be relatively safe from the dangers and horrors that life had to bring. Both had worked up sweats, playing with the other local kids, these two brothers considered exotic and mysterious to the surrounding youthful populace; a time of virtue indeed. Sebastian had broken away from the game of tag, and run the short trip home. There, he had made a beeline toward the freezer, and dug deep inside to retrieve an ice-lolly. He'd ripped away at the wrapper and jammed the frozen lolly into his mouth. And was instantly shocked when it stuck to his lips. Freezer burn. The lolly had been languishing there throughout winter, and had subsequently fallen victim to oxidation and dehydration.

Moments later, Ricardo had burst into the kitchen, he himself looking for immediate refreshment, only to find his older brother hopping around in agony with a multicoloured ice-rocket glued to his lips.

Sebastian had spent weeks suffering with the pain of two enormous blisters to his lips. Perhaps, the agent thought now, that that was why he didn't smile too willingly these days.

Fernandez turned from the cool relief of the window and away from the world of yesterday, and returned instead to the desk. The crime reports lay open, faces looking back, and bold ink listing the victim's lives in nothing but harsh black lines.

The door to the small office opened and a burly individual entered. The agent looked away from the information splayed out before him.

"Anything?" he asked hopefully.

Chief Laren Zager shook his head dismally. "No."

The chief looked tired; as if he'd served every single day since the Fairbanks Police Department had been established back in 1904. His blue eyes were red-rimmed, dark hair unruly, and a peppering of grey and brown whiskers sprinkled his lower face. He was a thickset man. In his late forties, large boned, muscular and somewhat handsome. He had a no-nonsense approach to policing, a fact that impressed Fernandez, yet had somehow retained a youthful outlook on life. However, this recent spate of killings had begun to stretch his normal exuberance to the limit.

"You sure our killer didn't take any trophies?" Fernandez pushed.

"None that either two-dozen cops or a pathologist can determine," Chief Zager replied.

The agent looked over the chief's shoulder and scanned the office beyond momentarily. Two dozen uniformed and plain clothes cops were actively at it. Most were double-shifting, some on a straight triple shift, and nearing exhaustion, yet all looked eager as they went about the business of tracking down this gruesome killer. With a staff of forty-four officers and three civilians, the police department was running at almost maximum capacity. Those that were not here, were either patrolling the city's streets, or canvassing locals, in the hope of identifying a suspect. Any suspect.

Chief Zager shifted his considerable mass over to the single chair next to Fernandez's adopted desk. The fan blew air into the guy's tired-looking face. Zager closed his eyes, seemingly enjoying a moment's respite from the strain of recent events.

Opening his eyes, he said, "Can't determine any lost possessions, external or internal, or otherwise."

The agent nodded. "That's a worry."

"Meaning?" asked Chief Zager.

"Meaning, that our unknown suspect is not necessarily about to fall into the pattern of a serial killer."

"Meaning?" Zager repeated.

"Meaning," Fernandez elaborated, "that it'll prove that more difficult to predict the killer's next intended victim or movements."

Zager coughed uncomfortably into his hand. "Agent Fernandez, aren't we forgetting the missing head from our latest victim? Doesn't *that* qualify as trophy taking?"

The agent looked towards the crime-reports. He had two dead women staring back at him. And a third headless body caught in all its macabre glory, sprawled with limbs at odd angles, printed out in high definition colour.

He picked up the report to their headless victim. Read some of the provisional information that was found there. And then frowned.

"What is it?" Zager asked.

"Toxicology found traces of barbiturates in her blood samples, right?"

"Right."

"Yet the other two came up clean?"

"Correct."

The obvious had eluded Fernandez until now. He silently rebuked himself for being so stupid. The evidence was practically staring him in the face. He took the case file of the headless victim, and then very casually handed it over to Chief Zager.

"Maybe you should channel all your resources into that

one," he said, matter-of-factly.

Puzzled, Zager accepted the proffer. "What do you mean?"

"Use all available manpower to find her killer."

"*Her* killer?"

"Yes."

"What about *their* killer?" asked Zager.

"Leave that to me," Fernandez replied.

Zager stood abruptly. "What do you mean?"

The agent spread his hands flat at either end of the table, in a subconscious gesture, staking claim to the two remaining case files. "I mean," he began, "you take care of that killer. And I'll take care of this one."

The sudden ramifications of what the agent was saying dawned on the police chief. He stood opened-mouthed for a second.

"You mean we have *two* killers here?" he finally managed to say.

"Yes – Chief Zager, that's exactly what I'm saying, two mutually exclusive killers. One unlikely to kill again, and one only just beginning."

Zager looked out towards the rapidly dwindling light that had now cast the city of Fairbanks into darkest shadow.

He shuddered. "Jesus tonight."

Chapter Three

Chamela - West Mexico

The *rat-tat-tat* of automatic gunfire sounded again. With it, Josh's heart tightened. Concern for the woman he loved had sprouted roots and fixed him to the spot. One of the Mexican newcomers laughed to reveal a mouthful of rotten teeth.

"Looks like your friend's been found," the Eastern European said.

More gunfire sounded, a lot of it now. And to the untrained ear it might have been a signal of bloodshed. However, Josh now understood that the weapons discharging were being done so in an indiscriminate fashion. They were shooting at shadows.

"Good for you," Josh whispered silently.

The European took a few steps closer. "I think your agency bitch just got her return ticket home."

This guy's use of the word 'agency' almost made Josh laugh out loud. How absurd. For him, or anyone, to think that either he or Anna were part of any legal or authoritative agency. Special Agent Josh Sawyer—FBI! Or, even more ridiculous, that either of them were part of a larger collective – the CIA. Ludicrous. Still, it seemed that this sudden promotion in stature had at least granted Josh a momentary pardon from a bullet between the eyes.

"I think you underestimate my partner," Josh replied, slowly shortening the distance. The Mexicans were remaining at a safe distance – for now.

Feeling as if he had the upper hand, what with superior fire-power, the European didn't waver or step back from Josh's slow advance.

"You underestimate our operation," he replied.

Josh stopped with only a few yards separating them. "Operation?"

He knew exactly from Anna's explanations what type of 'operation' was going on here, but was still curious to hear what this guy had to say. Even after 12 months of being on the run with the mysterious woman, Josh still struggled at times to fully appreciate the amazing talents and abilities that Anna possessed, talents and abilities that no other human could possibly understand.

The European grinned ruefully. "My friend – I am a business man, I do not care to divulge such information. Information that my competitors may use against me." He laughed then, as if knowing damn well that his words had no real meaning to them.

Josh felt sick having a conversation with this man. Without thought, he shifted his gaze towards the only other Colonial building within the town's limits, the one that sat purposefully over all the others.

Josh's nemesis caught the look. "My boss wouldn't be too pleased either if I openly talked about his business."

Irritated by the guy's constant use of this *business* euphemism, Josh pushed closer, new-found anger and determination breaking the bonds of fear.

"We all know what goes on up there," he said.

The guy simply shrugged his shoulders unapologetically.

"People like you make me sick," Josh stated.

"People like you wouldn't exist without people like me," he countered.

Josh couldn't argue with that. "No – I guess not."

The guy finally made the move Josh had been expecting.

He slipped his hand behind him and it returned a second later holding a large handgun. "Enough speak. Sorry – nothing personal. Business is business – right?" He levelled his arm towards Josh.

The blood rushed towards Josh's ears. Almost deafening him. And his heart now pounded with fear. He had a moment then, one that was either a clichéd paradigm, or one that was an utterly absolute truth, that his life flashed before his eyes.

Born to run. His father had once said this. How apt that Josh now found himself on the run. The irony of this did not elude him. Only 12 months ago, he'd been a simple college student, studying for a degree in Sports Science in the place of his birth – Chicago. This had all changed on that fateful night he met Anna Privalova.

The hammer of the gun clicked, which subsequently brought Josh back to the fore. Now, the weapon bore down on him.

Josh realised the gunfire coming from the shoreline had ceased some moments earlier. He looked beyond the barrel of the gun and towards the dark skyline.

There, a brief, fleeting movement.

Only he knew the significance of that. Night in this place was almost as impenetrable as the dark hearts that resided here. Yet a part of that blackness had shifted. A liquid shadow within a shadow. Josh just needed to buy himself a few more seconds.

"I'm wired. You shoot me now – they'll still catch you through voice recognition software," he said.

Ridiculous!

He almost laughed at its absurdity.

The European's face turned suddenly ashen. "What ... are you..?" Then realising he was only incriminating himself further he caught the rest of what he was about to say.

"Yeah – the agency is listening in right now. Probably triangulating our location as we speak."

Josh was getting good at this. The other guy just looked back blankly. "I'd be running now if I were you," Josh advised.

Silence followed: a genuine Mexican stand-off. The sounds

of music and laughter, which filtered in from the busy market square filled in the silence found here.

Then, a magnificent burst of fireworks lit up the sky, throwing the shadows around them into life. The shadows stretched – as if trying to break free from the buildings – before shrinking back into the surrounding brickwork.

When the spectacle ended, the small gathering found that they were one man short. One of the Mexicans had vanished. It took a moment for his two remaining compadres to realise. For a second both stood watching as the embers from the firework twinkled and fell towards the earth.

It was the one on the left who noticed first. He turned to make a comment, nudging his friend with his elbow, but simply ended up poking at nothing. He stopped jabbering then, the absence of his companion somewhat alarming.

Now, too, the Eastern European sensed things were somewhat amiss. He turned his attention towards the two remaining Mexicans and launched into a verbal frenzy. He spoke in Spanish, or so Josh thought, but the two natives paid little or no attention as they raised their weapons towards the gloom.

A burst of gunfire ripped through the night – both Mexicans spooked by something seen at the very edges of their periphery – and bullets tore fist-sized holes in the surrounding buildings.

With their attention turned, Josh made a run for the Jeep. He managed a few strides only before the European gathered his senses and cut off his path to safety.

The gun once again found its mark.

Two things happened simultaneously then.

One, the Mexicans were suddenly halved again in numbers. And, two, the European started firing at Josh in an indiscriminate fashion.

Chapter Four

Fairbanks - Alaska

Nyctophobia: a phobia characterised by a severe fear of the dark.

Alaska: the 49th state of America, with typically sub Arctic temperatures and long, bitterly cold winters.

Nyctophobia + Alaska = Special Agent Sebastian Fernandez's worst nightmare.

Night had so totally and completely thrown the city of Fairbanks into darkness, and would stay that way for the next 20 hours. A fact that had started to push Fernandez's heart-rate up and make fresh beads of sweat break out along the surface of his brow.

He was ashamed of this. It was a recent, unexplainable condition that had manifested itself with callous disregard. Now, night and its resultant dark had the effect of turning the usually level-headed and logically-minded agent into a gibbering mess.

Standing alone in the small office, the agent tried to remember when he had first fallen victim to this sudden and debilitating condition.

It had been 12 months ago on waking up in a hospital bed

somewhere in Glenwood Springs – Colorado.

The agent had been in pursuit of two fugitives—a young couple from Chicago. He'd teamed up with one of the local cops there, and between them they'd managed to trace the couple from Chicago, to the small skiing resort of Glenwood Springs. What had followed was still shady and uncertain in the agent's mind.

Fernandez had managed to corner the woman; he'd had little information of her past, even with the infinite might of the FBI. The cop, clearly working out of his jurisdiction, had apprehended the young male fugitive.

What had followed those next few hours on the slopes of the abandoned skiing complex had now escaped the agent, a complete mental block, of sorts. He had snippets of memory; the woman attacking him, her face distorted – or twisted in rage, or so the agent wanted to believe, and he had been caught in the aftermath of an avalanche.

Then nothing.

He had awakened some time later in a strange daze, laid out flat on a hospital bed, wrapped in tinfoil. Hypothermia, the cop had explained, due to his time spent trapped in the debris of a shattered cabin and the mass of ice and snow. The agent had pushed for the cop to reveal all – but had been met with a vague explanation at best.

Somehow the cop had managed to pull him free from the snow, and then carry him to safety. The cop's tone had warned Fernandez not to push for more. And as for the two fugitives, the cop said that they had both likely perished during the destruction wrought by the avalanche. Yet, three months later, and throughout the spring weeks that followed, no trace or bodies of the two had been found.

Fernandez had been discharged a week after waking within the hospital – his right foot strapped heavily due to a shattered ankle.

The agent had spent the next few months trying to locate the fugitives, but to no avail. Perhaps he thought, from time to time, usually in the late worrying hours of the night, that the two had actually met their fates on that strange night on the mountainside.

What *had* followed him from there was this sudden and irrational fear of the dark. Couple that with the oppressive weight of snow, and that was enough to break the agent out into a cold sweat.

Just the agent's luck then that he had been assigned this case, way out here in this almost perpetually dark and frozen wasteland.

He was tired now, and had been at it for what seemed like hours. The harsh blackness that pushed heavily against his back was not helping matters either.

He checked his watch and was dismayed to find that it was only 8PM. Which meant the night would continue to stretch out for hours to come.

Rubbing fatigue from his eyes, he stood and walked around the table to examine the photos from a new angle: a new perspective.

Okay – what the hell did these two have in common? The younger of the two was attractive, with youth on her side, and an innocence that should have been tested, yet now never would be. The two women lay with almost serene poses. One had been found in a nearby park. Simply sitting on a bench, her hand held out with mobile phone in her grasp. The other in her car, which had been found, parked up; her body slumped at the wheel.

Fernandez had used the agency's resources to trace the park bench victim's calls. His early hope of catching a voice or tracing a number from her call had been quickly dispelled. A list of uneventful outward bound and incoming calls had bore no leads. It seemed victim #1, as the agent referred to her, had led a simple and boring life.

Victim #2 was much the same. No illicit goings-on or wrongfulness. She had left her home, driving to work, headed for the Alaskan National Bank. Her role had been cashier on one of the terminals. Her manager had raised the alarm when she'd failed to arrive for work three days running. Her flatmates had stated that they had assumed she was staying at her boyfriend's home. Both flatmates and boyfriend checked out. No leads there either. Calls to and from her cell were no more mysterious than the first victim. Just a humdrum life of normality.

Nothing obvious connected any of the victims.

The autopsy reports were just has frustrating. Neither of the women showed any signs of cardiac arrest, or heart-disease, high blood pressure, or any heart-related illnesses. Nor had they suffered a sudden and fatal brain haemorrhage, stroke, sudden death syndrome – although they had indeed died suddenly – nor had they been stabbed, shot, strangled, or poisoned; toxicology reports drew a blank, and nothing from any of the first two autopsies could determine the actual cause of death.

So why was Agent Fernandez referring to them as 'victims'? Truth be told, the agent wasn't completely sure why. But the mystery of two, plus the headless body, had caused enough of a panic for the Fairbanks Police Department to call in help from the FBI.

Agent Fernandez was deeply regretting that fact already. He needed to find answers, and fast. Before the body count grew larger, and the people of Fairbanks started dropping dead in the streets.

Chapter Five

Chamela - West Mexico

Josh hit the ground with a bone-jarring thump. The bullets tore over him, missing his head by mere inches. He was up and running again in seconds. Another hail of bullets matched him step for step as he launched himself towards the 4x4.

Mercifully he made it to cover without being hit. A couple of bullets punched holes into the Jeep. For a second Josh feared the fuel tank would ignite, blowing them all across the Mexican border. The sounds of gunfire ceased then. Josh poked his head from behind the 4x4 to find the European in the process of reloading his spent magazine.

Across the open courtyard, the single remaining Mexican stood with his semi-automatic weapon clutched to his chest. He appeared to be chanting insistently. He was also spinning in circles as if trying to locate something that was constantly staying just out of his field of vision. A movement to his left set his weapon off again, as he fired towards this unknown, unseen enemy.

The European had finished reloading, and was about to empty his clip towards Josh and the Jeep, when the strangled sounds of struggle stopped him short. Turning his attention away from his target, he found himself suddenly alone. No Mexicans to be found – just their discarded weapons expelling wisps of gun smoke.

"Come out!" bellowed the European. "Cowards!"

A fine statement coming from someone in his line of work, Josh thought, finally rising from his position.

"It's over," Josh said.

The other guy swung his arm out to point the weapon at Josh, but his eyes continued to roam everywhere about him.

"Where is the bitch?" he asked, hysteria now heightening his tone.

"Who?" Josh asked, trying to get the guy's full attention.

"The bitch! The spook!" he replied.

Spook?

Maybe an apt description Josh thought, but not the CIA spook that this guy was implying. No, this was a spook of ethereal substance. And more deadly then any trained operative.

"She's right behind you," Josh said.

The guy spun away, to find the woman there.

Cast in shadows, it was her slim, lithe physique that gave her away. She took a step closer, but the night was not quite willing to let her go. Her upper body remained shrouded. Yet as she spoke, her white teeth were more than visible.

"You should have run, like my friend advised," she said.

Those teeth sent a shiver down the guy's spine. They looked all wrong. Too long. Too many.

"Brave words for a dead bitch," he managed to counter.

Whatever bravery he had possessed was now rapidly evaporating out of his words. They were weak and feeble. All threat lost.

Anna broke from the cover of darkness.

The guy's legs buckled, the vision before him draining all energy from his limbs. Terror threatened to pull him to his knees.

Then, unexpectedly, the guy started babbling for forgiveness. He dropped the weapon from his hands, clasping them tightly, his lips moving rapidly as he spoke. His words did not stop as the woman drew near. Rather, they grew in magnitude, as he tried desperately to seek for clemency, absolution, *mercy*. She stood before him – her appearance, the stuff of nightmares.

Knowing his time on this planet was short, the guy threw himself to her feet, kissing them, gibbering, with twin rivers of tears streaming down either side of his face. He looked up then, into the face above, and his bladder opened. Hands that had done hideous, unspeakable acts, things that no man with any thread of humanity would have done, grasped desperately onto Anna's clothing.

Josh watched as Anna's hands flexed. Her defined muscles tensed and in the next second she...

Josh looked away, unwilling to witness this pathetic man's final moment. When he did look back, the European's head had been tossed to one side, his lips now silent, face wide-eyed and ghost-white. His headless body had slumped into a sitting position, and a pool of arterial blood was leaking out around it, turning the dusty soil to deepest black.

In the next second, Anna was by his side.

"You okay?" she asked, her face beautiful again, yet worried-looking. The frightening mask that had presented itself from the dark, like a nightmare surfacing from the dark depths of troubled sleep, was now gone. Anna was before him, her face returned to normal and soft gentle hands reaching out to offer comfort.

It took Josh a moment to gather his wits. "Yeah – I'm fine."

"We'd better hurry, we'll have company soon."

Anna took a few fleeting steps towards the connecting alleyways.

Voices coming from somewhere within the maze of buildings drew Josh's attention away from the dead European.

"Wait," Josh warned. "We may need this." He stooped over the hideous remains of the body to pick up the handgun. Heat radiated from the grip. Josh felt his stomach lurch.

"Leave it," Anna told him.

"Anna, they ain't rushing here with welcoming arms."

Anna returned to his side. "Leave it. What good would it do

you?"

"I almost had my ass blown off back there. A little bit of added protection wouldn't go a miss."

Anna grinned mischievously. "Cute ass too."

Josh groaned. "I'm serious Anna. What if that guy had actually fired – at you?"

"Then he'd have missed."

"Really? What about Chicago? That wasn't a miss."

Back then, the Chicago detective hunting them had managed to wound Anna with a single shot. It had been a lucky shot, too – in Anna's opinion. Yet, the bullet injury had been the event that had finally destroyed any real hope of Josh maintaining his then reality. And Anna had come to realise that for him, unnecessary risks and fraternising willingly with danger, were two things best avoided.

Anna had to nod at his last comment. "Okay – fair point. But I don't want you with bloodshed on your hands."

"I can handle that," Josh replied, head held high.

"Really?" Anna said.

She brushed the gun aside and pushed herself close to him. Bringing their lips only inches apart. "And when was the last time you killed someone? Have you been sneaking out throughout the daylight hours and putting this illicit world of ours to rights?"

Josh leaned back slightly to catch her eyes. "I don't think we have time for this – do you?"

The sounds of rushing feet were getting louder. And the voices that preceded them were getting more animated.

"We'll make time," Anna said, bringing her lips to his.

Josh sighed. His arms remained at his sides, gun still held firm.

Anna released a slight whimper of enjoyment. False enjoyment. She was using her special ability to testify to the fact that Josh was still free from bloodshed. Josh just rolled his eyes at her obvious attempts at false affection. She lingered at his lips a second longer, then stepped back.

"No Josh, no signs of mass vigilantism. You're still as pure as the driven snow."

"Jeez—" Josh huffed. "Sometimes I hate it when you do that."

Anna nodded with sympathetic agreement. "It is a burden. That's for sure."

Realising that it was this very talent of hers, this amazing ability, that had actually brought them here, and understanding that the pain it must have caused to Anna, Josh reached out to take her hand.

"I'm sorry – that was insensitive of me," he said.

Anna simply nodded again. "Thanks – Josh."

She leaned into him, this time placing a genuinely loving kiss onto his lips.

They broke away.

Anna said, "They're getting closer."

Josh could clearly hear individual voices within the ruckus now. "Okay." He held the handgun for a second longer, and then tossed it to the ground. Anna was right. This last year had changed him forever, hardened him beyond what he thought possible, and shown him things he'd have thought impossible. Yet, he was still, deep down, the simple young man from Chicago. Not a killer. And hopefully never would be.

Anna pulled him away from the macabre sight of the headless body, and into the nearest connecting passageways.

Once they were safely away from any danger, Josh pulled them to a stop.

"Wait," he said. "What about the boat?"

Anna turned to look at him. "Gone."

"What about the cargo?"

Anna's expression turned earnest. "Safe – for now."

"Where?"

"Somewhere were they cannot be found."

"We can't just leave. What will become of them?"

"We're not leaving – not just yet."

It was Josh's turn to look serious. "What do you mean 'yet'?"

Anna's mischievousness returned. She smiled wryly. "Josh —
it's time we shut this operation down for good."

"And how do you plan on doing just that?"

She turned her attention towards the highest point of the
town. The black silhouette of the imposing mansion stood out
against the night.

"We're going there."

Josh followed her gaze. "Christ — Anna."

The old building loomed oppressively in the night. It
stood out from the surrounding darkness like a twisted and
misshapen lighthouse, which radiated deepest dread, rather
than brightness and expectation. What lights did flicker from
open windows appeared hypnotic; like a jack-o-lantern, ready
to draw upon innocent and unsuspecting victims, with only the
deadliest of intentions in mind.

Josh knew that these images were simply a manifestation of
his mind. The structure was no more foreboding than any of
the neighbouring buildings.

It was what he knew to have gone on up there that was
blurring his reality, warping his sensibilities, twisting his gut.
He felt sick to his stomach with the thought of what they might
find up there.

Anna was at his side, guiding them deeper within the maze
of brickwork. The sky was still a blank canvas — the moon and
stars seemingly unwilling to pay witness to what went on in this
ghastly place.

They climbed steadily towards the building. No resistance
was met. The outside dangers had been dealt with by Anna
over on the shorefront and then in the open courtyard. Now,
what was left would be holding down the fort.

Anna drew them to a halt.

"This could get ugly. You should either wait here or return
to the Jeep."

Josh shook his head. "You need my help. What if we find
more inside?"

Anna started to object, but then realising that Josh was not talking about more armed men, but rather more innocents, she nodded her head instead. "If that's the case, then you get them out as quickly as possible. Go to the Jeep or hotel and wait."

Josh almost dismissed the sense of returning to the hotel. Until Anna added, "There were a couple of foreign nationals. People not involved in what's happening here. It should remain safe."

"Okay," he replied.

His mouth had turned totally dry. Not from fear for himself. No, he knew Anna had his back. This fear was fuelled by the thought of what they would discover ahead. He was surprised that this feeling had gripped him so tightly.

Anna shifted away from him then, which forced him to push aside these fears, and instead, focus on the imminent future. Getting himself shot would not be beneficial to anyone – least of all himself.

He had a second to question how the hell he'd come to this – tracking down killers and criminals – before he lost sight of Anna. Not wishing to be left behind, he was forced to simply accept that a higher purpose had other things in mind. He quickly caught Anna up and then allowed her to lead the way.

The ugly building was a two-storey affair. Square in design, with the lower half a smooth white, and the upper half made from wooden slats that ran in a horizontal direction. The roof sloped upwards to a thatched point. Two doors, both arched, gave entrance. The windows top and bottom were secured by iron bars. Internal lights made the glass look liquid in appearance. A guard, with weapon hanging loosely in his grasp, stood on a balcony overlooking the front of the building.

"Now what?" Josh asked.

Anna placed her finger over his lips. "Quiet – Josh. Leave the guard to me."

Before he had time to protest, she was up from their hiding position and stealthily moving towards the front of the colonial house.

Chapter Six

Fairbanks - Alaska

The grittiness of fatigue turned Chief Zager's eyes red-rimmed and sore. He closed them, using his thumb and finger to rub at the tender orbs. A dull throb had also taken up permanent residence at the sides of his skull. Shifting away from bloodshot eyes, he then began to massage fingertips into his temples. His moment of relief was short-lived. The phone on top of his desk rang with a shrill of noise.

Snatching it up, he answered, "Yeah?"

The voice on the other end sounded like it was a thousand miles away, the pain in the chief's head filtering away the speaker's voice to nothing more than a whisper.

"Say again," he said, now shaking his head clear.

The caller repeated their message.

A shiver ran along the length of Zager's spine. "Jesus – another one? So soon."

The reply rendered the police officer mute. He dropped the handset away from his ear before placing it back into the cradle.

He tipped his eyes upwards. The FBI agent was clearly visible in his makeshift office through the break of white blinds. He was stooped over his desk, engrossed in the case files spread out before him.

Zager contemplated his next move. The call had come

through directly to him – not the agent. This was his town after all. He felt a slight amount of animosity towards the agent for being excluded from the rest of the investigation. Okay, the MO of the headless victim stood out from the mysterious circumstances of the others, but it was still too early to rule out that all three victims were somehow connected, unless, of course, Special Agent Fernandez was keeping information to himself.

Now, another call had come in stating that a fourth body had been found.

Zager stood.

The details from the call had been vague. A male victim, found slumped in a toilet stall, in a tavern not far from the precinct. The bar was familiar to the chief. A local hotspot for fist fights, DUIs, and drunken behaviour in general. A couple of uniformed officers were currently on site, having already cordoned off the scene, awaiting the acting detective and crime lab boys to arrive.

Until otherwise stated, Zager considered himself to be the acting detective. Therefore, he quickly gathered up his padded jacket, spoke to no one as he headed for the corridor, least of all the agent, and silently left the precinct behind.

The bar was only two blocks walk from the station, so the chief bypassed his state cruiser, and simply cut across the street and took a right onto the next avenue.

Already, a small gathering had formed outside the bar's entrance. Most wore thick overcoats and padded trousers. With hoods tightly pulled over their heads, Zager struggled to pull one noticeable face from the rest.

The lights from the uniformed cops' cruiser flashed blue phantoms of light over the surrounding buildings, momentarily pushing back the shadows, revealing narrow alleyways and empty side streets.

Zager was surprised to feel his chest tighten as he passed from the incandescence into darkness. He stepped across the opening of a shadowy alleyway, and subconsciously his hand moved to his sidearm. His hand wavered, eyes fixing themselves to the gloom, yet in the next second he was clear and moving into the periphery of the small gathering.

Some of the hooded heads turned his way as he pushed his way towards the entrance.

"Hey – Chief," someone called out.

Zager turned in the direction of the speaker.

The weather-beaten face of Kavik Tonrar looked back at him. Tonrar, one of the few native Alaskan Indians to be gainfully employed in Fairbanks, took a step closer to the chief.

"It doesn't make any sense," Tonrar said. "I was drinking with him just an hour ago."

Zager understood the Indian's meaning instantly. Tonrar spent most of his spare, and a generous amount of company, time, frequenting the numerous drinking holes found dotted around town. If one of the patrons inside was a local—and why wouldn't he be—then Tonrar would know everything there was to know about such an individual. When sober, Kavik Tonrar was a formidable force to be reckoned with. A shame then that it had probably been the mid-80s since the native Alaskan had last been steady on his feet. Now, the Alaskan looked even more haunted. As if the years of neglect had eventually taken their toll. In truth, Kavik Tonrar looked like a broken man – spiritless, his physical self slowly but surely losing what fortitude still remained.

"Who we got inside, Kavik?" asked Chief Zager.

Tonrar leaned in, closer to the chief's ear. "It's Jonny." The big Alaskan placed a shovel-like hand on the lawman's shoulder, squeezed in sympathy—or to hold himself steady with buckling legs, Zager was not sure—and then shook his head sympathetically. "It's a real mess in there."

Zager's heart quickened. He patted Tonrar's hand in simple gratitude and then pushed his way inside, nodding solemnly to the two uniformed cops that had taken up flanking positions on either side of the entrance.

The wooden floor echoed his footsteps. Stools sat vacant,

some with jackets still draped over them, and the square-shaped stalls were empty. Half-filled jugs of beer and taller glasses, with a mixture of spirits, littered the unoccupied tables. The sound coming from the jukebox added to the strangely otherwise silence of the bar-room. Billy Ray Cyrus was currently singing about his Achy Breaky Heart.

Jesus tonight, thought Zager, get over it, as he moved closer to the jukebox and its insistent wailings.

He stopped next to the music player, his intentions to pull the fucking plug. Before he had chance, however, a shadow filled the gap leading towards the washrooms. It was there momentarily, dark and ominous, and then only the faint light from beyond the entrance remained.

Zager's hand abruptly stopped. "Police," he announced, his hand now seeking out his firearm. No response followed. He moved away from the jukebox and negotiated his way around the many chairs that had been pushed back from beer-cluttered tables.

He reached the entrance. Nothing or nobody jumped out. Leaving the open plan of the bar-room behind, he entered the connecting passageway. It was a short run to two doors, directly opposite to each other. Either the word *Male* or *Female* was stencilled to a door.

Zager unzipped his heavy winter coat, giving himself better movement, and then unclipped the holster to his side arm. He did this without being consciously aware of it either. He wasn't a man known for pulling his gun on a whim. Hell, this was Fairbanks for Christ sakes, not Detroit or New York City.

Both doors stood ajar. The detective paused for just a second, and then pushed his way into the nearest washroom.

"This is Chief Zager, anyone in here?" he called.

Zager moved into the Male washroom, starkly aware that his back would now become exposed.

He smelled it instantly. Not the usual stench of stale urine or worse. It was the metallic odour of blood, and lots of it. A pool of it had spread out from one of the stalls, dark and sluggish, running between the cracks of the floor.

Beads of cold sweat broke out on the detective's forehead. He wiped his brow with the back of his hand. Then drew his firearm. The door to the central stall was closed. That left one on either side. The one on the left stood half open, revealing it to be empty. The right one, the one now closest to Zager, was open by an inch only.

Careful not to step into the pool of blood, Zager used the toe of his shoe to gently push the door open. Just a well-used and tainted toilet sat there.

Zager sidestepped and brought himself level with the shut stall.

The lock had engaged to red.

What the hell?

Zager paused, hand held out, almost touching the door. His hand closed into a fist, and he rapped gently on the door – tentatively; his subconscious mind clinging onto the notion that this would amount to nothing more than an embarrassing intrusion. The sheer amount of blood pooling onto the floor ripped any real hope free.

"Jonny," he called in a whisper.

Silence prevailed.

Zager pushed against the door – perhaps the lock hadn't engaged fully? The door was shut fast. Which didn't make any sense? How could it. If what lay inside had already been discovered.

"Jonny – you in there?" Zager said, a bit more forcefully.

A wheezing of breath came from within.

"Jonny!" Zager called now.

The chief abandoned any sort of bathroom etiquette, as he pushed his way into the next stall, climbed onto the toilet seat before pulling himself up to bring himself level with the wall that split the stalls in two. His legs almost buckled at the sight he found there.

All of Jonny's considerable 200lbs of bulk lay slumped on the seat, his legs propped up at two awkward angles, booted feet pressed against the doorway. One hand lay across his midriff, which was glistening bright red, and his other hand had curled itself into a macabre claw, balancing precariously on the toilet roll holder. Blood had run down the front of his clothing, into the pan, over the seat, and then onto the white tiling beneath.

A second wheeze of air sounded. The noise came out of Jonny's chest. Literally. His lungs were deflating as they lost oxygen, and the released air was escaping from the gaping hole in his rib cage. His clothing had been torn open to reveal his torso, and a dark red crust of blood had started to congeal around the terrible wound.

Zager couldn't take his eyes off the open cavity. An inky blackness filled the void where the heart should have been. The chief blinked heavily. Opened his eyes. Praying that fatigue was playing some sort of sick joke. No joke. Jonny was still slumped with his heart ripped out from his chest.

Jonny Tarver – a 200lb ex pro boxer, with the facial scars to prove it, and possibly the most physically capable man in Fairbanks, had somehow been beaten to death before having his heart ripped from his body.

How?

Why!

Zager climbed down from his vantage point. He moved over to the connecting corridor, his intentions on calling the forensics team and the coroner. However, as his hand moved to take his cell phone, the sound of footsteps echoed towards him.

Next, he was suddenly confronted by a hostile face. The newcomer had the advantage of having his gun on target.

***

Agent Fernandez stepped outside the precinct. The sudden drop in temperature almost froze the air within his lungs. He felt his eyes burn as the subzero temperatures bit into the tender and exposed tissue. His sight blurred and the lights of Fairbanks sprung to macabre life as the glare from streetlights and storefronts became twisted and warped.

He rubbed his eyes gently, gloved fingers working heat back into the tender orbs. He stepped away from the police department's entrance and took a few uncertain steps. Instantly, his flesh broke out in beads of sweat, and his heart knocked painfully against his chest.

The dark: a terrifying and living entity that struck fear into Fernandez's soul.

He stopped in his tracks. Sucked a lungful of air inward, its cold bite helping to clear his senses somewhat, and then continued towards the main high street.

He'd heard about this most recent incident over the chatter of excitement while sitting thoughtful inside his office. Some of the police officers had made a grab for coats and weapons. Fernandez had vacated his office in time to stop the assisting officers. A quick interrogation had led him to the knowledge of a fourth killing. A male victim this time, a fact that could quite possibly change the entire direction of this murder spree.

Fernandez had ordered, yes ordered, pulling rank and seniority over the uniformed cops, them to stay put; his immediate thoughts to maintain the crime scene and examine this latest victim in relative calm. He didn't want local cops reacting badly to the loss of a friend or relative.

He wanted peace and quiet.

And time to think.

To think about why he was starting to believe that these recent events here in Fairbanks were somehow inexplicably tied to the events that had happened almost a year ago now on the abandoned slopes of Glenwood Springs – Colorado.

***

The dark eye of the gun dropped away from Zager's head. Then the slight figure of the agent came into view. The agent and police chief stood momentarily silent—their primeval instincts all too aware that something of darkest dread had recently visited this place.

In the next second, Chief Zager breathed out a lungful of air, lowering his guard slightly, now in the unexpected company of an ally.

"It's a real mess," Zager said.

The chief sidestepped, giving the FBI agent the option to enter.

Fernandez paused at the entrance before holstering his weapon. He stepped inside, next to Zager, his attention instantly drawn to the pool of congealing blood.

"This changes everything," he announced.

"You think?" Zager responded grimly.

The agent took an exaggerated stride over the blood pool. His left foot trod awkwardly, straining beyond his normal stride, and he had to hop-skip slightly to find a secure footing on the opposite side. Zager simply stepped over to the agent, his long legs easily avoiding the crimson puddle.

"You looked inside?" the agent asked.

Zager nodded sombrely. "A real mess."

"From what vantage point?" asked Fernandez.

"There," Zager replied, pointing towards the walled partition.

Fernandez frowned. "So who locked the door?"

All Zager could do was offer the agent a shrug.

The agent reached inside his jacket. He produced his wallet, and took a moment to extract a dime. Using the coin, he slotted it into the lock mechanism, a groove similar to that of a flathead screw to be found there, and he flipped the bolt over to its vacant position.

Keeping the dime in hand, he then used it to push the stall's door open.

The stench of blood and guts wafted out in a noxious cloud. The agent gagged slightly.

"Jonny Tarver," Zager said.

It took a moment for the agent to process what was in front of him. A mess. A huge open cavity. Bones shattered. Blood black and gelatine. Jonny's eyes vacant. His mouth crooked and misshapen. A scream of silent horror etched into his face.

"What the hell happened here?" Fernandez asked.

Zager cleared his throat. "Someone ripped his heart right from his chest. Never seen anything like it."

Fernandez looked back towards the police chief. "No?"

The chief held the agent's look. "Never. Not in Fairbanks. Not even if one of the native wolves got its teeth into you."

The agent nodded in agreement. Something on two legs had caused this mess. With enough strength and cruelty to beat Jonny to death, and literally rip his heart out, and all within moments. This was a calculated act. Prepared with grace and dexterity, and timed to perfection, yet beyond the realms of the normal. It had then returned after the body had been initially found to lock it inside. A huge and unnecessary risk. Was the killer mocking them?

Something vicious had taken Jonny Tarver's life, without the attachment of humanity, or compassion, or sympathy. Something that had acted swiftly; something that had taken the life from the living in the blink of an eye.

Some-*thing.*

Chapter Seven

Chamela - West Mexico

Anna reached the overhang under the cover of darkness. She ducked into shadows. Then waited to see if she had raised an alarm. The guard above appeared oblivious to the presence of this silent stalker. Confident she had at least gotten this far undetected, she then slipped away from the overhang to hug the sides of the main perimeter.

The wall offered little if any resistance. Anna simply scaled its heights effortlessly, before dropping down into the open courtyard within. She held her position until she was certain the area was clear. Then she was up and running.

A thick wooden doorway blocked her progress. A simple drop latch opened the way. Anna used it. The door cracked open.

A lavish kitchen presented itself, old-fashioned and bright with cooking utensils, a stone oven, and washing basins. A large table, laden with foodstuff and empty dishes, made up most of the centre. Cutting knives occupied one corner of the table, arranged in ascending sizes, and laid out neatly.

Anna slipped inside. She took one of the knives, decided she liked the look of another, so swapped it for that one instead. She didn't bother to wipe her prints from the initial knife, neither worried about being identified to this place, nor fearful that it would lead to her capture. Come sunrise, both she and Josh would be long gone from this place.

***

Josh waited for what felt like an eternity. The guard on the balcony just stood there, statuesque, weapon now held firmly, eyes seemingly drawn to the night.

From his vantage point Josh thought the guard looked relatively young. Perhaps he was the son or nephew to the man who ran this place? This operation? For a second Josh felt remorse for the guard, maybe he was unaware of what went on in there, kept away from the festering heart of it. But then cold hard truth reminded Josh that such a fact was unlikely, considering he himself knew all too well what this place was harbouring within.

It had been complete chance too, how he and Anna had come about this place. Looking to stay out of trouble, they had found this town, not marked on any map, after taking a simple wrong turn from the main highway.

With dawn only hours away, they had decided to seek shelter and wait for the following night to continue their journey.

Only there had been evil waiting for them here.

Anna's ability had tuned into it instantly. That was her gift. And her curse. The ability to sense bad from good, and the capacity to offer swift and brutal justice when needed.

Josh heard voices coming from the building, casual in their nature. Anna had, as yet, not raised any alarm. A second guy appeared on the balcony, large in size and in stature. From his vantage point, Josh recognised him as the owner of the colonial house.

The leader of this operation.

A man responsible for endless suffering.

And the man Anna had come here to kill.

***

Beyond the kitchen now, Anna found herself on the outskirts of an open hallway. Connecting doorways branched off at intervals, all shut tight, and a grand stairway swept upwards to the next level.

She took the first few steps, with her weapon in hand, climbing silently upwards. A sudden blast of noise came from behind. Music, laced with static interference, filled the hallway. Anna spun back to find an armed man vacating a room. His weapon hung loosely in one hand, and a half-empty bottle was clasped tightly in the other.

Anna paused.

The guy took a swig from the bottle, and then grimaced slightly from the liquid's bite. He belched loudly, and then spoke over his shoulder in a monologue of drunken chatter.

Either the haze of drunkenness or the fog of tiredness forced him to rub at red-rimmed eyes. When his hand dropped away, he found himself suddenly confronted by a beautiful woman.

"Señor," Anna said, offering him a smile.

The guy looked back blankly for a second. He took a step back, eyeing her outfit, as if trying to place where and how she would fit into this place. Her dusky, Mediterranean complexion gained her a moment of credibility. The guy grinned foolishly, perhaps mistaking her for a maid or servant. Yet, as the blade in her hand rose, his grin slipped and his face bent into a crooked look of bemusement.

Anna could have ended things quickly. The guy should have been falling to the floor with his throat cut and his life's fluid pooling out around him. But Anna didn't think such a quick, merciful death was deserved. Not to anyone found in this place.

Instead, she flicked her wrist backwards, slicing a chunk of the guy's face away, leaving raw tissue and exposed bone.

The guy's hand went to his face casually. The cut so quick and precise, that his brain had yet to register pain. What remained in the bottle sloshed about inside. A warm trickle of blood ran from between his fingers. Now, the pain flared across his face. The bottle slipped from bloodied fingers and it cracked apart against the floor. His eyes sprang open, the alcoholic haze lifted from his mind, and he stepped back, ready to yell in warning.

The blade moved quicker this time, faster than the guy could follow. The point entered his mouth, slicing his tongue in two, before exiting in a spray of blood as it cut his remaining cheek in half.

Anna clamped her free hand over his ruined face, simultaneously pinching his nostrils shut and forcing his bloody mouth closed.

The guy tried to break free but Anna's other hand, fist tight with the knife, held him rigid, pressed against the middle of his back. He struggled to bring his weapon up, but Anna kneed him in the midriff, and the gun fell from his fingers with a metallic clatter.

In the end it took just a few minutes for the guy to drown in his own blood. Not before he'd been forced to swallow his own severed tongue.

Anna allowed the body to slip to the floor, holding the front of his shirt roughly, as he buckled first to his knees, then to his side.

The lights from the open room flickered. Anna stepped over the body. She bypassed the open doorway for now, and headed towards the main entrance. There she quickly released a complicated locking mechanism, should she require a swift exit later. Then she turned her attention back towards the open doorway and the noises emitting from within.

***

The two men on the balcony of the colonial house stood in conversation for a moment or two. The younger man nodding subserviently, hanging onto the larger guy's every word.

Josh maintained his hidden position—his heart rate climbing steadily as his fear for Anna's safety grew by the second. He took a couple of deep breaths in an attempt to calm his nerves. What finally pushed his heart to bursting point was the sudden and clear crack of a pistol-shot.

Josh looked towards the balcony. The two men had frozen solid. This unexpected noise had seemingly rendered them immobile. Then a second shot sounded and that broke whatever spell they'd been under. In the next second both had quickly disappeared inside.

Josh paused for just a heartbeat. Then he too was up and running. No way was he going to leave Anna at the mercy of those found inside.

He crossed the open ground, his left leg forcing him into an awkward gait – an old injury impeding his progress. Nothing or nobody stopped him as he reached the colonial building's main entry. It was a thick slab of dark ebony. A large oval handle offered access. With no real hope of gaining entry Josh tried the handle anyway. It turned easily – a well-maintained mechanism, and then, surprisingly, the doorway opened.

He found himself within an open hallway. His attention turned instantly to the bloodied and slumped figure on the floor.

Anna had been here.

No question of that.

The body and pool of blood on the floor had the clear characteristics of her signature.

He could here voices from above. Followed by heavy footsteps.

"Anna. . . ." he called, in a harsh whisper.

A muffled cry came from an open doorway just beyond the dead body.

Josh crossed the hallway, looking for danger as he went. The footsteps on the level above beat out a tattoo, which matched him step for step. He wasted no time waiting for their arrival, and instead entered the room beyond. A bank of low-definition TV sets filled his vision. Most were tuned to the same thing – the building's immediate surroundings. The screens offered views of different shades of greens, some bright and glowing, others almost black in appearance. The colonial house was wired from every angle, giving the occupants within a complete 360 degree view of the world.

Anna had a second guard gripped by the throat. His feet were kicking uncontrollably as he dangled a few inches off the floor. His body was going through its final death throes. A shot sounded as his hand twitched spasmodically, pulling once again against the trigger to his pistol. The bullet ricocheted off the floor to blow out one of the monitor screens. It exploded in a shower of sparks. The first few shots – the ones that had raised the alarm – had been aimed towards Anna, but her speed and agility had forced them wide of their mark, and now, finally, the guard lay still in her outstretched hand.

"Anna, we're about to have company," Josh warned.

Anna pitched the guard's body away; it landed on the other side of the room with a sickening crunch. The weapon fell to the floor with a metallic clang. She spun to face Josh. And made little attempt to hide her annoyance.

"I told you to wait," she snapped. "Can't you follow simple orders?"

"Orders?" Josh said. "Who the hell put you in charge?" A degree of animosity had hardened his words.

Anna read his unease. She stepped away from the bank of TV monitors. Took his hand. "Sorry – Josh. It just makes it harder if you're here."

"I don't need my arse wiping. I can look after myself."

"Really?"

"Yeah – really."

Anna raised her eyebrows and her lower lip pouted. "Perhaps you're right. But I didn't mean that exactly."

Josh felt his anger subside a little. "Then what did you mean."

Anna simply squeezed his hand. "Not now. Ask me again later."

She led him towards the hallway. They stopped just within the TV room. The colonial house had fallen suddenly silent.

"What do you think?" Josh asked.

"They could be waiting right outside. On the stairway. Or have bunkered down above our heads."

"So what do we do?" he asked.

"We need some sort of diversion."

Josh looked behind them. "Here – help me with this." He stepped back into the centre of the room. Then pulled one of two chairs away from the bank of screens.

"What have you got in mind?" Anna asked, now at his side.

"You go get him," Josh said, pointing towards the crumpled guard.

"What're you going to do?"

In a parody of Anna's Slavonic tones, Josh said, "Can't you follow simple orders?"

Anna laughed – a quick nervous snort. "Wiseass." She moved over to the body and scooped it up effortlessly.

"What now – boss?" she asked mischievously.

"On the chair," Josh advised.

Anna dropped the body onto the chair unceremoniously. It started to tip forwards, the top-heavy torso pulling it towards the floor. Josh placed his hand on the guy's forehead in an attempt to keep it on the chair.

"That cable – there," he said, drawing Anna's attention to a long extension cord. "Bring it over here."

Anna stood with her hands on her hips for a second in a prissy manner. "Are we doing a reversal of gender roles here, or what?"

Josh wasn't up for playing games. Half of Mexico could be waiting outside for them. "The cable, please."

Anna pursed her lips in a pantomime of childish insubordination.

"The cable," Josh demanded.

"Okay," she said, finally unplugging the cord from the wall. A row of monitors died instantly. She quickly pulled the electrical plugs from the socket end, and then handed it to Josh.

He wrapped the cable around the dead guy's upper body

and the back of the chair before tying it into a tight but crude knot.

"It'll do," he said.

He started to push the combination of the two towards the doorway. The wheels on the chair skittered along rather than rolled. And Josh found himself fighting to keep them on a straight trajectory.

"Christ – it's worse than watching you shop at Walmart," Anna said, watching him struggle. "Here – let me."

She took the back of the chair and pushed it closer to the open door. They gathered at one side. "Okay," Anna began, "what are we going on, three or after?"

"Three will do fine," Josh replied.

"Then what?"

"Then we finish this," he said. "Finish *them*."

Anna nodded. "Okay."

Josh took up position behind her. A clunk click of noise sounded.

Anna turned to find that Josh had retrieved the guard's fallen weapon.

"Josh – no," she said.

"We don't have time for this," he replied. "I can handle the ramifications of using this. But not losing you."

Anna almost protested, yet seeing his look of grim determination, she instead nodded in silent acceptance. She turned back to the opening.

"Okay – but try not to shoot me in the ass," she said.

"Will do."

"You don't have a full clip either," she explained. "So make them count."

They paused for the briefest of moments. And then Anna yelled, "Three!"

The guard and chair flew across the hallway, wheels screeching as they half rubbed and half rolled across the marbled floor. The chatter of weapons discharging filled the air. The dead guard bucked. The chair spun violently from side to side, and blood and flesh exploded in a violent spray of red mush.

Anna was outside already – a sudden blur of motion, clearing the lower steps of the stairway. Josh followed. He thrust his arm out, aiming the gun upwards.

The men had gone for the distraction. They were still firing towards the bullet-riddled body of the guard. Josh had time to squeeze off a shot, which missed by a mile. Still, this sudden and unexpected assault forced the shooter to duck his head down.

By which time, Anna had cleared the stairway, and was now within reach of their nearest attacker.

Some unaffected part of Josh's mind – the bit that was now becoming accustomed to this insane alternate reality that he now found himself in—was impressed by Anna's strength and speed.

She kicked out at the guy's weapon and sent it spinning away. His trigger finger went with it, too – torn away by the sheer force of her attack.

A second shooter appeared from behind the wooden baluster. The leader popped his head up from safety and then took aim. A fierce-looking handgun exploded with gunfire. Wood disintegrated all around Anna. A hail of splinters sliced away at her skin. She hit out blindly. Her hand connecting with something solid. The younger Mexican's head rocked back from the blow.

Josh was now midway up the stairway. He trained his weapon towards the leader and started firing indiscriminately. He wasn't trying to find his target, not a hope in hell of that, but he was successful in holding off another attack.

He reached Anna to find her hunkered down, blood blurring her vision. A few of the wooden splinters had embedded themselves into the skin of her brow. Blood seeped out, running into her eye, then down her cheek like red teardrops.

Josh ducked down next to her. The young guard from the balcony lay on his side with his head snapped back grotesquely. His eyes were staring up emptily at the ceiling above. Josh felt a moment of regret for the kid. Then a barrage of bullets exploded about them, which ripped any sentiment away, now leaving Josh with only thoughts of grim determination. He was ready now to do whatever it took to end this.

And end it forever.

Chapter Eight

Fairbanks - Alaska

What was left of Jonny Tarver was heading towards the morgue. Even though it was clear to everyone, heart ripped out and all, that he was dead, procedure had dictated that a medical examiner had been required to first examine the body to conclude that they were indeed dealing with the deceased.

A cold sweat had broken out over Agent Fernandez's skin while he had waited for the M.E. to do her job. He kept looking into the stall expecting the body to suddenly spring to life, catapulting itself upwards on unsteady legs, before leering towards them with bloody hands. Mercifully, the body had remained just that. A body. Finally, after what seemed like an age to the agent, the body was removed and loaded into a coroner's wagon.

Outside, the bar had become a hub of activity. Uniformed officers were currently collecting witness statements in subzero temperatures, the Crime Scene Unit were in the early stages of processing the bloody washroom. The bar manager—his face ashen—was leading one of Chief Zager's men through the basement, checking for any unexpected escape routes. Both had returned to Zager's side, reporting that neither the loading dock nor basement entrance had been compromised.

Zager had returned to the washroom. He'd checked the

security of the windows there, to find them sealed shut; decades of paint, layer after layer, had been applied over the years, amalgamating the window and frame, and nothing short of a stick of TNT was likely to open them.

Which told Chief Zager just one thing.

That the killer had left via the front of the bar, along with the rest of the patrons.

"What do you think?" Agent Fernandez asked, leaning into Zager's ear.

The two lawmen were huddled together on the outside of the police cordon. The patrons from inside had been herded inside the makeshift pen, bar staff included, and a small group of officers were conducting initial identity checks.

Zager and Fernandez were currently scanning over the small crowd, looking for any signs of duress. It was their hope that the killer, if still contained here, would panic and bolt for freedom. A group of Zager's men had been strategically placed throughout Fairbanks, ready to give chase if necessary.

In truth the people all looked uncomfortable. All ready to run for freedom, the cold driving them away. Icy winds cutting into exposed flesh.

The large figure of Kavik Tonrar loomed over the crowd, his head and shoulders raised above the general populace. He was stomping his feet and wrapping his arms around himself in an attempt to keep warm. The large Native Alaskan Indian caught sight of the two lawmen stood just outside the perimeter. He headed towards them, his hefty and threatening size forcing the crowd around him to move out of his way.

He stopped a few feet from the lawmen, yet remained on his side of the cordon.

"Hell of a mess," he said, with a backwards nod.

Chief Zager nodded. "You okay?"

Fernandez looked on intently, understanding that someone of Tonrar's size could, theoretically at least, be capable of the horrors to be found inside.

Tonrar kicked his foot at nothing in particular. "Fine," he

said. "Better than Jonny, anyway." The Alaskan didn't look fine. His face looked sunken, eyes dark and hollow, and incapable of maintaining eye contact for any real length of time. Perhaps finding his friend in such a state had shocked him to the core. A deeper presence was haunting the guy, plaguing him, and seemingly draining him of his living spirit.

Zager slipped effortlessly under the cordon. He placed one of his hands on the Indian's big shoulder.

"We have counsellors at hand, if you need to speak to someone," he said.

Tonrar looked away embarrassed. "Don't need no counselling, Chief."

"Can't have been easy—finding Jonny like that," Zager suggested.

Again Tonrar looked away, his frosted breath trailing away from his lips as he released a weary sigh. "Guess not."

"Sir, you were the first on the scene?" asked the agent, eager to interview this witness himself.

"Scene?" Tonrar echoed, his eyes now finally focusing directly onto the agent. "Wouldn't have called it a scene myself. Bloodbath is more in tune with what happened."

"And what did happen?" Fernandez pushed.

Another trail of breath pursed from the Indian's lips. "Hell if I know. One minute I was sharing a beer with Jonny, the next, he winds up dead. Heart gone. Simple and as fast as that."

"And you didn't see anything?" asked the agent.

"Like what?"

"Like, someone following him into the restroom. Did he have any enemies? A beef with a local, perhaps?"

Tonrar laughed, humourlessly. "Jonny had a beef with everyone. With the world. Doesn't mean he deserved—*that*."

Fernandez asked, "You see any newcomers in town? Or anyone out of place?"

"Apart from you, you mean?" Tonrar said, focusing once again onto the agent. "No—nothing, nobody new."

Fernandez looked beyond the large guy, scanning the

remaining crowd. Most were huddled together, in groups of two or three. The uniformed cops were slowly working their way through the gathering, taking each individual away from their respective groups, to question them alone. Fernandez had to admit it, there didn't appear to be anyone that stood out. No solitary creature looking anxious or ready to make his or her escape. Not one person stood alone; no one showed a key mannerism that would indicate a sense of not being part of the larger collective. Out of place.

In fact, Agent Fernandez realised, everyone looked relatively at ease with each other, considering the horrific event, and freezing conditions, that bound them here.

The agent was just about to turn his attention away from the gathering, when a small figure appeared suddenly from behind a young couple.

The child looked over at the three men. A hat was pulled down tight over the girl's head, pink stripes and a white bobble, and deer hunter flaps covered her ears. She was wrapped up in a small duffel coat, shiny black buttons gleaming like liquid shadows, and a pair of bright yellow boots reached to the point of her knees.

She was holding a teddy bear in one hand, and stroking its head with the other. Black gloves covered her hands.

A pair of uniformed cops moved over to the couple. One cop led the male adult a few paces away, and the other took the mother in the opposite direction. The kid stood alone, no sudden fear of being left **unattended**.

Fernandez was just about to call to one of the cops; his intentions to get either the mother or father to take the child in hand, when, unexpectedly the child threw the teddy bear onto the ground. It landed with a wet flop. The agent frowned. The child hadn't done that by accident. It had been an aggressive gesture. And it was meant for the agent to see.

The child took a step closer and used her boot to kick the toy a few feet closer. Somewhere along its lining the stitches must have split, because a slight trail of stuffing trailed out behind it.

Fernandez felt himself shiver. The kid's actions weren't making any sense. And the parents didn't seem to either notice or care.

The agent ducked under the police tape, and then took a few steps closer. A sudden chill took over. The kid was looking directly at Fernandez, her eyes full of intent, challenging almost, as if daring the agent to take another step. Just one more.

He did just that.

The night seemed to darken then, blacker than imaginable, as shadows swelled out like running tar to cover everything it touched.

The next step took the agent within a few feet of the discarded toy. The agent's veins turned icy cold. The object on the floor was not a stuffed toy. Stuffing had not fallen from burst seams.

Open-mouthed, the agent looked back towards the girl. Her small arms were at her sides, her hands not covered by gloves, but by a layer of thick, congealing blood. Almost unable to believe the ramifications of what he was seeing, Fernandez returned his gaze to the object before him.

What actually lay before Special Agent Fernandez was the torn and bloodied heart of a human being.

Chapter Nine

Chamela - West Mexico

The quiet before the storm. A well used analogy. Its meaning: a period of relative calm before an act of destruction. Josh found himself more correctly in the eye of the storm. The initial barrage had finished. The sounds of discharging weapons echoed loudly.

Anna was reloading her weapon, one taken from the dead guard, who now lay broken and splayed out before them.

Across the hallway their attacker was also out of ammo. Josh chanced a look over the splintered baluster. The large guy from the balcony was hunkered down, hands busy reloading a fresh clip. The weapon in Josh's hand was spent too. He hadn't hit a thing, having emptied the entire clip into the wall or ceiling.

Josh heard Anna chamber a round into her pistol.

"I'm going to draw his attention," he announced.

Anna said, "Like hell you are."

Josh slipped behind the cover of the baluster. "How many bullets have you got left?"

"Enough," Anna replied shortly.

"We need to finish this now," he said.

"Josh – where is he going to go? We have him right where we want him."

Not convinced of this fact, Josh gave her a short shake of his head. "No—he'll have back up soon enough. We'll be the ones cornered."

Anna frowned. "We took care of the guards. Who's left?"

"The cops," Josh stated.

"What cops?"

"All of them," he replied. "You think they're blind to what's been going on in here? They must know."

Anna's mouth opened, an argument ready to form, but nothing came forth. Josh was right. The police in this town would most likely be involved, if not directly, then at least to a point where they turned a blind eye. But not when bullets were flying and bodies dropping. Even a corrupt police force had to maintain the pretence of control.

Understanding that the fight could easily escalate into a full-on war with the authorities, Anna nodded solemnly, knowing that this battle of theirs had to end now.

"Okay, what do you suggest?" she asked.

Josh gave her a fleeting look of bravado. "I draw his fire. You shoot him. Simple plan."

"That's it?" Anna said. "Really?"

"What else do you suggest? We ask him to give himself up."

A barrage of bullets tore wood and debris all around them. Seemed the guy was not about to do just that.

Pinned down, they huddled against each other until the hail of red-hot lead faltered.

"Okay, Josh, lets see what you've got," Anna said.

Josh nodded. He crawled away from the cover of the baluster, bringing himself up to the dead guard's body. Gripping onto the guy's shirt, he pulled the dead weight back towards Anna.

Anna laughed—a brief exhalation of fear and bitter amusement.

"You going to dress up in a disguise?" she asked.

Josh looked back blankly. "What?"

"You think he'll fall for that. You as one of his men?"

Josh just shook his head in dismay. "Hardly."

One year ago, Josh would not have been considered as

physically strong. Not by any stretch of the imagination. Tall and ropey, with defined muscles and athletic build, yes, but hardy possessing the natural strength or bulk that some men are born with. Nor did he have a streetwise toughness, or mean edge to his persona, or any general level of hostility.

Yet, now a federal fugitive for twelve months, Josh had hardened to a level that went beyond his natural expectations. His shoulders had broadened, biceps that were once mere knots on string had swelled into large lumps of muscle, his face had lost its boyish adolescence – it now had hard angles and lived in. Handsome he was, without doubt, but ruggedly so now.

And it was this recent change in fortitude that allowed Josh to manhandle the guard's corpse into a sitting position, thrust his arms around the cadaver, and then climb to a standing position. Hauling the limp body to its feet, Josh stood, taking cover from behind his shield of skin and bone.

Bullets tore into flesh as chunks of gore exploded in a bloody mess. Holding on tightly, Josh took a step away from Anna, drawing more bullets towards him. One hit the guard just below the elbow, and the power of the projectile almost tore the lower arm free.

Like two haplessly uncoordinated dancers, both Josh and the corpse shuffled and stumbled forwards, taking bullets and wooden splinters as they went.

A bullet ripped into the body's head, its skull bursting open with a sickening crack. The stench of blood filled Josh's nostrils. He hunkered behind the cadaver finding safety behind the greater mass of its torso.

Just when he thought the shooter was about to finally find his mark, substituting dead flesh for the living, Josh heard a shot ring out from over his shoulder, coming from Anna's direction.

The ruse worked.

The shooter took his eyes off Anna long enough for her to take careful aim. A cry – guttural and agonising – sounded as a bullet ripped into the guy's shoulder.

He staggered back, almost dropping to his knees, as the pain of torn skin and shattered bones burst into his brain. A survival instinct took over all rational thought. He swapped targets in a heartbeat. Pulling hard on the trigger. Firing a short barrage towards Anna.

She ducked instinctively, allowing the guy to stumble out of harm's way, as he slipped awkwardly through one of the connecting doorways.

A deafening silence prevailed.

Josh held his breath for a moment before allowing the bullet-riddled body to slip to the floor. The corpse slumped into a macabre sitting position, its arms and legs twisted in broken angles.

Anna was at his side within moments.

"You okay?" she asked.

"Fine," Josh replied. His teeth chattered slightly, his body dumping high levels of adrenaline throughout his veins.

"I think I hit him," Anna said.

She took a step away from Josh and moved towards the opposite side of the landing.

Josh followed closely behind.

"Wait," he said, as they drew closer to the doorway. "What if he's simply waiting on the other side?"

Anna stopped. Her gun pointed straight out before them. "I'm out of ideas, Josh. Our friend's time is about to end." She stepped through the threshold.

Josh almost cried out for her to wait, expecting a weapon to appear and fire at point-blank range. The expectant boom of gunfire never came. Anna simply and silently disappeared into the room. A second later, Josh joined her, leaving the dead behind him.

What hit him on the other side was somewhat unexpected. A photographer's studio. Lightening pods set up in specific locations to capture, in finest detail, the centre of the room. The conditioned part of Josh's mind wanted to see a green screen, or something similar, a neutral background for a subject to stand before, but the reality, the obvious requirement needed for such an operation, sat unceremoniously before them, simple and crude, and robbed any hope that the horrors of this place were possibly misconceived.

A squat bed with rumpled sheets lay in the centre of the room. The burning bulbs of the lights illuminated the figure splayed out across the glistening bed sheets. Here he had fallen, the leader of this operation, the man responsible for countless lives ruined, pale and fearful, an arm raised in a merciful plea. Blood was leaking into the sheets, turning instantly black, as it spread out like the blossoming, yet malignant petals of a flower.

The sick irony of where this guy had fallen struck Josh in the pit of his stomach.

Here, in this exact place, was where this town had lost its humanity. A place that had robbed the townsfolk of the rightful privilege to life, and had stolen the innocence of those who had been forced to come here.

Josh widened his vision, to look beyond the centre of the room. A group of tripods set up a perimeter around the bed. Perched on top were high-definition cameras, some that looked like simple digital ones, ones that any ordinary family may have stored somewhere in a drawer at home, others looked to be more high-end, with telescopic zoom lenses, which peered towards the bed with black, empty eyes.

Beyond the camera arrangement a bank of laptops and desktop computers sat in a neat row along the back wall. Some of the screens were illuminated with streaming videos. Josh caught a glimpse of one, and was instantly forced to turn away; the images captured there an awful collection of pain and suffering.

A rage like no other built within Josh. He felt his vision mist, and the veins in his neck began to throb heavily with each passing heartbeat. Another moment of awful imagery, which in reality lasted no more than a mere second, filled Josh's mind with pictures of people that were beyond reason. The look of pleasure that some portrayed sent a deep agonising pain into his soul.

Anna sensed Josh's loathing. His anger. His wish to put what they had discovered here right. To end it now. Burn this dreadful place to the ground. And all those in it. Then scatter the ashes to the four corners of the world.

The handgun weighed heavily in her hand. She looked at it for a second. Tried to work out how many bullets remained.

At least one.

One would be enough.

Something shifted inside of Anna. She turned to Josh to find his resolution clear. His eyes looked close to tears. His fists clenched tightly. He was using all of his will to focus on the pathetic subject on the bed, and keep his eyes away from the streaming images that occupied the rear of the room.

Anger flared throughout Anna's soul. She had used every ounce of her fibre these last twelve months to keep Josh safe. Nurtured his innocence, and fought hard to stop their recent past events from robbing him of his treasured purity. But now, here he was, witnessing first hand the horrors that man was capable of.

A feeling inside of Anna snapped then, deep within her being. It was instinctive and so primeval she could not even articulate it into a rational or civilised thought. What she did understand was that she needed to allow Josh to end this. Allow him this act that, although brutal in itself, would help purge him of the horrors to be found here.

"Josh," she said gently.

He turned to her, his eyes filled with pain.

"Take this," she said, holding the gun out to him.

Josh dropped his gaze. Locked onto the gun, and what significance Anna's proffer meant. He nodded simply, and took the weapon in his own hand. He didn't feel repulsed by the slickness of the grip. Or the heat that radiated from it. Nor by the very nature of what this implement was designed to do. Instead he took comfort in it. Held onto it tightly. Felt it was able to deliver the wrath that his soul so desperately needed to assert.

Josh stepped closer to the bed. The man laid out on top was speaking in quick tones, begging for mercy in one breath, then instantly swapping tack, and admonishing them for daring to challenge him. He was above and beyond reproach.

Josh tuned out the guy's insistent ramblings. Instead, he took one final quick, fleeting look at the images running across the monitor screens. The pictures would haunt him for the rest of his days. He locked eyes with the guy on the bed. They were filled with anger. Incensed hatred. Not a hint of remorse or a show of penitents revealed itself, even now, so close to the end.

Josh levelled his gun at head height, focused on what had to be done, and then without forgiveness, he fired at point-blank range.

Chapter Ten

West Mexico

The town of Chamela had been left behind in what seemed like one, continuous, never-ending strip of darkness. No floodlights illuminated the way, cats eyes did not warn the driver that they were in the correct lane, dark mountains loomed on either side and, where they met, they created a natural basin that was flooded with deep, near impenetrable shadows.

Anna had the Jeep's headlights turned to full beam. Even 400Watts of power struggled to cut through the night, barely burning a channel narrow enough for Anna to guide the vehicle to safety.

Laughter came from the rear of the Jeep – bright and innocent, and in stark contrast to the oppressiveness that surrounded them. Anna took a moment to look through the rear view mirror.

Josh was sitting in the rear. A small child flanked him on either side. They were both boys, dark skinned with eyes almost as dark as the night itself, and hair that looked as if it had been coloured by charcoal.

The three of them were playing a game of snap with a pack of picture cards. Each had a handful of cards, and was taking turns to place them on a pile in the central armrest just behind Anna.

Josh was acting the fool. He was snapping his hand at any given opportunity, trying to match anything, yet only gaining more and more cards, allowing the two young boys to get the better of him.

He was doing an admirable job at keeping them entertained, considering they did not speak – *snap* not included – a word of English.

At Anna's side there sat a young girl – her skin ghostly white in contrast to the two boys. She had bright blue eyes, blond hair and a small peppering of freckles across her button-like nose. A remarkably pretty girl. And totally out of place from where she had been rescued from.

For these three children, none older than their tenth birthday, had been the well-guarded, and well expected, cargo from the small boat that had beached on the dark shores of Chamela. This is what the town had taken such lengths to hide, the trafficking and illegal exposure of children.

The little girl had only spoken once, to tell Anna her name – Isabelle – and had then simply shut down, her eyes seemingly focusing on the distant horizon. Anna had tried to coax her out of her mute silence, but had not, as yet, been able to draw the girl back to the living. Josh had maintained a distance from her, instinctively knowing that the child would be twice as wary towards men as she was to a woman.

The girl was now finally snoozing. Her head was slumped towards the side window, and her hands clasped together in her lap.

The game of snap was drawing to an end. Both boys had become suddenly tired, small mouths opening in enormous yawns. Josh gathered the cards together and then carefully placed them into the pack. The two boys saw this as a signal that it was time for sleep. In an almost synchronised fashion, they huddled closer to Josh, and fell instantly asleep.

Josh sat there in awkward silence for a moment, not wanting to even twitch, and wake either of the two.

"You okay?" Anna asked quietly.

Josh looked up. Made eye contact through the rear view mirror. Anna's eyes looked full of concern.

"I'm fine, thanks."

Anna nodded. "You'd tell me if you weren't – right?"

"Right," Josh echoed briefly.

A few moments of silence passed before Anna spoke again.

"You did the right thing. Back there. In that room," she said.

Josh nodded absent-mindedly.

"Hey," Anna said, drawing his eyes back to the mirror. "I meant it. That was brave of you. The whole thing. A lot of people wouldn't have done what you did."

Josh looked quickly from one small face to the next. *Of course they would* – he was about to say, but of course it was *men* that had done this to them in the first place.

"What else would we have done – reported them to the authorities?" It was a bitter statement laced together with sarcasm.

"I guess not," replied Anna, understanding that the authorities must have been aware of what was happening up at the colonial house. "I still want to thank you for what you did. Not easy. Any of this."

Anna paused, returning her attention to the dark road ahead. She waited a few moments in the hope that Josh would open up about those final events at the house.

"Where do you think a person like that comes from?" he asked finally.

Anna checked on her small passenger first. Making sure the girl was still asleep at her side. A gentle wheezing was coming from her chest. The girl's eyes were rolling slightly underneath the lids. Anna hoped the kid was having a dream, and not running from the stuff of nightmares.

Anna almost reached out to wake the girl, to save her from the dark horrors of her mind, but, in the next second, she fell silent, now finally slipping into a deep, dreamless state of sleep.

"Truth be told – Josh, I don't know where someone like that comes from."

Over the last twelve months Josh had learned to trust in Anna's amazing ability to tap into the human psyche, and somehow determine, without question, if the individual was inherently good or bad. A saint or a sinner, if you like.

"So you think he was a bad man? Nothing more than that?"

"You mean hu*man*? Like you?"

"Yes."

"Absolutely not. No. Don't ever think that again. He was broken. Sick. A man of no conscience."

"Explain that to me," he asked.

Anna continued. "The human mind is a very complex thing. The most amazing machine. I guess it's inevitable that such a machine will break down from time to time."

"And that's what you think happened back there – in Chamela, people just simply broke down?" asked Josh.

Anna shook her head vigorously. "Not quite I'm afraid. Most probably thought nothing of it. Too busy leading their own lives. Blind to the facts, hiding behind an ignorance that suited them. I don't believe the entire town was a festering place, full of malice."

"No?"

"No," Anna replied. "People get scared, fearful of those that hold on to all the power. Most townsfolk were probably too frightened to speak out."

"It doesn't make it right though," Josh added. "They could have done something. Anything."

"True," Anna agreed.

"Still, there's no need now. We took care of things. *You* took care of things," she added.

Josh looked down, unable to hide his unease.

"Josh, what you did, to that man, it was the right thing to do. You know that—right?"

Josh puffed out his cheeks, a sudden near-exhaustion overwhelming him.

This had been the first life he had taken.

This last year had offered ample opportunity for Josh to be

put into such a situation, to take a life, caught or cornered, forcing him and Anna to fight their way out, yet providence had always found another, less destructive way for them to find safety. But this was different. They hadn't been fighting for themselves. No, they had been the protectors. And it was this thought that strengthened his resolve. What he had done was more a way of cleansing the human spirit, his spirit, and had not come close to the actions of a murderer.

Still, the thought of blood on his hands sickened him. He felt unexpectedly alone all of a sudden.

Anna felt his unease. "Hey—I love you; you know that more than anything."

Josh caught her gaze in reflection. "Yes, I know that."

"Let it go—those feelings of doubt. You still have a good heart and soul, never forget that."

She lowered her tone to barely a whisper. "What he'd have done to these children, what he'd already done, didn't warrant such a merciful death. He should have suffered. I would have made sure of that. You at least saved him of that indignity."

The Jeep came to a crossroads as the valley levelled out to reveal an open expanse of wasteland. Anna brought them to a gentle stop. All three kids were still asleep. The engine idled quietly underneath the hood.

"Which way?" asked Josh from the rear, thankful for a required change in conversation.

Anna scanned first one way then the next. "I think it's time we headed north."

"North?"

"Yeah—time for a change of scenery. I've had enough of this place. Long days. And short nights."

Anna turned the steering wheel to join the connecting highway. No headlights or tail-lights could be seen for miles around. Seemed like they had the night all to themselves.

"What's our plan?" Josh asked. A small digital clock flashed in darkest red on the dashboard. "We have about three more hours before daylight. Not going to get very far."

"Far enough," Anna replied, adding pressure to the gas pedal.

The Jeep lurched forward as it gained speed. They had the highway to themselves, no point in not utilising such a fact. The Jeep continued onwards, twin headlights cutting through the darkness, its precious cargo ready now to be delivered into the light.

Chapter Eleven

Fairbanks - Alaska

Agent Fernandez was back in his office. He was using every ounce of his willpower to focus on the simple task of bringing the mug of coffee to his lips. The dark liquid inside sloshed about, before overflowing as it ran down the sides in a thick drool. To Fernandez it looked similar to arterial blood. Sickened by his own thoughts, he placed the mug at the corner of his desk.

He took a step away from the desk. Moved over to the office window. It seemed like the night would never end. The sky was still an impenetrable black. The cloud cover over Fairbanks blocked out any hint of stars, making Fernandez think that this town had been cut away from the rest of the world, and left drifting off into a bleak and empty abyss.

The door to his office opened.

Chief Zager's considerable bulk filled the doorway.

"Anything?" asked Fernandez.

Zager shook his head, and his shoulders dropped slightly. "Nothing as yet. No missing persons report. Either here in Fairbanks, or neighbouring towns."

Fernandez wasn't surprised. The next town was what – fifty miles away, separated by subzero temperatures, a wind that felt like it could flay skin, and snow deep enough to bury a man to his waist. It was hardly likely someone would abduct a child and bring them here, to then simply let that child roam free.

Which brought Fernandez to the next problem – why couldn't he actually bring himself to think of the young girl as a child?

What had happened less than two hours ago was still vivid in his mind.

A scream had pierced the night. One of the female witnesses had seen the bloodied and torn heart so hideously cast away.

Fernandez had his weapon drawn by the time the horrified cry had ended. He scanned the crowd, quickly, committing each face, and immediate reaction, to memory.

The woman he had considered to be the child's mother was looking at the severed organ, her face blanched of colour. He expected her to rush towards her child and snatch her up in protective arms. Only the woman remained frozen in place, unable to move.

The agent looked quickly to the other witness, the father, surely he would react and make haste towards the girl. But no, he too stood mute, rigid, either unwilling or unable to move.

In the next second, the child pushed her way through the group before slipping easily underneath the police cordon, and then took to the dark streets.

A moment of confusion struck Fernandez dumb. What the hell was this? Why weren't the child's parents screaming blue murder to get her back? It hit the agent suddenly. Their faces were drawn to the torn heart on the floor, blood still oozing from the torn arteries, and their attention was fixed firmly on the horrors of that. Neither had even glanced towards the child.

A quick examination over the rest of the gathering gave Fernandez his answer. The child did not belong. Not here, and not now, in this small group of witnesses.

In the next instant, the agent was pushing his way through the bystanders, clearing a path of bodies as he took off in pursuit of the mysterious child.

A moment of realisation almost made him stop in his tracks.

The night, and the fear it instilled, lay just beyond the safety of the police barrier. He felt a cold sweat blossom on his skin. The frozen air around him almost froze him solid. Dark buildings appeared to contract, the agent's vision distorting his immediate surroundings, and the warped images threatened to trap him in a stone cocoon. Using every fibre of his being the agent forced his fear of the dark away, focusing instead on the slight, dwindling figure of the girl. She was heading deeper into town.

With his resolve restored, Fernandez ducked under the cordon and gave chase.

The kid was fast – perhaps she had an intimate understanding of her immediate surroundings, Fernandez thought – as she quickly disappeared from view. A couple of tall buildings, separated by a narrow alleyway, offered her an instant getaway.

"Hey—kid!" Fernandez yelled.

He was initially concerned for her safety. The night was not known for its kindness in this remote part of the world. Freezing temperatures, wild, indigenous animals, and all the usual hazards that the night held, made it a dangerous place for anyone, let alone that of a small child.

The agent reached the dark entrance. An impenetrable blackness stretched out before him. For a few seconds, Fernandez felt unsteady on his feet. His vision swam out of focus, and a sudden buzzing noise filled his ears. He shook his head, clearing away the phantoms of fear. He managed to get one foot in front of the other. His first step felt weighed down as if he were wearing lead boots.

His next step felt that little bit easier. He entered the alleyway. The lights from the connecting streets offered some illumination, which bathed this end, and the opposite end of the narrow passageway, in a yellow murky luminescence. Where the tendrils of light failed to reach, a deep and impenetrable gloom was left.

Steeling his resolve, the agent took another step. His feet kicked up a light smattering of snow, and the soft soles of his shoes slipped slightly on the ice found underneath. He chided himself silently for not being more suitably prepared for the harsh conditions.

"Hey—kid," he called again.

What was wrong with this child, thought the agent. Why would anyone – a child in particular – enter such a dark and intimidating place? Hadn't she heard of the Bogeyman? What kid hadn't for Christ sakes?

The agent shivered; an expulsion of fear, coming from the centre of his being, and nothing whatsoever to do with the ice-cold air. As ridiculous as it seemed, maybe it was what hid in the dark, and not the dark itself, that had recently started to plague the agent's mind. There was something buried inside his memory. That wanted to surface. Needed to be seen. Yet, was lurking in the darkest recesses of his mind, and refusing to be drawn into the full light of his consciousness.

A face flashed before his eyes then, twisted and hideous. A visage that could only have been formed by the very imagination of hell. Teeth, elongated and sharpened to points, parted impossibly wide, as the macabre jaws threatened to close around the agent's throat.

He cried out, inadvertently stepping backwards, his foot slipped and he tumbled to the ground. The air in his lungs exploded in a wheeze of breath.

When he finally gathered his senses he found himself splayed out on the ground, his clothes sodden from the snow and ice, with his arm raised out before him in a protective gesture.

Nothing was coming at him with fangs snapping together. No horrors had been conjured out of the night ready to besiege him. The alleyway was empty.

Fernandez climbed to his feet. Then peered into the gloom for a long time. Nothing. No movement. No sound. He stepped away from the entrance, the streetlights bathing him in a murky glow.

He realised then that what he'd just witnessed was a burst of memory – flashing to life, having finally broken free from the agent's mind. What he had just seen was from twelve months ago on that fateful night in Glenwood Springs. It had been the woman coming out at him from his darkest memory, her face twisted and hideous.

This sudden realisation made the agent understand that the events happening here and the ones almost a year ago were somehow related. These bizarre deaths, and those that had led to his pursuit of the woman – Anna Privalova, were inexplicably connected.

And if he had any chance of stopping these murders in Fairbanks, then he needed to first understand what had happened to him so many nights ago.

Only one man could help the agent.

Someone else who had witnessed those strange happenings in Colorado, someone who had flatly refused to disclose anything about the woman, or the aftermath of those events.

The problem was that three thousand miles separated the agent from the one person he needed help from.

No matter. The agent would get answers. He would walk those miles if it granted him an understanding. He would put an end to these killings. And in doing so, vanquish the demons of the past.

Agent Fernandez had made his way hastily back towards the precinct. Eager now to make a call. Hopeful that the man he needed to speak to would be there to answer it.

Now safely back inside his office, the agent pulled his cell free from his jacket. He took a moment to scroll through the list of contacts. Quickly finding the one he needed. Punching DIAL he waited for the connection to be made. An unfamiliar voice answered.

The agent held a brief conversation with the speaker on the other end. By the time he'd hung up, his heart rate had climbed steadily. The man he needed, desperately needed, was not there, nor would he be.

Maybe never.

Chapter Twelve

Chicago - Illinois

Being dead isn't a nice feeling, Harry Balooga would tell you. That is, if you were dead too.

No bright lights had materialised before him at his moment of death. Spectral figures, with open arms, had not gathered him up in loving embrace to carry him into the afterlife. Nor had his life flashed before his eyes, capturing key-moments of his existence in movie-like slow-motion, before slipping quietly and serenely into the Great Beyond.

Nothing of the sort, really.

Harry Balooga had been ripped from the living world with all the finesse of a high-speed pile-up. The wail of a banshee had split the night's silence, loud enough to tear open the fabric of the universe, or so it seemed.

The ambulance, with Balooga's convulsing body strapped tightly to the gurney, and paramedics working to clear airways and maintain blood circulation, had torn through the early evening traffic, scattering vehicles in its wake. A torrent of rain, which had dropped from the heavens to cover Chicago in a distorted and dismal blanket, forced the ambulance to slow intermittently, throwing a blood-red mist behind it as brake lights burnt suddenly.

Inside, the paramedics were desperately trying to restart

Balooga's heart. Not an easy task, considering the amount of damage the patient had self-inflicted on this major organ.

Twenty years of stress and overindulgence had pushed Balooga's blood pressure and cholesterol count towards the realms of the superhuman. Two decades of policing had played their part also.

Detective Harry Balooga had not lived a life of halves.

Chief of Homicide, he had partaken in his fair share of sleepless nights, bad dietary habits, pressure, and general misuse and abuse of anything that remotely qualified as the physical. A big man in size, who had seemingly gained an extra pound of weight for each and every investigation solved, or an additional two pounds for those cases that were not.

This constant barrage of stressful living had eventually taken its toll. Balooga had collapsed at home, clutching at his chest, struggling to draw breath. Horror had moulded his facial features into a ghastly mask. Fear had been present too, the mortality of his own being instantly understood, but it was not the thought of an imminent death that pushed knives of terror into the detective's chest, but rather, the knowledge of what lay beyond this mortal realm.

Because Harry Balooga had seen, with his own eyes, what insane and fantastic horrors the afterlife had to offer.

He too had witnessed the spectacular events on that fateful night in Glenwood Springs. A night when the very fabric of his known universe had been torn open, spilling forth an alternate vision of what could come, if or when his final heartbeat was nothing more than a distant echo.

The ambulance came to a stop. The rear doors opened. And the gurney was rushed towards awaiting doctors. Rain caught Balooga's exposed face, and formed tiny pools of water, before slipping down his cheeks in rivulets of tears.

***

This had all happened six weeks ago.

Now, the detective sat upright in bed, his hospital room quiet. The chair at the bedside unoccupied. Similarly, the small wardrobe that had housed his meagre clothing stood empty.

Balooga looked out of the room's window. Sighed once. Then taking a deep breath, he slipped his legs over the edge of the bed, pushing his bare feet into a pair of hospital issued slippers. His heels hung over the backs by an inch, which forced Balooga to shuffle around, rather than walk, giving him the archetypal gait of a sick patient. The overzealous staff had point-blank refused to allow him to wear his own threadbare slippers, for fear of him tripping over his feet and suing for malpractice at the forefront of their minds no doubt.

Standing upright, Balooga caught his reflection in the window, the dark beyond giving the glass a mirror-like effect.

His usually round face looked somewhat deflated. Once meaty jowls had sagged into Basset Hound chops. His usually shaven head bristled with wispy grey hair. He smiled in an attempt to pull the skin around his face tighter. A demented-looking hobo looked back at him.

"Fuck it," he said, gathering up his small pile of belongings.

He pushed his meagre amount of clothing into a carryall. Pulled the drawstrings tight. A familiar face appeared at the open doorway.

Detective Sanchez, Balooga's partner for the last 2 years, stopped with a squeak, finishing parked halfway inside the hospital room.

"Chief—your chariot awaits," he announced, his face bright and mischievous, his hands firmly wrapped around the push handles of a wheelchair.

Almost a head shorter than the larger patient, Sanchez looked back with a wry smile on his dark, Hispanic face. He was dressed in a rumpled suit, shoes that had seen many miles, most of which had been accumulated while canvassing local neighbourhoods during the initial phase of an investigation, and a loosely knotted tie.

All things considered, Sanchez looked like he'd jumped right out of the pages of *Cop Monthly*.

Balooga glanced at the chair with disdain. "I ain't sitting in *that* thing."

Expecting exactly this, Sanchez laughed openly. "It's hospital policy. You gotta sit your ass down in this or they'll not let you out of this room."

"They can shoot me. I'm walking out of here," Balooga said.

Sanchez pushed the chair further into the room, blocking off the detective's immediate escape. "Maybe we should rethink that," Sanchez advised, flipping his eyes sideways, towards the general direction of the nursing station, towards the individual that his superior had come to loathe.

Nurse Edmondson.

Balooga shivered involuntarily. Over the last six weeks, Nurse Edmondson had become his mortal nemesis.

Head of his rehabilitation programme, Nurse Edmondson had conducted business with the same conviction as a drill instructor. Initially she had berated the detective for his lack of self-aware health choices; too much self-indulgence, in diet, managing stress levels, lack of exercise, poor sleeping habits: typical cop's life, in simple terms.

A cocktail of medicines had followed next, with the primary task of getting the detective's sky-high blood pressure back under control. A daily dose of Angiotensin-converting enzyme (ACE) inhibitors had been administered to help lower his blood pressure. Balooga had taken these 'unpronounceable' pills, wondering what the hell had happened to simple good old-fashioned beta-blockers, with feelings of disdain. Only hours after taking these little blue pills, the detective was rendered immobile by an acute bout of nausea and tiredness, forcing him to sit it out, whilst trapped in this hospital room, unfocused eyes washing blearily over the small TV screen fixed to the wall at the foot of his bed.

Almost six weeks of daytime television had reduced the usually active detective into a lobotomised wreck.

The midday hours were now spent with the unemployed,

unfaithful, those of unknown paternal status, and every unstable American that the country had to offer. Balooga felt by the end of his first two weeks of hospitalisation that he knew every DNA paternity and lie-detector test there was to know.

His saviour from this daily torture had come in the form of exercise. Something the detective was not altogether familiar with. Just a small routine to begin with. A few ambling steps out of bed, slippered feet shuffling inch by inch along the hospital corridor. Once this small measure had been achieved, Balooga had been assigned his own personal physiotherapist—Caesar.

Caesar, or so he presented himself, was a small nervous bundle of energy. Full of bright smiles and enthusiasm, the physiotherapist had arrived promptly on a daily basis, eager to put the recovering detective through his paces.

Balooga had grown to hate his 2 o'clock appointments with Caesar, to the point where he'd pushed himself beyond his limits, if only to see the back of this irksome individual. The insistent hand clapping, words of encouragement, or over-exaggerated congratulations, for doing nothing more remarkable than putting his slippers on, had almost driven the detective towards justifiable homicide.

A meagre two flights of stairs had been Balooga's escape. Once he'd successfully ascended these, he would be deemed fit and well enough to leave hospital. Balooga had confronted this challenge with gusto. Not wanting to remain either in hospital, or worse, in the company of Caesar, he had quickly summoned his will and climbed the two-dozen or so steps with the same eagerness as that of a rising spirit, climbing towards opening heavenly gates.

Now, Balooga had to just tackle his departure from the hospital, and he would be home free.

Detective Sanchez pushed the wheelchair further into the room, forcing Balooga to take a lumbering step backwards.

"Come on Chief," Sanchez said, gesturing towards the chair. "We can be out of here in no time at all."

The large detective gave a weary sigh. "Okay, okay." He

threw the carryall over his shoulder and then unceremoniously dropped his ample weight into the chair.

The padded seat squealed momentarily in protest to this sudden burden. And the momentum created almost drove the chair back into the Hispanic detective's legs.

"Let's roll," Balooga ordered, without a hint of mirth. "I've had enough of this place for the rest of my life."

"Roger that, Chief," Sanchez said.

The smaller detective back-pedalled while simultaneously pulling the chair and its load into the hospital corridor. From their vantage point both detectives could see the nursing station at the far end of the corridor. Before Sanchez could move them closer, Balooga gripped onto the rubber of the wheels, halting their progress.

"Maybe we should go the other way?" he suggested, not wanting to run into Nurse Edmondson.

"I heard that," quipped Sanchez.

The Hispanic detective took small moon-walking steps backwards until he'd pulled Balooga and the wheelchair into the connecting corridor.

Just a few utility doorways and a service elevator filled in where white sterilised walls could not be found.

Sanchez made a beeline towards the elevator. He brought the chair to a stop, parking it at an angle, and then punched the CALL button. A whir of vibrating cables sounded from beyond the elevator doors. Both detectives watched as the light at the top of the door dropped from the highest floor down to theirs, signalling the booth's arrival. The metallic doors opened on rattling castors.

Sanchez entered backwards, pulling the wheelchair and detective with him. The doors rolled shut again.

From his position, Balooga reached out to press the button to the ground floor. The light behind the button turn milky white.

"Okay," Balooga said, as the booth began its descent, "let's get the hell out of Dodge."

Chapter Thirteen

Chicago – Illinois

Harry Balooga dug his bare feet into threadbare slippers, enjoying the comfy familiarity of them. He sighed with pleasure. Finally freed from the tyranny of Nurse Edmondson and her oppressive rehabilitation regime, Balooga was now alleviated by the intimate surroundings of his home. Ester, his beloved wife, was currently fussing around Detective Sanchez, offering homemade cookies and an extensive choice of exotic teas. Their voices were filtering through from the kitchen.

An exceptional amount of time had been taken up on their inability to agree on the correct preference of biscuit or most fancied hot beverage.

Balooga smiled slightly to himself. The offer of tea and biscuits had been Ester's ruse to draw Sanchez away, her real motive to explain, in no uncertain terms, that her husband was not to be bothered, or burdened, by current events happening within the homicide department.

Work, as she put it, could go and take a high jump.

Balooga felt a moment of sympathy towards the young Hispanic detective. Ester would not grant Sanchez his pardon until this message had been made crystal-clear.

In truth Balooga would have welcomed the chance to be occupied by a homicide case, to help bring about an end to the six weeks of mental inactivity and boredom.

Unfortunately, the sickness certificate that his doctor had issued would guarantee that he remain away from work, and all its troublesome issues, for some time to come.

A notion that made Balooga almost as scared as the thought of a secondary, and quite possibly, fatal heart attack.

Two more months stuck at home would maybe drive Balooga to a case of murder – suicide. He loved Ester with every ounce of his being but regarded the idea of being stuck in-house – together – with the same trepidation as that of being with a death row inmate.

The reappearance of the young detective drew Balooga away from these worrying thoughts.

"Hey – Chief, how's it hanging?" Sanchez asked, carrying with him a cup of tea and handful of plain biscuits.

"So, you finally made your choice?" Balooga responded, nodding towards the light snack.

Sanchez grinned sheepishly. "It was a tough decision. Think I made good in the end."

Balooga just laughed quietly. "She means well. Doesn't want me returning back too early, and taking on a full workload."

Sanchez sat on the sofa facing the large detective. "I got your back, Chief. You take as long as it takes to get fit and well. No worries. We can handle things."

Balooga nodded. It was this very fact that now worried him. These last few years had been difficult for him to begin with. The world was moving too damn fast. The detective was already beginning to feel like a fossil. Old-school policing, and its mentality, was fast becoming obsolete. The kids coming through to the ranks of detective looked like they'd just finished high-school. They all arrived with a dossier an inch-thick full of certificates, with eager and expectant fresh faces, fast-tracked into the rank of detective through education alone.

Balooga was a dinosaur, almost extinct with his old-school attitude and street-wise approach.

Seemed these days the general thought was, if it couldn't

be done on an iPhone or social networking device, then it just couldn't be done.

In his mind, his absence, whether that be through illness or not, was an open invitation for his superiors to let him go and make way for more forward-thinking individuals.

Balooga sighed. "It's going to be one hell of a long summer."

Sanchez brushed off his partner's negativity. "Hey – you'll be swinging nine-irons by the end of week two and wondering why the hell you gave a damn."

"You think?" Balooga asked hopefully.

"I know it. You'll probably hand in your badge and retire to Vegas or somewhere hot. Enjoy the easy life. What do we get for all our troubles anyway, Chief?"

Balooga remained thoughtful for a moment. Truth be told, he'd never really gone into policing for a fat pay cheque or health benefits. He loved the streets. Loved working them. Lived for the rush of solving a crime, and the gratification of putting a violent scum bag away. Balooga was Chicago Police Department through and through. He really did have blue blood running through his veins.

The thought of that being taken away from him prematurely was terrifying. What would he do instead, security at Walmart? God no.

The sudden electronic sound of a phone ringing turned Balooga away from his sour thoughts.

Sanchez reached into his jacket. Read the number on the display. Groaned openly.

"Captain Applegate," he announced, referring to their immediate supervisor. "Gonna have to take this, Chief, see what's a cookin'."

The Hispanic detective stood, patted Balooga with affection, and then headed for the door, duty calling him back to the world of the living.

Balooga sat there in silence for a while. Ester was still in the kitchen, probably aware that her husband needed time alone to come to terms with this unwanted predicament.

Had she known that in less than an hour her husband would receive a phone call, from someone in his recent past, who would yank him brutally from his respite, to thrust him headlong into a nightmare of darkness and mayhem—then she may have called Sanchez back and begged him to put her husband under house arrest.

Chapter Fourteen

Mexico

The shower was more of a drip. Hardly the cascade Josh had hoped for. Longed for after such an arduous road trip. He wasn't all that surprised considering the motel room had cost the equivalent of thirty dollars for the night. The small, worn-out room had two beds, singles, and this, the washroom. No bath. Just toilet and a grimy looking shower stall.

The two towels that hung from the back of the door were already damp with use. Proving chivalry was not dead, Josh had offered to take his shower last, allowing the two Mexican boys, then Anna to go before him. The girl Isabelle had declined the chance to wash herself clean. Josh wasn't at all surprised the girl didn't want to expose herself to such a thing. Not considering what she had already been through whilst in the company of men. He had made a real effort to keep his distance, not coldly so, he tried to offer her a warm smile or word of encouragement when possible, yet allowed Anna to comfort her for the majority of the time.

The two boys were enjoying watching the old TV set, which was tuned into a local Mexican channel. The animated voices of cartoon characters could be clearly heard from beyond the washroom, as they spoke in an over-exaggerated Spanish chatter.

Josh finished his shower by trying to position himself under the steady drip and remove the remaining soap suds. He dried himself as best he could, and then climbed back into his worn clothing. They felt dirty against his freshly scrubbed skin.

He ran his fingers through his damp hair, brushing his fringe backwards, and then exited the washroom.

Anna was sat on the other bed, with the young girl, laughing openly at the vivid pantomime images that played out across the TV screen.

"Better?" she asked.

Josh shot her a quick smile. "It was hardly on par with the spa at the Hilton, but I guess it will do."

"Really," Anna said. "The Hilton? Right. That the kind of place you're used to, Josh Sawyer? All fluffy bath towels and white robes?"

She made a show of looking around the head of the bed, searching around the pillows.

"No Sir, sorry, no little bars of chocolate here," she joked. "Hey Isabelle, you seen any chocolate, or have you secretly scoffed it already?"

Anna's face turned into a picture of scrutiny as she looked at Isabelle's mouth for signs of chocolate smears. "Nope – Isabelle hasn't had it either."

The little girl had barely registered Anna's interest in her. Her eyes stayed fixed to the TV, and her expression remained mute towards the antics of the cartoon.

"Maybe we could pop out and grab us some chocolate and candy?" Josh suggested.

Isabelle just stared ahead.

Anna gave Josh a slightly apologetic look, as if it was her fault that the little girl had not offered up any kind of enthusiasm.

"No worries," Josh added, "we're all probably too beat to go out again anyway."

Anna got up from the bed. She ruffled the girl's blond hair then crossed the small room to stand beside Josh.

"We need to talk," she whispered.

Josh simply nodded. "Where?"

"Outside," she responded.

Josh asked quietly, "What about them?"

Anna took his hand, leading him to the main door. "Kids we're going to grab some fresh air. We'll be right outside by the window."

Now Isabelle finally pulled her attention away from the TV. Her eyes looked panicked.

"Don't worry sweetheart," Anna soothed. "We will stand right at the window so you can see us."

The girl seemed genuinely distressed at the thought of her leaving. Anna crossed to the window and drew the grey – possibly once white, but not for a decade – net curtains to one side. It was a risk. Someone passing by outside could look in and see the children sat there. It was a risk worth taking. Anna and Josh had to think of a way to get the kids to safety. And they needed to discuss it openly without fear of upsetting them unnecessarily.

"See," Anna said, hinting towards the bare window. "You will be able to see us the whole time."

From somewhere deep inside her, Isabelle found the courage to nod in agreement.

"We'll be two minutes – that's all," Josh added.

He opened the door slightly, did his best to scan the immediate surroundings, without alarming the girl, then stepped outside. Anna followed him and then clicked the door gently shut.

They stopped outside the window and looked in. Both waved. Isabelle just looked on. Her small face worried. Josh gave her the thumbs up gesture. Her face was deadpan.

"We have a real problem," Anna said, turning her face sideways so her words were masked.

Josh continued to look inside the motel room.

"Really," he responded. "Why?"

Anna ignored his sarcasm.

"Josh, what are we going to do? We can't take them with us."

"Take them where, Anna? We have no idea where *we're*

headed."

"Fair point. But we need to keep moving, as always. We can't guarantee their safety. They need to go home – be with their families."

"Agreed," Josh said. "But where the hell do we start?"

"I don't know," Anna admitted gloomily.

Initially their withdrawal from the motel room had gone unnoticed by the two Mexican boys. So engrossed with the cartoon they had been. Now, as the credits rolled upwards, they looked eagerly around the small room.

Josh tapped gently against the window getting their attention. He waved and, unlike Isabelle, they waved back. Then using his fore finger, Josh began to draw lines through the grime found on the window. He started with a triangular shape, but replaced hard angles with softer rounded shapes. Next, he traced out the lines of a Mexican hat, before adding a proportionally reduced body.

The boys clapped their hands animatedly as they realised that Josh had actually drawn one of the mice (although to Josh it looked more like an aardvark) from the cartoon they'd just been watching.

Even Isabelle seemed to be watching now.

Impressed with his effort, and his ability to captivate such an audience, Josh started on a second drawing, next to the first.

"Okay – Picasso, where were we?" Anna asked, unable to hide her amusement at his limited artistic ability.

"We were – *are* somewhere – I'm just not sure where though."

Anna turned so she had her back to the window. She scanned around their surroundings. The motel's reception area was set back away from the main body of the building. The word RECEPTION flashed intermittently in red neon. It didn't appear to have any real rhythm to it. And Anna guessed it was more likely a faulty electrical connection. Back towards the highway stood another neon sign with MOTEL written in a swirl of loops, but the power supply must have been either off or damaged beyond repair, as the sign stood in darkness, barely distinguishable.

The parking lot was occupied by only a handful of vehicles. Two SUVs had taken up residence at the opposite end of the complex, and an old beat-up Chevy with slightly deflated tyres was parked three doors further up from where Josh and Anna were staying. The complex had an eerie near-abandoned quality to it. This suited Anna perfectly.

She looked beyond the motel complex out towards the distant mountains. A glimmer of first light was rapidly approaching.

Josh was midway through his second dust drawing. The kids inside were watching intently.

"Okay – we need to think fast," Anna said, her attention back to their conversation. "We need to keep moving. They need returning to their rightful guardians."

"But where would we begin?" Josh asked, adding a big pair of googly eyes to his drawing.

"In truth, I don't know," Anna responded. "We can't simply walk into the cops and say we found them. There'd be too many questions raised."

"What if we handed them over to a charitable organisation? Maybe they would be able to track their parents down, or at least notify the authorities?"

Anna considered this for a moment. "Good idea. But I'm just worried about dropping them off with someone who isn't qualified to deal with the trauma that they've been through."

Josh laughed slightly. "Anna – we're hardly qualified to deal with that ourselves."

A true statement Anna realised. "You're right. The police will have the best resources to both deal with their emotional state, and make a start at finding their loved ones."

Josh stopped with his drawing for a second. "I hate to say it, but after what we just left behind us, I don't really trust the Mexican authorities. Some of them must have known what was going on in Chamela. How could they not?"

"You're right Josh. Corruption runs deep in this place. We need to look further a field."

"Like where?"

Anna pointed out towards the night. "Like home," she said.

Josh followed her finger. For a second he thought she meant as far as her homeland, Russia. But then he realised that she was actually pointing northwards, towards the American boarder.

"What – you're kidding, right? We can't go back there, remember. We're wanted criminals. They'd shoot us first then ask questions."

"I'm aware of the situation," Anna responded.

"Then what are you talking about?"

Anna paused for a moment, sure in the knowledge that Josh would not like what she was about to say.

"Well?" he pushed.

"Not all of the authorities over there are against us. We do still have one ally. Someone we can trust to do the right thing, and have all the connections required to find their parents."

"Who?" asked Josh.

Anna flashed him a mischievous smile. "I think you know who, Mr Sawyer," she said, addressing him in the same manner as the person in question.

Josh's jaw dropped. "You're kidding right?"

Anna's smile broadened. "Josh, when do I ever kid you about anything?"

Josh groaned with dismay. He returned his thoughts to his drawing, finishing it off to the best of his ability. He took a step back. Part of its design was not quite right. What he should have been looking at was the mouse's nemesis. A fat cat named *Eduardo*. He had the dimensions right, and the cat's bloated face looked somewhat similar. Yet it still didn't quite resemble the intended thing.

The girl on the bed stood. Josh looked at Isabelle through the grime coated window. She stood uncertain for a second before taking a few steps towards the window. She studied the drawing for a second. Then reached out with a small hand. Her finger traced straight lines, three on either side of the cat's face, using the same method as Josh, dragging her fingertip over the dust found on the inside of the window.

Whiskers.

Isabelle had drawn the long whiskers that Josh had left out.

Josh nodded at her and smiled.

She met his eyes. And for the first time held his gaze. The corners of her lips bent ever so slightly. The smile, if that's what it truly was, lasted for the briefest of moments. In the next second, Isabelle returned to the bed, sat at its edge, and continued to look at him with only concern in her eyes.

Josh felt his heart drop.

"Okay – I guess we need to make that phone call," he said.

Anna kissed him gently on his cheek. "We'll be okay. You'll see."

"We need to be. For their sake," he said, looking from one small face to the next.

He sensed Anna move around him. The door to the motel room opened and in the next second Anna was back inside, leaving Josh alone.

He stayed there for a minute or two, enjoying watching as Anna goofed about with the two boys, and in doing so, did her best to keep Isabelle entertained.

Josh sighed in resignation. For the first time in twelve months they would have to rely on someone else.

Josh just prayed that the man in question would be up to the task.

Chapter Fifteen

Flight 263A from Chicago

It had come down to simple logic in the end. Once he had disconnected any emotional or duty bound feelings. What could he have done anyway – be in two places at once? Impossible. He had spent the best part of the day trying to determine where he was needed most. In truth, both parties required immediate assistance, their cause equal in necessity, and both requiring urgent assistance.

The thought of innocents dying had first pulled him one way. Could what little understanding he had really help in ending a recent spate of gruesome killings? On the other hand, what could he do to resolve the problem others had presented him with? Did he have sufficient leverage to rectify that issue? No – was probably the truth.

Harry Balooga looked out of the small oval shaped window. Just a thin wisp of clouds could be seen. The sun was rapidly dwindling somewhere on the horizon. Soon night would fall. He had the sudden worrying thought that this would be his last trip. Ever. Had he really made the right choice?

He turned away from the window and the rapidly descending twilight. A small cell phone lay clasped in one of his meaty hands. Even though it had not left his grasp for almost a day now it still felt alien in the detective's hand.

The device – as Balooga referred to it – had been bought for him by his wife, Ester. She had insisted that he take it, explaining that they required a constant connection while Balooga was recuperating in hospital.

Balooga had accepted the device begrudgingly – not really wanting to be at the mercy of the device 24/7. He had seen first-hand how these things could quickly dictate a person's life. He had all too often commented on how such a thing owned the owner, rather than the owner owning *it*.

And now here he was allowing such a device to shape his life. Initially, only Ester and his partner had been given the number of his cellular. However that number of people had quickly doubled in a matter of hours.

The first call had come in late in the afternoon. From a source that Balooga had not expected. The caller had sounded somewhat relieved at first, seemingly grateful to be speaking to an old acquaintance. Yet as the conversation lengthened, the caller had grown hostile, and had even hinted that it was the detective's own unwillingness to disclose prior information that had led to this spate of recent killings.

The conversation had quickly descended into an argument. Nevertheless, by its end, Balooga had felt an unnerving amount of responsibility directed towards him. Yes, he did know something that might be of importance. But no, he wasn't willing to divulge such information. Not unless it was in a face to face capacity. Such knowledge could only be shared in the direct proximity of the recipient.

If the first contact had been unexpected, then the next, almost immediate, was downright astonishing.

No call this time. Just a simple automated voice-mail.

Balooga had listened to it several times. It wasn't a complicated piece of information either. But considering the previous conversation, he could not at first rule out some sort of hoax.

The detective had spent the next hour frustratingly trying to find out any of the caller's details. He had navigated his way through a set of complicated—to an old technophobe, such as him—menus and had eventually found a number.

He had gathered his senses and dialled the number back. He wasn't surprised when what seemed like a completely random stranger answered him back. He didn't even bother to try and make himself understood once the speaker started to reply in a garbled litany of Spanish.

All Balooga did was listen.

The traffic noise and general cacophony of sound that filtered through the receiver told him everything he needed to know.

The second caller had used a payphone.

He wasn't surprised by this. Wouldn't have expected anything else. The second caller would not have wanted an easy trace back.

Without even being aware of it, Balooga had checked his wrist watch. Five hours of daylight remained. Maybe more in the location of the caller?

A few hours later, and Balooga was in mid-flight.

Simple logic had determined his decision. Agreed, both problems were mutually exclusive. Yet they could only be resolved by direct intervention from the other.

The window at Balooga's side dropped into darkness. Night had finally fallen. The detective paused for a second, and then using the cell phone, he dialled the number to the payphone.

It rang just the once.

"What time do you land?" asked the speaker at the other end.

Balooga almost laughed at the speaker's over-confident manner. But he'd expected as much.

"In twenty minutes," he replied, simply.

"We'll be waiting."

In the next instant the phone went dead.

PART II

Fairbanks

Chapter Sixteen

Fairbanks International Airport

Agent Fernandez checked his watch. Only 9:32PM. And already the agent felt as if he'd been trapped in the bleakness of night for an eternity. What meagre amount of light the day had offered was now little more than a distant memory. The large windows before Fernandez were simple black panels, offering no real concept of the outside world. A few lights blinked intermittently in the distance.

On this side of the airport terminal things were relatively quiet. The general populace were not privy to this private lounge. Most would be waiting to either embark on their journey, or be waiting anxiously for returned loved ones, in the main part of the airport. Only a few people shared the small lounge with the agent, and most were dressed in military uniform.

Agent Fernandez was awaiting the arrival of a flight that was not 'officially' listed on any manifesto. A small privately flown jet was headed towards Fairbanks, chartered by the Bureau, and carrying on board a small group of individuals that Fernandez felt both relieved and terrified about meeting.

He checked his watch again. If the aircraft stayed on schedule then it would be due for arrival in less than fifteen minutes.

He felt relieved that Balooga would be on board. In part,

because the detective had some of the answers that Fernandez was looking for, parts of the puzzle that were missing from his memory. But also, because Agent Fernandez felt he had a partner, of sorts, in Balooga, someone to share this burden with, and also an individual of strong character and will. An ally. Balooga had proven this on their first encounter, when they had hunted down the two fugitives together, as far as Glenwood Springs.

Which brought him to Josh Sawyer and, more importantly, Anna Privalova.

If Fernandez had surprised the Chicago detective with his unexpected phone call, then Anna Privalova had shocked the agent to his very core with hers. She had called the agent directly. Fernandez had been rendered speechless, as she had demanded Balooga's cell number. She wasn't about to take no for an answer, either, having already been abruptly cut off by the detective's place of work. Balooga was not currently on active duty, she had been told. Fernandez was not ready to disclose such information.

However, he was equally in need of help. No question about that. Intuition told the agent that if he helped her to achieve her objective, then she would be obliged into helping him with his. And therefore he had compromised and given up Balooga's number. The understanding being that his help would be repaid, with the assistance in solving this recent spate of killings.

Yet more importantly and, the real reason why Agent Fernandez had relinquished such information, was in the hope that he would now—almost a year on—finally catch his prey. Thus vanquishing these demons of old. And render this perplexing fear of the dark from his very being.

Fernandez moved over to the large windows. The sky was a solid slab of blackness. No stars twinkled. Light that had successfully travelled a billion miles from the furthest points of the universe was now unable to penetrate just the thinnest blanket of clouds that covered Fairbanks.

Only a single light blinked in the distance. Fernandez focused in on it. For what seemed like an age, the light just sat in the sky, a tiny white eye that blinked rhythmically. Eventually, the light intensified, finally splitting apart and blossoming into a multicoloured spectacle.

Red and green navigation lights, found at the wingtips, spread out from the central white one, and red anti-collision lights at the top and bottom of the fuselage turned the vision into an illuminated crucifix, floating spectrally down from the dark heavens.

Fernandez shivered. Not wanting to admit his fears, he put it down to the freezing temperatures outside.

The light grew in intensity, and ultimately the small aircraft took shape. A Learjet: a small aircraft that had been commissioned by the FBI to carry agents quickly into the field of operation.

There would be no agents arriving on board this time. Fernandez was not about to be relieved of his duty.

No such luck.

The aircraft glided silently towards the blacktop—a small addition to the main runway that was not accustomed to civil passenger jets. The US Air Force operated from this smaller airstrip, fighter and cargo planes taxiing to and from various parts of the northern hemisphere, and exempt from the usual constraints of passport and courier control, an open portal that Fernandez had utilised to gain entrance for the passengers that were now arriving. A list of phone calls, and promises made, had been required from the agent to allow special use of this military terminal.

The small Learjet touched down, finally, the roar of the jet engines clearly heard as they reversed thrust to bring the aircraft to a standstill.

A few moments of inactivity ensued. Then the fuselage cracked open and a set of steps descended from the belly of the aircraft. White light from the cabin filled the doorway.

A figure appeared then, the lights from inside temporarily

blocked out by the individual. The figure stepped down onto the tarmac.

About two inches of reinforced glass and a further hundred yards of darkness separated the agent from the new arrival. It mattered not. The agent still felt his blood chill. He held his gaze for a few seconds longer, before having to look away, yet, he'd sensed that the passenger had been able to pick him out, out amongst the many shadows of the night, fixing in on his position with the natural ability of a wild and hungry killer.

The agent turned his back on the arrival of Anna Privalova, and readied himself for what was about to come.

Chapter Seventeen

Airport Runway

Josh thought he must have officially become the most wanted man on Earth. He must be, considering the entire army had assembled here waiting to arrest him.

He was making his way across the black tarmac of the runway. Ahead was the large figure of Detective Harry Balooga, with Anna's slighter build lagging just behind the lawman. Josh looked anxiously from one uniformed person to the next. Army fatigues surrounded them, as men and women carried out maintenance or service duties to the small fleet of fighter jets or troop transports that were grounded there.

"Relax," Anna said, slowing her pace, allowing Josh to join her.

"Really..?" Josh breathed, his voice barely above a whisper.

"This is a throughway for Air Force operations," she explained. "They're not here to throw us in the brig. Not yet anyway."

"You sure of that?" Josh asked. He took a closer look at their uniforms to find the US Air Force's recognisable insignia.

"Relax Josh, we made it. Safe and sound."

Josh nodded absent-mindedly.

Less than twenty-four hours had elapsed since Balooga had joined them in Mexico. It had been a subdued reunion. The

Chicago detective had offered both a cautionary greeting. Then he had simply given these two fugitives a list of directions. They had left the outskirts of Benito Juarez International Airport in their wake, steering the dust and dirt covered 4x4 along Highway 57.

The thickset detective had rode in silence initially, up front in the passenger seat, Isabelle now squeezed in on the back seat along with Josh and the two Mexican boys. The dark skinned boys were snoring softly within minutes of them hitting the busy highway.

The young girl had sat there visually uncomfortable so close to this sudden male newcomer. Anna had sensed this instantly and she'd made repeated attempts to engage the girl in conversation – asking what she enjoyed at school, her favourite doll's name, siblings' names, anything to tentatively pry information regarding her original whereabouts or parents' location or guardians.

Nothing worked.

The stranger – the large detective – had added a new strain to the already odd mechanism that they had formed since escaping the town of Chamela. This uncomfortable stalemate had finally been broken once Balooga had started to talk.

"So, got ourselves a real situation here then?" he said, his voice light and easy, conscious of the child's sensibilities.

Anna snorted a short laugh. "Something like that."

Balooga nodded. He turned the rear-view mirror his way, until he caught the reflection of all three kids. "I'd say so."

"It's wasn't exactly planned when we first got here," Anna responded, tilting the mirror back her way. Headlights from the traffic behind filled the glass in a white glare. "We just chanced upon it – nothing more."

Balooga's mind was working overtime trying to fill in the blanks. "Orphans?"

Anna was thoughtful for a moment. "Perhaps. Maybe something a bit more sinister," she prompted.

Balooga looked ahead. "Like?"

Josh huffed irritably from the rear. "You know – like *Chitty Chitty Bang Bang*."

The detective frowned, turned his ample bulk in his seat.

"What the hell does that mean?"

Josh chanced a glance towards Isabelle. The little girl was staring out of the side window, the flow of faster traffic in the outside lane drawing her attention. Not wanting to drag up fearful images of her recent abduction, he lowered his tone.

"You know, the guy with the long nose and cage?" he asked.

Balooga frowned, unaware of Josh's meaning.

"The Child Catcher . . . " said a small voice.

Both men turned to find a pair of bright blue eyes flicking between them. Isabelle repeated, "The Child Catcher—from *Chitty Chitty Bang Bang*."

The memory of that dreadful colonial house, and what it stood for, filtered into Josh's mind. "Yes—honey, that's what I meant."

Rather than Isabelle shying away from the conversation, she now looked interested.

"What happened? To him . . . " she asked.

An explosion of pink mist filled Josh's mind. Not sure of how to explain recent events, he sat silent, struggling to find the right words for a child to understand. Without putting the fear of God into her.

Anna spoke up. "Josh slayed him, honey. You know, like a knight would an evil dragon."

The little girl's mouth dropped slightly, and her eyes lit up a little. "Really? With a magic sword?"

Anna nodded eagerly. "With a magic sword. Cut that dragon's head clean off. No more evil dragon to bother the kids living in the nearby villages."

Josh looked between the two. Anna was smiling openly at the girl through the rear-view mirror. He was surprised when he turned his attention to Isabelle to find her mirroring Anna's expression.

"Sir Josh, the dragon slayer," she said softly.

Josh sat there, his heart melting at how the girl's limited realisation of what they were saying took shape.

"Regular hero," Anna said. "Shame he rides a donkey instead of a horse though."

Isabelle giggled slightly. "That's not true."

"'Tis too," Anna said.

Josh sighed miserably. "Couldn't afford a horse. Had all my gold stolen by a big miserable…" A sudden look in Balooga's direction, "… bald troll!"

Finally getting in on the act, Balooga raised his hand. "Hello," he said, in a comical, grumpy voice.

Isabelle was beside herself now, enjoying the silliness of the conversation, and her mind a million miles away from her recent horrors.

"What did you spend all the gold on?" she asked, her defensive manner abandoned.

Balooga had to think of that one. "Ah—a . . . new . . . nose."

"What?!" blurted all three in unison.

"A new nose, you know, because the old one was all full of hairy warts." They all laughed at the absurdity.

Once the laughter ceased, a new, more relaxed silence fell upon them. Occasionally during their late journey towards the Mexican border, the little girl would turn in the direction of Josh and whisper, "Sir Josh, the dragon slayer," from time to time.

Now, Josh felt the little girl's hand clasped in his as they made their way together towards the airport terminal.

He looked down at her little face. She tilted her blue eyes to him. And smiled warmly. "Sir Josh," she said softly.

Josh nodded. Although deep inside, he felt a sudden fear begin to build. Balooga had managed to fill them in on some of what had transpired in this cold and dark place, while the girl had slept at their side during the flight.

Josh hadn't liked what he'd heard. Not one bit. It sounded too familiar to the horrors they'd fled from last year. Unexplainable deaths. Missing people. Stolen hearts and the beginning of something immense.

Chapter Eighteen

Police Department

For the first time in days the precinct was relatively calm. Most of the attending officers had gone home, exhaustion turning already pale skin whiter, eyes dark and red-rimmed, and weary souls in need of rest. Only a late night cleaner occupied the walkways between cluttered desks, the drone of a vacuum cleaner filling in the silence.

In stark contrast, the small office that Agent Fernandez had taken up residence in was a swell of bodies.

The agent had positioned himself against the office window, his back pressed against the night. Even his fear for the darkness paled compared to his trepidation towards the woman who now sat just across the room.

Anna and Josh were seated at the table, the macabre photos of the murdered victims hastily cleared away, the young girl's well-being now considered, even though Isabelle was asleep, curled up on two chairs that had been brought in from the main room.

The Chicago detective was perched at the edge of the table, his back to Josh and Anna, and his attention focused on the FBI agent.

In an attempt to break the silence, Fernandez asked, "So, the two Mexican children, they made the trip okay?"

Balooga nodded. "Handed them over to the contact you named in San Diego."

Fernandez seemed pleased with that. "Good, they have the required support to deal with emotional trauma and also the right contacts in finding their parents or guardians. They're in safe hands."

Anna said, "We owe you our thanks for taking care of the boys for us. They're a resilient pair, should find a way through the coming weeks without too much lasting damage."

"Right," replied Fernandez. The agent's eyes flicked towards the sleeping child. "But we still have a problem."

"Problem?" echoed Anna.

The agent cleared his throat. "This is not the place for a child. Not now. Not with everything that's going on."

Anna's voice grew with tension. "Then what do you suggest we do. Leave her?"

Fernandez raised his hand. "I'm not saying anything of the sort. But my contacts in San Diego were much better equipped for dealing with such a thing."

"Maybe they were," Anna conceded. "But the child stays with us, for now."

Josh spoke. "It was the last thing we needed too. We're hardly in a good position to be playing parents of the year. Every law enforcement agency wants us in prison."

Fernandez couldn't argue with that. He had been forced to go to the top to get the two fugitives this far. Two field agents had met them at the US border. The children had been granted entrance to the United States under the humanitarian act, stating that their lives were in danger if they remained in Mexico and were not granted clemency.

The children's passage had been the least of Fernandez's problems. Getting the two fugitives back into the States had been even harder. The field agents had explained to border control that the two had surrendered themselves voluntarily to be extradited back to Chicago for the ongoing investigation of three previously unsolved murders.

It was a ruse that had eventually paid off. They all gained entry – the children not expected to present any form of ID or passports, nor were Josh and Anna, as they were handed over immediately to the two field agents for arrest.

Two hours later, at just turned midnight, they had arrived at the agency's safe-house, where the two Mexican boys had been handed over.

Isabelle had held onto Anna's hand for dear life. She was not willing to be left alone here. Anna had tried to reassure her that this was a safe place, full of people wanting to help return her to her rightful family. The little girl had visibly tensed when she'd asked if she wanted to see her mom and pop again. Tears had sprung from her eyes. Not an emotional response in desperation at being returned to loved ones, but a fearful one. It was at that moment when Anna considered that perhaps Isabelle had not been taken from such a safe and loving environment. She decided not to push her on it. Instead she had given her a hug and promised to keep her close, for now. Anna could have used her ability to pry deeper into the child's being, but she felt that would almost be like a betrayal of trust. Maybe the time would come when Isabelle was ready to open up.

An hour later they were in the air. The Learjet cutting its way through the night, the two jet engines screaming their way towards the furthest tips of America, intent on delivering its cargo before the sun broke beyond the distant horizon.

Now Fernandez found himself with the unwanted burden of a missing child.

"You should have left her in San Diego. She'd have been well looked after."

"Perhaps," agreed Anna. "But she's fragile. Scared. We've gained her trust. Therefore, she stays with us. For now."

The agent grumbled. "I still don't like it."

Anna shrugged her shoulders dismissively. "That's the deal. You want us. You get her too."

Did he really want *any* of them here? Fernandez considered. Admittedly, he had asked for the detective's help, but more in understanding what had happened in the past, and not necessarily to get physically involved in the events that now had Fairbanks quaking in fear.

"Okay," the agent said, "moving forward, I need to figure out what is going on here. Why people are dropping dead, seemingly unharmed, or . . ." he looked towards Isabelle to check the child was asleep, ". . . or why the hell someone would have their heart ripped out?"

Josh stiffened noticeably at the last comment. "What do you mean, their heart ripped out? You mean—eaten?"

The agent shook his head. "No, not eaten. Just, well, ripped out. Discarded."

Anna stood, moved closer to the agent. "Are you sure of this fact? The heart has been found?"

"Yes," Fernandez replied. "Torn clean out. But otherwise intact."

Both Josh and Anna sighed with relief.

Anna spoke to Josh. "So we can rule out one of my kind."

"I guess so," responded Josh. "They would have consumed the heart to grant them powers from the host—right?"

"Right," Anna said.

Balooga asked, "So what *do* you think?"

Fernandez tried to clear his head. They were all openly talking like they were crazy. Insane even. Had he really requested their help? Was he crazy too, for believing something of a supernatural nature was here in Fairbanks, slaughtering its citizens?

Yet instinctively he knew what they had all experienced together, twelve months ago in Colorado, was somehow inexplicably tied to the events that were happening right here and now. All he could do was extend his curiosity, suspend his beliefs, and see what they came up with.

Anna's voice brought him back from his worrying thoughts.

"My type would not have discarded such an important prize. That would be the whole reason for taking a victim in the first place."

"Is that true, Anna?" asked Josh. "What about the need for food?"

"Then there would have been no need to take the heart. Pointless. And risky."

Christ, thought Fernandez, *they're now openly talking about murder!*

The agent turned towards the Chicago detective. "You buying any of this?"

Balooga simply nodded. "We've both seen with our own eyes what fantastic and unexplainable things the world has to offer. We can't argue with what we have witnessed already."

"I think this was a mistake," the agent said. "I shouldn't have brought you here."

"It's no mistake," countered Anna. "From what you explained on the trip over here, I would say you've definitely attracted one that has a penchant for human flesh."

Fernandez asked, "But even if that's so—and I'm not saying that it is—then why were the first two victims left intact?"

Anna replied, "Why skin one animal for its fur, yet eat another in its entirety? This hunter requires different things for different purposes. And not all of the mortal flesh."

"I don't get you," Fernandez responded.

"Let me explain." Anna drew alongside the agent. "This thing has chosen Fairbanks for many reasons; its isolation, a habitation that near guarantees it remains well hidden. Not many would be willing to stray out into the frozen wasteland, but most of all, the fact that this town offers it an array of prey to choose from."

"But you could say that about any town or city. What's so special about Fairbanks?"

Anna laughed at the agent's misunderstanding. "What does Fairbanks offer that most cannot?"

The agent looked outside at the frozen landscape. "Snow and ice?"

Now Anna shook her head. "No, Agent Fernandez. Far more precious than that."

Fernandez continued to scan the dark horizon. He was

almost at the point of telling her he didn't know, when the sudden realisation dawned on him.

"The night," he said.

Anna turned to meet the agent's gaze. "Exactly. The night."

"So what are you saying? That we are looking for one like you?"

"No, agent. But we do share just the one similarity. Neither of us can survive in daylight."

The agent shivered involuntarily. With over twenty hours of darkness per day, then yes, this entity had chosen the right hunting ground exactly.

Chapter Nineteen

Fairbanks – The Outskirts

Although she had never visited the city of Fairbanks before, Anna instinctively knew how the general layout of commercial, residential and utility services would affect the general topography.

The centre of Fairbanks would consist of mostly commercial enterprises, banks, shops, most with high-street brands, the mall, no doubt, and an endless list of fast-food chains, and a variety of restaurants.

Beyond that would be the towering walls of apartment buildings, where the most affluent high-flyers watched over the city, bankers and financiers, ready to quickly make an extra buck if the opportunity arose.

The inner-city would give way to the blue-collar sector, hard-working families, with even harder jobs. They were the real people that kept the city of Fairbanks from becoming a solid icy slab. Dotted throughout this suburban area would be many mom and pop stores, hardware, groceries, essential requirements for the average family to survive.

Finishing off the map would be all the main service utilities. Massive factories that provided water, gas, sanitation, and electricity, distributed in a network of cables, tunnels, pipes, most buried deep underground and inaccessible from the subzero temperatures and harsh winds that raged above.

Only the airport and a few remaining businesses could be found beyond the main perimeter of the city.

Anna was at one such business – an old sawmill that had once helped build Fairbanks and its infrastructure. Now, the mill was little more than an empty shell.

She had come alone; the rest of the group now nearing exhaustion. Josh and Isabelle, along with Balooga had managed to find accommodation at the same hotel where Agent Fernandez was staying. Anna had been worried about Isabelle and her reluctance to be left with Josh alone. But since learning of his heroic slayings back in Mexico, the little girl had taken a shine to him. She still acted timid and shy, but Anna understood that was more to do with the child's natural demeanour, rather than anything she really feared.

As for Anna, she felt like she'd had her shackles removed. The limitations that Mexico had imposed upon her had now been lifted, and she could finally embrace what was almost an eternal night here in Fairbanks.

She was dressed in thick clothing, the cold still capable of chilling her, but less so than her human counterparts. The hood of her coat hid her features within its folds.

The roads she had travelled on had been near-deserted at this late hour. Just a few patrol cars moved from street to street, their sudden arrival signalled well in advance by the bright glare of headlights. Although not a suspect for the recent killings here, Anna had still taken to the shadows when the police cruisers rolled by. The crunch of chains sounded as tyres cut through the ice and snow, before red tail lights dwindled in the distance, taking the threat of discovery with them.

Now Anna stood on the outer perimeter of the old wood mill.

The main building had fallen into disrepair, the tiled roof either reduced to gaping holes or sagging dangerously low. Most of the windows were empty hollows, their glass panels lost to the elements years ago.

What would she find inside? Her adversary, or … adversaries? She hadn't discounted the fact that they may be dealing with more than one.

The first two deaths had been done without any bloodshed, none that had been determined as of yet anyway, and there had been no apparent violence. The torn heart and headless victims were in complete contrast. And although Fernandez had been certain that the headless victim was a separate entity entirely, Anna had not yet reached that same conclusion.

Maybe they were all done by separate killers. Perhaps Fairbanks had now become the epicentre for mass murderers, converging here en masse to carry out their grisly dealings. Truth be told, the city definitely had one killer here – Anna.

She herself had taken the lives of many, over countless centuries, but only from the wicked and immoral. Blood was her necessity. Only the very life force that ran through human veins could keep her hunger at bay. A task to control now more complicated by the man she loved.

Josh had stood by her over the last twelve months; indeed, he had discovered her true identity on their very first encounter, back in Chicago on that fateful night. Although initially repulsed by her needs, he had eventually come to understand that Anna used her abilities to sift through the souls of saints or sinners.

Anna would not, could not, take the essence of an innocent being. A need, deep within her core, had formed over the years, which gave her the compulsion to preserve someone of righteousness: a good soul.

Josh was not the only one who knew of her secrets. The detective, Harry Balooga, had also paid witness to her true form.

Indeed, the detective had played a vital role in them defeating Anna's adversary from years gone by – a shape-shifter, like her, but one with a heart as black as night itself. Without the detective's help, Anna was convinced that she and Josh would have perished on that mountainside in Colorado.

Even the FBI agent had played his part. Tracking them to

the abandoned skiing resort. Only the agent had been trapped in an ensuing avalanche. And although the agent had caught a glimpse of what Anna could become, the resultant trauma of being buried alive had subsequently suppressed any memory. A complete mental blackout. Yet, even with this self-induced amnesia, the agent's instincts had led him to believe that whatever had happened to him there had somehow followed him here.

And he was right too. Not Jonus, Anna's old adversary and the one they had defeated on those icy slopes, but someone else, or something which had the same degree of malignancy running through its veins.

Anna could sense it. The air was rank with the promise of death to come. What had already happened here was just a prelude. More was to come. A lot more.

Anna closed her eyes and breathed deeply. She focused her thoughts and feelings. A picture formed in her mind, a dark river running like congealing blood between the homes and buildings of Fairbanks. The river was lapping upwards as it coursed through the streets and alleyways, clotted waves dragging anyone or anything that chanced upon its path, down into the black churning mass, to be swept away by the fetid waters. The river pushed its way onwards in sluggish fashion. It did not run out to sea, to become a bottomless swell, but rather it stopped here at the sawmill, pooling around the old building to form a bloody and stagnant tarn.

Anna opened her eyes.

The festering malignancy had brought her here, to this place.

It was inside. Waiting.

In the dark.

Chapter Twenty

Alpine Lodge Fairbanks

Balooga eyed the plate with feelings of guilt. A small mound of crispy bacon sat perched over a fried egg. Two half-cut pieces of toast, buttered a quarter inch thick, fanned out on either side of the bacon and egg.

The hotel's restaurant was mostly abandoned, to the point were the waiting staff outnumbered the patrons 2 to 1.

For the fifth time in as many minutes, Balooga picked up the menu to read the calorie intake of the dish: 320 to be precise. Hardly worth noting, right. Yet, no matter how many times he readied his knife and fork, he just couldn't bring himself to begin eating.

It was guilt that stopped him. He knew such a dish would be bad for his cholesterol, even just the one. His thoughts returned to his wife every time the prongs to his fork almost skewered the red meat. Her look of fear at losing her husband to a fatal heart attack played on the detective's mind.

He put the fork down, disgusted with himself for even thinking about betraying her.

"Food that good…?"

Balooga looked up to find Agent Fernandez by his side.

The moment of guilt flushed Balooga's cheeks red. "Something like that," he replied, pushing the dish away.

Fernandez took a seat opposite the detective. "You can't sleep either?"

"Weird – right? Considering it's almost always dark here."

The agent nodded. "It's a seasonal thing. Come back here in the summer and you get almost six months of perpetual daylight."

"Joy," Balooga said.

"Not the ideal conditions for our new friend?" Fernandez added.

Balooga smiled bitterly. The agent had bided his time, waiting for the most opportune time to prise the information that he so desperately wanted free.

"You could say that," Balooga responded.

"Is she out there in the dark now, slaying the innocent?"

Balooga held the agent's gaze. "Is that what you think? You think I'd have brought her here to add more bodies to your list."

Fernandez offered a slight shrug of his shoulders. "Is it?"

"You need to look beyond what the agency teaches you, and let go of all those logical beliefs you hold so dear."

The agent spread his hands. "So fill me in, detective. What have you let loose in Fairbanks?"

"You were there – back in Colorado. You already know what she is. You just won't allow yourself to admit it."

"All I saw were two wanted killers remember. That's why we tracked them across country."

Balooga nodded. "Initially – yes. But we both know Josh Sawyer is no killer. Never was."

"You sure of that?" Fernandez asked.

Balooga understood all too well what the dragon slaying analogy back in Mexico had meant. Yes, Sawyer had taken a life – maybe not his first – and that, in itself, raised suspicion about his involvement in the three killings back in Chicago. Yet, the detective's gut instincts told him that the young man was not capable of such atrocities, not under normal circumstances anyway.

What had recently happened in Mexico were hardly normal circumstances.

"We were wrong about Sawyer," Balooga said. "He may have bent the truth originally, to protect the woman, but not about his involvement in the killings. Sawyer didn't kill those guys back in Chicago."

"Then why have the charges not been dropped? My information leads me to believe he's still a wanted man."

"My belief goes beyond what the legal system deems as either guilty or innocent. I'm sure a competent prosecution team could tie the boy to those killings – as an accessory or conspirator. But what I witnessed back in Colorado, led me to believe that the kid is of good heart. Simple case of wrong place, wrong time."

The agent remained quiet, thoughtful for a moment. "But what of the woman. What does your gut tell you about her?"

It was the detective's turn to take a moment to gauge his response. "Can't say she's the innocent type. I know without doubt what she's capable of. Even so, I do believe she does what she does with a degree of compassion."

"Compassion?" echoed Fernandez. "Are you serious?"

"Then you tell me – Agent, who has she killed that *we*, as law enforcers, wouldn't have put behind bars ourselves?"

"Are we condoning vigilantism now, detective?" Fernandez asked, unable to pick an innocent name out amongst the memorised list of victims.

Balooga laughed slightly. He had once asked a question similar from the woman in doubt. Her reply had been simple.

"What are we, Agent Fernandez, if not some regulated vengeance committee?" Balooga replied, drawing up the woman's response from memory.

The agent shook his head. "This is getting us nowhere. I asked you to come here to help me understand what might be happening here, with what has happened already in the past. The two seem somehow connected."

"And I brought you the one thing that can offer you your

answers."

"I was hoping you could give me those answers," Fernandez said.

"At best, I could offer some sort of summary. Only Privalova can give you the answers you seek."

The agent checked his watch. There would be at least another five hours before the sun broke briefly from the darkness. This left plenty of time for whatever was stalking Fairbanks to claim yet another victim.

"Then let's hope she makes it through the night, so she can reveal all," Fernandez said, drawing away from the table.

Chapter Twenty-One

Sawmill

Anna found herself hesitating, unwilling to take the first step. Her special ability had brought her here. Yet her instincts were telling her to stay away. Turn back. Do not enter.

Was she scared?

Anna was not without caution. She was to be feared, yes, but not without frailties or weaknesses. Super fast and strong, but not invincible. She could be harmed. And killed, if the right circumstances prevailed.

Sunlight.

If caught out in daylight, she would burn, for all her kind were susceptible to the harmful UV rays generated by the sun. Only one had ever been impervious to the sun, a Viking Chief named Ragnar, and Anna had taken his soul, only to be cheated out of her prize by her hateful adversary – Jonus. For Jonus had taken the secret of daywalking to his icy tomb, when defeated by Anna and Josh, a year ago now.

So the one man she feared was buried under a hundred tonnes of snow and ice thousands of miles away.

Then why did she falter?

Whatever lay inside was not one of her own kind.

There was only one way she would find out.

Anna readied herself.

She pushed through a gap found in the old fencing and stepped into the shadows of the building. An inky blackness laid claim to this place.

The stench of blood hit her, only for Anna to realise moments later that it was actually the metallic rust of the machines inside that filled her nostrils. She took a moment to allow her vision to readjust to the gloominess of the place.

In places, where the roof had collapsed, weak beams of moonlight filled in the void, illuminating the interior of the ruin.

The majority of floor space was filled with the bulk of machinery—connected together in a series of massive pulleys and drives. Most machines were made from wood and iron, fashioned from the very land that surrounded the old building. Conveyors that had been flayed from animal skin stretched from one dark end to the next.

Some of the machines looked medieval in design. One such device had two rollers, layered with cog-like teeth, that came together to strip bark from logs. Anna imagined the sound it would have made while in operation, and the noise formed was like that of screaming torture.

She sidestepped around the machine to push deeper into the mill, her footsteps cushioned by generations of compressed wood shavings.

The centre of the building came into view. A huge circular saw glinted gloomily in the darkness. Easily the width of a man, with serrated teeth cut out along its entire circumference, the blade still looked capable of tearing through anything that was put in its path.

As she approached the saw, Anna added extra caution—her instincts somehow aware that this monstrous blade signified the very heart of this place.

She arrived at the saw, stooped over and silent.

What was she expecting?

That the machinery would spring to life, leather pulleys and belts snapping taut, and old motors suddenly whirring with the power of life. Would rusty chains rattle as they uncoiled themselves, before seeking out flesh to wrap around, strapping their prey down against the dark-stained saw-bed, before those brutal spinning teeth did their work.

Nothing of the sort.

Yet Anna still felt as if this place had a life of its own.

She stood then, understanding that whatever had once lurked here was now recently gone. She took a few more minutes to survey the abandoned property. Nothing of any real significance revealed itself. Twin tracks, for the loading and unloading of timber, long ago rusted, led Anna to the front of the old building. There, the twin rails snaked lazily into the surrounding woodland.

Anna considered following them for a while, but surely they would lead to nowhere in particular. Whatever had once brought timber to and from the old sawmill must have been decommissioned almost a century ago.

The danger she'd sensed on arrival was residual. Held here over time, bound to this place in memory, the horrors that had befallen this place were now remembered by time alone.

Anna was about to turn her attention elsewhere, when a small mound caught her eye. It was formed just within the overhang of the roof. She stepped towards it, and reached out to take a sample. A jacket. Wet and soiled. More clothing had been piled, or discarded, as Anna now thought. A pair of baggy pants, expensive looking, laid on top of a dress, which was difficult to make out in colour, but fitted and padded around the bosom. Clothes worn by young adults, possibly a couple? More items were found underneath. Followed by an assortment of footwear, a shoe here, an insulated boot there.

Some of the garments looked as if their wearer had torn themselves free from them, ripped to shreds, buttons popped free, or zippers burst open. No blood was present. Yet, this odd mix of clothing meant something significant. More than a hobo's odd collection, or dumped previously by their owners, way out here on the outskirts of town.

Anna dropped the ripped garment. A different object caught her attention now. She picked it up – knew exactly what it was without being able to read the information found printed there.

How had such a thing found its way here? Completely out of place with the rest of the discarded clothing.

She left the building behind her, eager to return to town, to show what she had found. Her belief firm now, Fairbanks had indeed attracted a force of supernatural significance.

Chapter Twenty-Two

Police Precinct

Agent Fernandez had the object in question clasped between his fingers. His other hand was flipping through the case files laid out across his desk.

Anna stood just within the room. Less than an hour of night-time remained. Then finally, Fairbanks would be bathed in the harsh glare of sunlight for just over 3 hours, from which Anna would have to seek refuge. She was willing the agent to conclude his assessment so she could leave now, while she still had time.

"Well..?" she asked, impatiently.

"Wait," ordered Fernandez.

The agent seemed nervous having found himself suddenly alone with her. He kept looking out towards the main office space, as if the presence of others would offer him safety. The main part of the precinct was empty, returning duty officers still making their way back, readying themselves for the onslaught of more long hours of policing.

The agent eventually refocused on the task at hand to finish his examination. "It doesn't match any of our victims. And why would it. Where did you get this again?"

Anna huffed irritably. "I've already told you, on the outskirts of town, out in the woodland area. An old sawmill."

"Somewhere a homeless person could seek shelter in, you mean?"

"No – agent, that's not what I mean. The place was no warmer than open fields. Just secluded. Out of the way. Perfect."

"Perfect for what?"

"A gathering," Anna said.

The agent rolled his eyes. "What sort of gathering? Of people?"

"Something like that," Anna responded. "Look – if it's not in there, then we need to look elsewhere." It was clear the agent was not about to match the information on the piece of card that Anna had found to any within his case files.

"It's not a match," the agent finally admitted.

"Then we need to look at the source. Where the item was issued."

Fernandez groaned inwardly. He checked the time, apparently aware of the advancing sunrise and its implications to the woman.

"There isn't enough time," he said.

"Agreed," Anna replied. "You can drop me off, and pick Balooga up on the way."

"What about Mr Sawyer – he's coming too?"

"If you wish. Hurry now."

The agent nodded. Snatched up his coat. Then paused for a moment. Should he bag and serialise this recent find? Would it become evidence, or had the woman simply brought him nothing more than a red herring. Another dead end. The piece of card meant nothing individually. Yet the strangeness of where it had been found, along with the rest of the clothing, did offer a certain level of interest.

In the end the agent simply dropped the toe-tag inside his jacket pocket. Not convinced that this unusual item would lead them further towards the killer, or otherwise.

A trip to the city morgue would be required to either shed some light on matters, or add another layer of the unknown, to what was already fast becoming an unfathomable mystery.

Chapter Twenty-Three

City Morgue

The key turned and the locking mechanism tumbled over to its engaged position to secure the doorway. The key was one of many, bunched together in a solid jangle of iron, like that of a jailer's. The attendant moved away from the secured access, his footwear squeaking slightly as rubber soles connected with the sterilized flooring.

The occupant inside lay silent and alone, having just been returned to its current resting place. The cadaver's final visitors would be making their return trip home now, teary-eyed and thoughtful, having just formally identified a lost loved one.

There would be no further visits. None would be required. The body had been identified. A young man, physically in his prime, yet taken suddenly by a brain haemorrhage that had burst overnight; taking the man in mid-dream, his thoughts slowly drifting away until all that lingered were the dying impulses of a broken mind.

Earlier, the young man had made the short trip to the coroner's table, dissected and prodded and poked, before his return here to the cold confinements of this storage space – to be locked away again until the undertaker arrived, ready to take the body away, to prepare it for its final journey.

Josh felt uncomfortable and out of place here. He didn't see what value he could add by being here either. He knew nothing of anthropology or pathology. Even so, Agent Fernandez had requested his attendance. Likewise, Balooga's attention had been required, and the Chicago detective looked no more at ease than did Josh.

A merry old bunch, mused Josh.

"Why are we here again?" he asked. "Don't we have enough dead bodies to keep us busy with? Without shopping for more."

Josh's feeble attempt at humour fell on deaf ears.

Neither the agent, nor detective seemed up for conversation.

"C'mon guys, what did Anna find to have brought us here?"

Earlier, Anna had arrived at their hotel room. Josh already showered and dressed, having slept little, worrying constantly about Anna's well-being and Isabelle's mental state. The young girl had slept fitfully in a small cot at Josh's side. Anna had silently eased her way inside, and advised Josh that she would keep an eye on the girl while he was required to meet with the agent and detective downstairs in the lobby.

Not long after they had arrived here – at the city morgue.

Joy of all joys.

Josh resigned himself into going along with whatever the agent had in mind.

They traversed the inner sanctum of the morgue, unabashed, the staff here already familiar with the agent who had been brought in to help them with their recent murder spree. The agent eventually led them to an office, where the morgue techs were busy coordinating the beginning of the day. The agent disappeared inside, leaving both Josh and the detective to ponder on events.

"What's this all about?" Josh asked. "Did Anna find another body?"

"No," was Balooga's simple reply. Then he seemingly changed his mind at the last minute, "Maybe . . ."

"Which is it—Detective?"

"Wait," he advised, seeing that the agent was finishing up with the morgue tech.

Fernandez reappeared, his face flushed with anger.

"What?" asked both Josh and Balooga in unison.

The agent moved away from the office and the techs inside. He looked towards first Josh, then Balooga.

"This," he said, raising the toe-tag, "is apparently not of sufficient importance to warrant reporting to the FBI."

Josh couldn't make out the finer details on the identification marker. "Who does that belong to?"

The agent handed it over. *Cynthia Reid #11365* the tag read.

Josh raised his eyebrows. "Well?" He handed the ID tag over to the detective.

Balooga eyed it with some caution. The last time he had found a fragment of paper with a name on it, it had led him halfway across the country in hot pursuit of the young man who was standing beside him, along with a list of murder victims, all of which were still unsolved.

"Who is she?" Balooga asked.

"A missing person," the agent responded, surprising them both.

Balooga said, "That doesn't make any sense. How can a dead person be considered missing?"

"When the body ups and disappears," Fernandez replied.

"Meaning?" Josh asked.

The agent laughed bitterly. "Meaning—exactly that. Mrs Cynthia Reid simply vanished. Walked right out of the morgue one night."

Both Josh and the detective looked back bemused.

Fernandez said, "Okay – we all know that can't have happened. But the techs are adamant that her body just vanished – unclaimed and unaccounted for."

Balooga scanned around them. The place was an advertisement for organisation. No mess. No chaos. An orderly place, like you would expect.

"Did they misplace it?" Balooga asked, unable to find any obvious reason for such a thing to happen.

"They looked," Fernandez explained. "High and low. It's a federal offence to steal a body, doesn't bode well for any organisation that loses one either. Talk about red-faced."

Josh asked, "So what did they do?"

"Nothing they could do. No official procedure for such a thing. So they filed a missing person's report to the police department."

"And they didn't think to include that in this case?" Balooga now asked.

"Why would they?" Fernandez replied. "She was already dead."

Josh asked the obvious question nagging at his senses. "Then how did her ID tag find its way out on the outskirts of town, in an old abandoned sawmill?"

The agent looked equally puzzled. "Maybe the clothing belonged to the bodies on arrival. And they should have been destroyed, but ended up there?"

Balooga nodded. "A possibility. Hell, stranger things are afoot. Perhaps an indolent city employee tossed them there instead of following procedure."

"Still doesn't tell us where our missing body is though," Josh reminded them. "Or how the hell someone managed to get one out unnoticed?"

The agent stood silent momentarily, and his two companions appeared to sense he was holding some information back.

"What?" quizzed Balooga.

The agent cleared his throat. "The tech mentioned a break in, a few weeks ago. Said nothing was taken. Our missing Reid had not had her post-mortem back then. She had not been included in the system. Seemingly died of natural causes, old age. She was a recent inclusion. Brought in that evening no less. The acting coroner had not even determined if a post-mortem was even required."

"And?" prompted Balooga.

"And there was only a bit of damage to the place; broken glass to one window, things slightly out of place. "

"A set of missing keys?" Balooga asked, hopefully.

The agent shook his head sympathetically. "No such luck."

"Then what?" Josh asked.

"Some of the enclosures had been opened, gurneys pulled out, bodies disturbed. Yet all were accounted for."

"Why would someone do such a thing? What were they looking for – a person in particular, or jewellery?" Josh asked.

The agent had no answer.

"What side of the wall was the glass found on?" Josh asked.

The agent groaned visibly. "Where is this leading to? You implying **she** simply walked out of the morgue. By her own accord I'm guessing?"

Josh shrugged. "Not walked exactly. Maybe crawled. Out the window."

Now Fernandez looked exasperated. "And how would she have done such a thing?"

Josh was about to speculate, when a sudden boom sounded from deeper within the basement. The noise had been hollow and metallic, like a hammer hitting against an empty drum.

"What the hell was that?" Josh now asked.

The sound came again, chilling them in place.

Next, a cry of surprise filled the barren passageways, which quickly trailed out into a blood-gurgling scream.

Chapter Twenty-Four

Alpine Lodge Fairbanks

The opposite side of the bed had felt warm when first climbing in. The side that Josh had occupied previously. Now, as Anna awoke, the sheets were cold and empty. Anna felt damp from sweat. She had spent the last few hours in that place between sleep and consciousness. Her light slumber had been plagued by the faces of the damned, and she had tossed and turned, the bedding now sodden from her exertions.

She awoke fully. The drapes were still drawn and, through their gap, she could see that white daylight was rapidly fading back to night. A wall light above her gave the room more definition. Anna had not wanted to throw the room into total darkness in case Isabelle had awakened.

She need not have worried. The little girl was still fast asleep in the cot at Anna's side. The child must have been exhausted, Anna thought, realising that Isabelle had now slept straight through with both Josh and herself.

It made sense all things considered. The child had gone through a lot these last couple of days, and it was more than understandable that she would have been drained. Even for a kid of her age, one who would have normally been gifted with an unlimited amount of energy.

The blanket from Isabelle's bed had slipped sideways and

left the child's skin exposed to the cold. Anna climbed out of bed to tuck her in. As she leaned over she caught sight of a little furry head, orange in colour, and peeking out from under the girl's chin.

A small teddy bear lay cuddled under Isabelle's white arm.

Anna wondered for a second where the bear had come from, the child had not previously been in possession of such a toy. The moment of speculation ended when Anna remembered that the hotel's foyer had a small gift shop attached.

Anna smiled. Josh had taken the child to buy the teddy bear before they'd settled in for the night. Sweet.

Crossing the room, Anna switched the TV on and set the volume to low. She didn't want Isabelle waking to a silent and empty room, if she stirred while Anna was busy showering. The TV screen flickered with the multicoloured mayhem of a kid's cartoon.

Anna entered the washroom, stripped off her underwear and then climbed into the shower cubicle. A hot spray of water cascaded over her flesh. She closed her eyes for a while and lost herself in the simple task of bathing.

Soap suds gathered in a spiralling swirl around the plug hole, and Anna watched as they were slowly drawn into the opening. The sight reminded her of the dark vision that had led her to the sawmill. And the conclusion of the odd pile of clothing found there.

There was still something that made her feel uneasy about the clothing. Had people really gone to the trouble of throwing their best clothing away?

Why would they?

The jet of hot water tapered into a drip, as Anna climbed from the cubicle to begin towelling herself dry. She re-entered the main room with the towel wrapped around her torso.

Isabelle was still snoring softly.

The TV program had finished and was now advertising breakfast cereals, or toys, or toys that came with breakfast cereals.

Anna felt a rumble in her stomach. She would need to feed soon, or the hunger that was always present would start to blur her reality.

A new show started on the TV.

Anna watched half-interestedly as she dressed. It was a cartoon she recognised, the main protagonist being a dog named *Scooby Doo*. The show had been big in the 70s and the clothing they wore had stayed fixed firmly in that era, with the gang dressed in flared pants, psychedelic dresses and tops dyed in bright pastel colours. It wasn't long before they were being chased by a lumbering creature of some sorts.

Anna watched as the Frankenstein-like monster, recently raised from the grave by some evil spell, had Shaggy and Scooby cornered in a derelict mansion. The monstrosity was wearing a tattered jacket, pants that stopped above the ankles in a torn mess, and shiny black shoes. Anna understood that this is what the creature had been buried wearing.

And the sudden realisation of what that implied hit her squarely in the chest, draining the air from her lungs and forcing her to draw breath.

That was what she had discovered the day previously; a pile of discarded funeral clothing. This now added significance to the finding of the ID tag. Both clothing and tag had been taken from the human remains of the deceased.

Or, as Anna sat there thinking about it, maybe not taken at all. But rather, discarded.

Although seemingly preposterous to think, that is what Anna believed had happened. Somehow the dead had risen, and stripped themselves of the life they had once known, and taken to the night.

And not just one or two.

But many.

Chapter Twenty-Five

City Morgue

The fear in the morgue felt palpable. Josh could almost taste it. A change in atmosphere, which seemed to be working on Josh on some instinctive, animalistic level, that had set his senses buzzing. He felt like time had slowed, a symptom of his brain dumping high levels of adrenaline into his veins, and he could almost pinpoint every sound that echoed throughout these sterilised corridors with incredible accuracy.

The three of them, Josh, Agent Fernandez and Detective Balooga had rounded the corner to find a morgue tech clutching at his throat. The floor beneath him was rapidly turning to a crimson colour, and the tech's bloody scream had become a wet rasp as his life's fluid pooled out around his feet.

A moment of rationality, even while presenting Josh with such a sight, expected an attacker with weapon in hand to step forth. Yet, as the tech slouched to the ground, only the cadaver that occupied the gurney seemed to be present in the room.

Then the body twitched. A sudden jolt of movement, that caused its back to arch clean off the metallic surface.

Josh looked towards the downed tech, then back towards the trembling figure.

Was this some sort of sick joke? He turned quickly to read his companions expressions. If it were some twisted prank then they weren't in on it. They too looked terrified.

The body had gone into a full spasm now; heels were kicking against the steel, blood and body fluids splashing out over the drip tray.

An arm slipped free from under the cadaver's shroud. Fingers that were curled into a claw appeared red, and they opened and closed, rhythmically, as if the body was slowly working life back into them.

A gasp of air then.

Not the dying tech's but the body on the table. It gasped again, ruined lungs trying to inflate, yet only succeeding in producing a sick wheezing of escaped air as the organs collapsed in a flap of dead tissue.

It mattered not.

The body sat upright.

Its eyes looked glazed, irises wan and threaded with slivers of bloodshot. The skin appeared to be made up of two halves—a pallor yellow at the front and a mottled red at the rear. Gravity had pulled the blood inside the body downwards, its back and rear legs a sickly collage of dark reds and bruised purples. The shroud that covered it had slipped away, half covering the dead tech at the foot of the table. In its place sat an open cavity, darkly outlined by dried blood and gristle, and horrendous to look upon.

What had once been Jonny Tarver sat upright.

A second tech entered and was instantly grabbed at by the corpse's reanimated arm. The hand slipped easily round the tech's slender throat. The woman screamed—a garbled and choking sound that rivalled the rattle coming from the ruined chest cavity.

Josh's instinct drove him forwards, his intention to help the woman. An audible snap sounded as the tech's vertebra shattered into two. The woman was pitched forward with ease, and she collided into Josh, sending both to the floor. Josh felt the air from his lungs explode as the dead-weight of the tech flattened him. His vision blurred, yet he still had time to see the hideous corpse begin to climb up from off the table.

He pushed against the tech, his arms straining with the effort, and his mind screaming out. He managed to twist his head, and yell, "Shoot it!" towards the FBI agent.

***

Fernandez had become transfixed. He had witnessed the entire episode with his own eyes, yet his mind did not want to believe such a thing was possible. It was only when some unaffected part of his brain registered the cry for help, when his hand eventually moved towards his gun.

Josh was pleading for him to shoot what was now climbing from the coroner's worktable.

Jonny Tarver's waxen body slipped from the table. His feet slapped against the cold floor, toenails grey, and skin already shrunken inwards to reveal every vein and sinew.

The thing tottered backwards slightly, its rear bumping against the stainless steel worktop, and instruments in metal trays clattered noisily to the floor. The sound was deafening.

Fernandez had his weapon drawn. He levelled it towards the ruined chest. His thumb flicked the safety off. Pressure applied to the trigger. Yet, he could not bring himself to pull the trigger. His mind had slipped between reality and fantasy, as he desperately tried to resolve the startling images before him. His analytical brain was trying to find sense where logic had abandoned it.

How could this be?

A second cry, this one at his side, finally pulled him from this confused state.

"What are you waiting for, shoot the fucking thing!"

It was Balooga at his side, trying to force the agent into taking action.

The corpse before them had found its feet, and was now getting ready to spring forwards, hands already stained by the splattering of blood.

The weapon bucked in the agent's hands, followed by a clap of gunfire. A chunk of flesh from the corpse's shoulder disappeared in a shower of gore. The wall behind it turned instantly red. The bullet slowed the thing, causing its body to twist awkwardly, knocking it out of its rhythm.

Balooga was down on one knee in an attempt to drag Josh clear.

This sudden movement caught Tarver's attention. His eyes flicked downward and his colourless lips twisted themselves into a ghastly leer.

Balooga pulled at Josh, eventually getting a grip and yanking his arm free. Josh slipped clear of the dead tech, quickly climbing to his feet. They stumbled backwards to clear the agent's line of sight.

The corpse made a lunge towards them. A second bullet tore a fist-sized hole in its lower-abdomen—entrails slipping forth in a wet trail of rotten meat.

The corpse slipped in its own mess. One foot cut a red smear across the flooring, and it tumbled backwards, the back of its skull catching the edge of the steel table.

The three men were backing away from the terrible sight, step by step, unwilling to look away.

They took the corridor backwards, expecting the body of Jonny Tarver to come hurtling towards them at any moment. More movement, on the edges of their periphery, forced them to turn that way.

A second figure was shuffling their way. This one looked fresh. A young woman. An incision had cut flesh down to bone, and her skin had been peeled away, her right breast hanging oddly at the end of a massive flap of raw tissue. The dark hair found between her legs played out starkly against the whiteness of her skin.

Josh felt a second of embarrassment for the naked woman. Until she opened her mouth and an unearthly shriek of anger burst from greying lips. Her teeth came together with a crack, white spittle forming at the corners of her mouth, foaming onto her chin like a rabid beast.

The agent had his weapon in her direction now, and Josh was willing him to pull the trigger—hell, empty the entire clip in the woman's skull.

Fernandez must have been in tune with Josh's thoughts, because he dropped into a shooter's stance and aimed steady. The single shot nearly took the woman's head off. It caught her at the top of the forehead, leaving a neat hole there, but reducing the back of her head to a messy pulp of brain tissue and bone fragments.

The woman dropped to the floor, her arms and legs twitching spasmodically.

The commotion had drawn other members of staff. Some had fallen foul of the arms and teeth of the cadavers, throats ripped or flesh torn open; others had run out into the frost-bitten streets, screaming for help or otherwise.

More bodies had sprung back to life. Some just sat there, their dead brain matter unable to fire up the signals required to give them direction, whereas others were seemingly dexterous enough to give chase to some of the fleeing staff members, bringing them down before they'd made good their escape, bloodied teeth and nails gouging out eyes and tearing screaming tongues from mouths.

It was the stuff of nightmares.

Chapter Twenty-Six

Richardson Highway

Voices chattered over the airwaves in a high-pitched squeal. Police cruisers were radioing in their present locations and giving nearest estimates on their imminent arrivals. All six police cars had taken to the streets—911 calls coming in all at once in a sudden flood. The entire town had gone into a state of panic. A mass of people had inexplicably gone on the rampage, smashing store windows, tearing up highways in mass packs, driving oncoming traffic into each other, or attacking pedestrians at random in a frenzied mob.

Chief Zager had his foot set firmly over the gas of his cruiser, doing his best to keep the big vehicle on the right side of the highway. A heavy storm had blown in, covering Fairbanks in a near-complete whiteout. His high-intensity spotlight was cutting a white beam through the deluge of falling snow. The wind outside was howling, which sounded to Zager like the demented wail of the insane.

The chief drove the cruiser up Richardson Highway. The chains on the tyres were doing a good job, keeping the vehicle straight, but the added traction required was keeping the cruiser to a slow crawl.

The voices on the airwaves seemed to be getting more erratic. Zager picked up the handset to his radio and hit the transmit switch.

"This is Chief Zager. Despatch, do you copy? Over."

The radio hissed in a squeal of static. He tried again. The call went unanswered. The storm was making transmitting difficult to achieve.

Zager dropped the handset into the passenger seat. The radio continued with its one-way chatter. The voices were becoming more desperate sounding by the minute.

"Dammit!" Zager snapped.

He took the bend in the highway faster than he should have and almost lost the cruiser to the ditch at the side. The driver's side wheels dropped momentarily, slush and ice doing their best to drag the vehicle to a halt, before the chief yanked on the steering wheel to bring the cruiser back onto the highway.

He flicked the windscreen wiper switch over to its fastest setting. A blur of rubber cleared the gathering snow from his sight.

Movement, out in the blizzard, caught his attention. A large, thickset shadow was staggering parallel to the highway, its back bent against the wind, face hidden deep within the folds of a hood.

The chief hit the siren and flashed his lights for a couple of seconds; this sudden spectacle drew some attention. The figure stopped abruptly, unseen eyes now focusing on the vehicle.

Zager slowed the cruiser until he had the figure in range. He dropped the side window in an attempt to train the spotlight onto his target of interest. The white light caught the figure in a glare of blinding white light. One of the individual's arms shot forward in an attempt to cover its eyes.

The hand looked bright red.

"Jesus tonight," hissed Zager, seeing the hand was covered in blood.

The other arm had come up in a defensive gesture. A short axe lay clutched against the individual's chest. Clearly, even across the torrent of snow, Zager could see that the axe had blood splattered across its blade.

The riot shotgun was lodged between the driver and passenger seats – bolted upright, yet instantly accessible by one simple tug on the stock.

Zager yanked the weapon free. He simultaneously stopped the cruiser, sliding the vehicle sideways, and cracked open his door. In the next second he was out in the storm. Wind ripped at his clothing. He wore a thick overcoat with reflective panelling down the front and back, and boots laced beyond his ankles.

The riot gun weighed reassuringly in his arms.

Snow was falling heavily and, after taking only a dozen or so steps, the highway disappeared under a white deluge. Zager chanced a look backwards to find comfort in his ability to see the spotlight – a solid translucent beam able to guide him back to safety. At the opposite end of the light the figure stood stationary. A fact that unnerved the chief.

"Police!" he called, hoping to make a connection.

The figure didn't flinch or move a muscle.

The chief rubbed stinging wet shards from his eyes, uncertain now if the individual before him was a simple trick of the eye, conjured up from the blizzard and his own tired mind.

"Hey—you need assistance?" Zager called to the individual.

He was only ten yards away from the figure and clearly heard now, even over the howl of the wind. Zager could feel his heart knocking inside his chest. Some of the voices coming over the radio had sounded terrified—screaming for help, or their lives even. Zager was ready for anything.

Something bad had descended over Fairbanks along with the snow storm.

"Need help..?" Zager asked.

Movement to the left of Zager ran between the trees. He caught sight of it as it traversed from one tree to the next. The movement had seemed awkward, not with any stealth or cunning, but simply random in nature, and the steps taken to get from one location to the next had been laboured and uncoordinated.

Had someone lost themselves in the forest, delirious or

injured, now close to falling victim of hypothermia?

"Did you see that?" Zager asked the person before him.

No answer.

The chief pulled his flashlight free from his belt. He clicked it on. Aimed the beam towards the trees.

There.

More movement.

Two shadowy figures staggering from tree to tree.

"This way!" Zager yelled, getting their attention.

Heads snapped up, their struggle in the snow halted momentarily as each of them homed in on the noise. The police officer called out to them again, and they focused in on Zager.

They came then. Fast. Quickly leaving the cover of the woodlands, cutting two deep trenches of snow as they came. The one at the fore appeared to have more strength. Long legs carried it into the small clearing. There, it stopped, as if waiting for the second to catch up. The second figure closed the gap. They paused then, seemingly unable to pinpoint exactly where the voice had come from.

Zager yelled again. "This way!"

As one, the two figures focused in on the noise. They kicked up snow as they hurried towards the chief and his silent witness.

Zager got a look at the first individual. A man, he was middle-aged and overweight. Blood had crusted on the guy's collar, and his jacket had one sleeve almost torn away. He was struggling with his footing, one bare foot digging into the snow, the other, slipping uselessly as the flat sole of a dress shoe found little purchase.

The chief moved instinctively then, to help. Yet, as he took his first step, a powerful grip stopped him short.

The silent witness was now at his side. Axe raised high, with a look of murderous intent clear in his eyes.

Chapter Twenty-Seven

Alpine Lodge Fairbanks

Anna was quickly packing their few meagre belongings into a backpack. Isabelle sat at the edge of the bed, the stuffed teddy bear clutched eagerly in her arms. The little girl's eyes looked frightened. Josh had returned and practically ordered them both to get ready to leave. He'd scooped Isabelle out of bed and started to pull her clothing over her head. Still sleepy-eyed, the girl had allowed him to do so.

Now, she watched as both Josh and Anna hurried to get their stuff packed and ready.

"What the hell happened in there?" Anna hissed, trying to prise information out of Josh.

He looked anxiously towards the little girl. Keeping his voice low, he replied, "Place went crazy. Like the goddamn walking dead!"

"What do you mean?" Anna pushed, needing to know.

Josh didn't know what to say. That the dead had risen from their slumber? Insane. Yet, he'd just witnessed it with his own eyes. The dead resurrected. Just like Lazarus. Only that biblical character had not turned upon his fellow man and torn at flesh with bared teeth.

"There's no time to explain. Not now. Not here," he said, snatching up the backpack and throwing it over one shoulder.

He moved towards Isabelle. Anna stopped him short.

"Here—Josh, let me," she said, reaching out to take the girl in her arms. "Hold on—honey," she advised, hugging her tight against her chest.

Josh moved back to the doorway. He laid his hand on the handle, yet paused as he listened for what lay beyond.

"We're safe," Anna said, sensing nothing malignant was lying in wait.

"Okay," Josh nodded. "We need to be quick. Balooga and Agent Fernandez are waiting just outside. Once we get down to the lobby don't stop for anything. Keep going. They're parked just across the street."

Anna didn't like Josh's worried tone. Something bad had happened at the morgue. And it had put the fear of God into him.

Josh pulled the door open. Together they all stepped outside. The passageway was empty; doors spaced equally and opposite to each other were shut tight. A few TVs could be heard playing in rooms or the sounds of voices coming from the connecting doorways.

Josh took the lead. He kept a few steps ahead of them, his body tense, ready for any sudden or unexpected movements. Mercifully, none came. They reached the elevators unscathed. Reaching out, Josh pressed the call button.

"Let's take the stairs," Anna advised.

He nodded. No point getting cornered in such an enclosed space. Good call. He followed Anna and Isabelle down the first flight of steps. The lobby came into view once they'd descended a second flight.

The reception desk stood empty. The girl that had previously occupied it was not in sight. Nor were there any patrons milling around the front desk, people waiting to be seated in the adjacent restaurant, or any general foot traffic coming in or out of the main entrance. An unnerving silence had taken up residence in this place.

The small party of three traversed quickly through the

abandoned lobby area. Then found themselves out in the darkness.

A blinding sheet of snow was falling from the skies to cover everything in a white blanket.

Josh heard the honk of a car horn.

"Over there – look," he said, pointing towards the parked vehicle.

Anna spotted the car as well. She held Isabelle closer, wanting the child to gain warmth from her body heat.

"Come on," Josh said. He took a few steps away from the entrance, his feet kicking up white puffs of snow as he went.

Anna was right behind him. Although still uncertain as to what was going on, she felt a moment's relief as they closed in on the stationary vehicle. Inside, she could make out the faces of Detective Balooga and Agent Fernandez; they looked worried and eager to leave, and Anna heard the engine rev in anticipation of their arrival.

We're safe, for now, she thought.

Not true.

She caught up with Josh, following him in the trail he had cut out in the snow, and then took the lead, leaving him quickly behind.

The little girl in her arms let loose with a scream, high-pitched and terrified.

Anna chanced a look behind her.

Spewing forth from the hotel foyer came a mass of bodies. Eyes like black mirrors and mouths stretched hideously wide. Some of the people at the front wore hotel uniforms. The white shirts normally found worn underneath company jackets were stained red or torn open to reveal bite marks or deep lacerations cut into skin. Behind them came a bedraggled mixture of people. Some wore casual clothing, street wear, or formal attire; others appeared near naked, skin as white as the snow at their feet, with just under garments or bathing robes covering them from the freezing temperatures.

The mass gathering homed in on the group of three – their

forbidden needs driving them on with only one thought in mind.

Feed the hunger.

Anna managed to bundle Isabelle into the rear of the car. She almost tore the door from its hinges getting the child to safety. Her next immediate thought was Josh. She spun around to see he had fallen behind.

"Run—Josh!" she yelled.

One of the infected was almost on top of him. Its arms were reaching out, fingers hooked into claws and a look of bloodthirsty madness twisting its features into a hideous mask.

Anna reacted instinctively. She pushed herself away from the car, propelling herself forwards with a speed unmatched. The thing's head snapped back as she landed a crushing blow. It fell at her feet with hands still clawing at the air. She brought her foot down hard crushing the skull with a sickening crunch of broken bone. The head disappeared in a burst of red liquid. Its hands stopped in mid-movement, and it lay there frozen in its death pose.

"Josh—come on," Anna called, grabbing his arm.

Josh slipped on the icy snow and almost took them both down in a heap. Yet somehow Anna managed to hold her footing and she half dragged him towards the vehicle.

Too late.

A swarm of bodies had started to gather around the car.

With no other option and, with Isabelle's safety in mind, Anna yelled for them to go. Get the hell out of there she ordered the agent.

The vehicle launched forwards mowing down the nearest bodies. Two went down together with demented cries, faces contorted and full of rage. The front tyre rolled over one, and its face ripped open in an explosion of torn flesh. The agent had the gas all the way to the floor. Within seconds he had steered them away from the baying mob and into the security of the deserted streets.

Anna heard the engine noise grow distant. She willed them

to safety. Now, they had to get themselves away from the mob. Anna scanned the surrounding streets. All looked deserted. The wind was raging and snow was being dumped in great droves to cover everything in a white, frozen layer. This bleached landscape threw her internal compass and sense of direction off kilter. They needed to get back to the precinct, but Anna didn't want to lead them directly back, taking the crazed horde with them.

"Josh, follow me," she said.

He was right behind her. His footsteps filling in were she had already trodden in the snow. They made it to the end of the street, unharmed, but the mass gathering was close behind them, matching them step for step.

"Can we lose them in this?" Josh asked, his eyes were tight slits against the raging blizzard.

Anna brought them to a stop. The street branched off in different directions. They needed to find shelter—and fast.

"This way," she said, her mind made up.

They cut into an adjourning street, their footsteps clear in the snow, and an easy path for those behind them to follow.

Josh brought them to an abrupt halt. "The mall!"

"What?" Anna asked.

Josh brought himself closer, so he could be heard over the wail of the wind. "The mall. That's where we can lose them."

Anna considered this for a second. "Good idea. But where the hell is it, Josh?"

Josh grinned. "Follow me."

He took off in the opposite direction, heading for a street back the way they had just come.

"This is insane," she yelled after him.

He didn't stop. Just bent against the wind and continued. Anna had no choice but to follow.

They were backtracking. Quickly. Trying to outrun the horde before they were cut off from their escape route. Josh was pushing hard.

Years before they had met, he had been a competent runner,

short-listed for the Olympics, only to fall foul of a DUI driver. The resultant crash had put paid to Josh's Olympic dream. His left leg had taken most of the impact, shattering bones, and ending his legacy before it had even begun. Yet, now, with the threat of the infected, he was doing remarkably well. His arms and legs were pumping through the snow with notable ease.

They re-entered the main street to find the majority of the infected closing in.

"Which way now?" Anna asked.

Josh took a lungful of air. Gathered his senses. "We passed it on the way to the morgue."

"How far?"

"A mile. Maybe more."

Anna gripped his arm. "You go. I'll hold them back. Give you a chance."

Josh almost swore at her. "Like hell. There's too many."

Anna quickly scanned along the highway. What the hell were these things?

Josh brought her to her senses. "This way – now." He pulled his arm free, grabbing her hand in the process and leading the way forward.

They tore down one of the connecting main streets with the mass gathering close behind.

From nowhere, as if conjured out of the very darkness, a naked female leered out of the blizzard, breaking through the white curtain of snow, and made a grab for them.

Josh and Anna skidded to a halt. Before Anna could react, Josh stepped forwards in a protective gesture. The woman opened her mouth in a piercing scream.

A primeval force took over Josh then. He reacted without thinking. Without planning. Without any consideration for his own safety. He took a step closer and threw a wild, but effective, swing at the woman. His balled fist caught her just below her chin, crushing her throat with the impact. Her scream stopped suddenly.

Wasting no time, Anna finished her off. She sidestepped

Josh, two easy steps, and then drove her foot into its chest. Bones shattered, piercing the heart, whether it beat with life or not, and the woman fell backwards, reclaimed by the night. Anna moved a step away and rammed her boot into the thing's already damaged throat. The woman's head practically shot away from the rest of her body in an explosion of blood.

"One for the good guys," Anna said, rejoining Josh.

"Heard that," he said.

More shrieks of madness called out from the connecting streets.

"Hurry," Josh said, retaking the lead.

Anna followed. Somewhere deep inside her, she was impressed by Josh's ability to maintain focus under such conditions. He was turning into a real man, capable of things he could not have ever imagined. Finding a hidden strength that was only now being tested.

They found themselves at a sudden T-junction. Josh paused for just a heartbeat. "This way," he said, taking the turn to the left.

"We're moving further away from the precinct," Anna advised.

"Don't worry," Josh countered. "Once we lose them, we can backtrack."

Anna simply shrugged. "Your call."

"Trust me," Josh grinned.

"Always," Anna replied.

The mob had fallen behind slightly. Maybe they had chanced upon the woman's body and were currently gorging themselves on her warm flesh.

Bon appétit, Anna thought, before following Josh deeper into the whiteout.

Chapter Twenty-Eight

Richardson Highway

Chief Zager felt himself pushed back with force. The axe bearer had stepped before him, with the weapon raised high above his head. It was a protective stance. One designed to keep the police chief safe. Zager recognized the person then. And shuddered involuntarily having suddenly witnessed the madness in the individual's eyes.

"Kavik – what the hell are you doing?" Zager yelled.

The large Alaskan Indian ignored the question, turning his back on the chief, the axe raised, and his focus on the advancing pair.

Zager had the Remington 870 shotgun aimed downwards. Now he brought the weapon up, chambering one of the 20 gauge cartridges in a single fluid motion.

"Kavik Tonrar—put the weapon down," he ordered.

The Alaskan's hand wavered for a second. Had the chief finally got through to him? Was Kavik drunk to the point of madness?

Perhaps – but the Alaskan was not letting go of the axe. Rather, he seemed to have found his grip on the weapon again, as it fixed above his head, ready to carve downwards like that of an executioner's.

Something inhuman screamed then. A horrible sound that

shattered the night and spoke of terrible suffering. For a second, Zager believed that Kavik Tonrar had finally succumbed to an inebriated insanity, his brain finally slipping into a permanent state of intoxication.

Yet as Zager considered this, he realised that the maddening cry had come from across the frozen fields, from one of the other individuals.

The middle-aged man closest to them unleashed another ungodly sound. He came at them then, his feet simultaneously finding purchase, propelling him forwards, then slipping and almost bringing him down. He clawed his way towards them. The crazed howl growing with every yard gained.

The man looked beset with rage, and Zager had a moment to consider if the Native Alaskan had recently attacked the middle-aged guy. Perhaps Tonrar had finally gone off the rails and assaulted these two in the forest. And now they were seeking their revenge. If that were true, then the chief had to take Tonrar in. Zager stood there trapped by indecision.

"Okay—everyone take it easy." Zager advised, trying to calm the situation.

The Alaskan didn't flinch.

In stark contrast the middle-aged guy bared his teeth and snapped his jaws together wildly.

Then all hell broke loose.

The guy launched himself at Tonrar. And the Alaskan moved forward to meet him. They came together in a clash of bodies. The guy was trying to claw at Tonrar's eyes, while the Alaskan in turn was swinging the axe in a wide arc to keep him at bay.

The second individual had now cleared the tree-line. A young man dressed in simple jeans and T-shirt. He must have been near frozen. He appeared unfazed by either the scuffle before him or the subzero temperatures.

Instead, he looked towards Zager with fury in his eyes. The man bore a slight resemblance to the older guy – perhaps his son, or nephew—with a chubby face and expanding waistline.

Zager stepped sideways in an attempt to get both Tonrar

and the older guy within his sights. Now, in this new position, he witnessed a ragged hole that had been torn from the guy's neck. A huge wound, with muscle and tissue present. The flurry of snow broke for a second and Zager had a clear view into the injury. The guy's vertebra was poking out from the crust of blood.

Zager felt hot bile in his throat. The injury was horrific. No one suffering with such an injury should have been capable of walking, let alone taking on such an imposing figure as Kavik Tonrar.

"Jesus tonight," breathed Zager, chilled to his bones.

The young man was within distance now. His mouth opened and a red chunk of flesh fell from his engorged lips. Zager watched in horror as the meaty morsel tumbled into the snow, leaving a red smear and bloody hole in its wake. It was coming then. Fast and direct. Arms out and fingers hooked into claws.

Zager didn't have time to think. Not to rationalise the situation anyway. Instinct took over. He aimed the shotgun and fired. An explosion of snow and soil erupted. The warning shot didn't slow it any. It just seemed to infuriate him further. Zager fired again. Again a warning shot. And again it did little to deter.

"Freeze!" Zager demanded.

The young man was on top of him in the next second. Zager felt the Remington pulled from his hands with tremendous strength. The weapon fell to the ground. Next, claws were reaching out to find a softer purchase.

The fingers stiffened though. Opened out straight. As if they'd gone into a sudden spasm. Zager watched in mesmerised amazement as the head flipped upwards, leaving behind a shower of red liquid, as it tumbled away from the decapitated body. The young man's body went rigid. It released one final gasp of breath—air from the severed larynx bubbling out, before toppling backwards to leave a blossoming stain in the snow.

In the next moment, Tonrar was shouting for them to get the

hell out of there.

Zager had just enough time to see that the Alaskan's axe had made short work of the middle-aged guy, and then he was being pulled roughly back towards the cruiser, with the sound of more insanity coming from somewhere deeper in the woods.

Chapter Twenty-Nine

Fairbanks Correctional Facility

To leave skin exposed to the cold was a foolish thing to do, especially here in Fairbanks at any time of the year, and more so now during the winter solstice. Yet here, in this strangest of places, many stood around with arms bare, or topless even, regardless of the fact that temperatures had dropped far beyond the negative.

Most, if not all, of the flesh revealed was decorated by either the vivid colours, or the deepest blacks of a tattooist's needle. Not all the designs were recognisable to the average person; most were exclusive in understanding to but a few, tribal or gang signatures that granted their bearer's exclusivity to groups that were structured by ethnicity alone.

Here, especially in this part of the facility, there would not be multiculturalism, that most tolerant practice societies now embraced.

No. The gangs and groups of this place stuck primarily to the same colours, blacks with blacks, Latinos with Latinos, and whites with whites. Only a few groups broke this racial divide, multicultural in their gathering, but these groups were already segregated from the main populace, as the crimes committed by such a gathering were not tolerated by men of forged principle or code.

Some crimes were simply too grave, even for those that had been locked away by the rest of society.

The exercise yard was a swell of overworked muscle and graffiti-scarred flesh. Many were working biceps into lumps of steel, or broad chests into slabs of hardened granite. The metallic clank of dumbbells and squeal of heavy weights rubbing against iron bars filled the yard with the sounds of focused aggression.

Some were shooting hoops into baskets, and the sounds of applause or jeering added to the clunk and clatter of the bodybuilding enthusiasts.

For this was the place of exhibition. Bodies that would have placed well in national tournaments swaggered under the floodlights, the hard angles of over-defined muscles cutting deep shadows in ink-stained flesh.

This was also a place where an individual could—no, wait —were demanded that they displayed their place in the group's hierarchy. The gang leaders of such groups stood nonchalantly, surrounded by the lesser positioned, as they commanded the day to day objectives with a seemingly casual indifference, yet deep down with the same conviction as that of a military chief.

A small group had gathered at the perimeter of the fence, looking out, over a short distance, and into an adjacent holding pen, similar to theirs. Yet holding men that had no moral compass or social placing. Even here in this place of ruthless killers and hardened criminals.

The smaller exercise yard harboured the sex offenders, and it was here where the boundaries of ethnicity had been broken – for a person of such immorality belonged to no civilised or uncivilised even, assembly.

Ordinarily, the warden of this prison would have split the exercise times into two distinct periods, his wish for conflict no more than his want for chaos, yet with the temperature dropping rapidly and darkness almost upon them, he had been forced to allow the inmates to congregate at similar times. High intensity floodlights shone brightly, masking the onset of dusk, and bathed the inmates in an artificial glow.

Now, that decision to allow all prisoners to exercise together was rapidly becoming the igniter required to set off an explosive disturbance.

The gathering in the main yard was growing as more flocked there, with baying breaths and hateful voices, and scarred knuckles pounding on the chain-mail fencing to rattle the razor wire, which topped it. The mob swelled further. Their loathing for the segregated prisoners, able to break the normal rule of the yard, very clear. Blacks, whites and all mixture of ethnics were mixing as one—chanting now, faces angry, and their hate turning to bitter resentment.

The guards that topped the perimeter of the yards grew nervous. The lead guard spoke into his radio—for perhaps now was the time to end yard duty, and safely get the prisoners back inside their cells. The two-way radio crackled in the guard's ear. The commands received were hard to make out over the ruckus of noise which came from below. He hit the transmit button for a second time and the squeal of interference added to the already deafening sound.

Then silence.

The mob fell quiet instantly—their growls of revulsion quelled as one. An eerie calm took place over the madness that had been growing.

A small number of gasps of surprise broke the silence, but they were short-lived and only a few.

Suddenly, from nowhere, a little girl had appeared in the smaller yard.

Some of the prisoners there gaped open-mouthed at the unexpected arrival. Had she materialised from the sick thoughts of those around her. Was she conjured from the memory of crimes committed, and had now somehow, amazingly, grown substance?

Some of the prisoners closest to her reared away, as if she possessed the power to admonish their crimes by presence alone. Others swelled closer, their appetite for the forbidden stronger than any conscious reasoning, or the sense of what was right and wrong.

The main body of men in the larger yard now started to call out. Perplexed and bemused by this arrival, yet paternal instincts finding its voice, as they yelled out warnings to the little girl of the immediate danger she now found herself in.

The girl appeared unfazed by her surroundings. Rather, she looked at ease and not worried about the men that had started to gather about her. She smiled at one or two; and these individuals pushed against others to get even closer.

More cries of warning sounded out. Even the guards on the wall were warning the child to get out of there, but went unheard, as the group of inmates gathered around her.

Then something peculiar happened. The first few to reach the girl dropped suddenly to the ground. They clutched at stomachs or held hands to their throats as the floor around them turned red.

The rest scattered. They bolted for the fencing, or entrance, as more fell to their knees, clutching at ruined flesh, which gushed with blood, and screamed for help or mercy, or both.

The little girl moved effortlessly from body to body, her teeth and nails tearing through clothing and human skin with the same strength as cold steel.

The ones that had fallen first had now stiffened, their legs no longer kicking nor bloodied hands grabbing to hold horrific wounds together.

Yet, moments later, they stirred again. Bodies jerked back to life, as heads snapped upwards, and eyes that had been empty only seconds ago, now burning with a need and desire; a desire that could not have been fantasized about whilst the recipient was still capable of drawing breath. They climbed unsteadily to their feet. Then took faltering steps towards the remaining inmates.

The rest of the prisoners were brought down, either by the reanimated inmates or the girl herself. And within minutes the smaller exercise yard had been cleansed of its burden.

Eyes feverish and yearning for more turned upon the prisoners trapped within the larger yard. The main group had now started to back away from the fencing, putting distance between themselves and the horde of bloodthirsty convicts. Some of the prisoners had stripped the iron bars of their loads, and they stood with makeshift weapons in hand, readying themselves with iron clubs or poles.

The horde screamed as one then—a blood-curdling noise that opened bladders and sprung tears from the faces of hardened men.

The little girl raised her arms aloft and the noise ceased abruptly. Now, the mass of bloodied figures stood still, their torn faces turned towards the cowering prisoners. Then the girl spoke a single word and the horde launched itself towards the fence. They climbed quickly, topping the barrier in seconds, before throwing themselves into the tangle of razor-wire. Clothing and strips of flesh were torn off, and they fluttered wildly like hideous banners, caught in the frozen winds of twilight.

A few gunshots rang out as the guards tried to maintain order. But madness had taken over this place, and the shots were quickly silenced as the prisoners set about their custodians with murderous glee.

As the cries for help dwindled, the resultant stillness claimed the souls of the sinful, offering neither mercy nor the understanding of forgiveness. And the unmoving darkness delivered an uncompromising vengeance that none could escape.

Chapter Thirty

The Mall

Josh had Anna in his arms. They were hiding out in the mall. They had successfully lost the maddened horde in the swirl of heavy snow. Only a few wet foot prints gave any indication of their passing, and they were rapidly drying as the mall's air-conditioning system was still running at full pelt. For now.

In danger of being charged with looting, Josh and Anna had swapped their damp clothing for dry ones, courtesy of a clothes shop that had surrendered its merchandise once Anna had gained easy access. Considering the mall had a few infected people wandering about it, they figured if The National Guard were to show up with weapons drawn, then they would have more to worry about than a couple of outfits taken by two desperate survivors.

They were now hidden in the back kitchen of a restaurant. The smell of spices and the rich aroma of meats filled the area with the pleasant odours of recent cooking. It was hard to believe that many would have been dining here as little as a few hours ago. Now though, the restaurant stood empty, tables cleaned and chairs neatly lined up, ready for tomorrow's feast, an event that would now probably never happen. Not in any ordinary sense anyway. Maybe those that roamed about outside had another type of feast in mind.

"You okay?" Anna asked.

Josh wiped his lips with a napkin. Grinned ruefully. "Guess we need to add stealing food to our long list of felonies now?"

Anna laughed quietly. "Maybe we could plea bargain, and see if we can get off lightly?"

"Yeah," Josh agreed. "Admit our culinary transgressions and see if they'll drop all the murder charges."

Anna shrugged her shoulders. "Maybe they would, but…" she pulled on her top, a thick jumper with snowflakes on it, "I think we're likely to do hard time for our crimes to fashion."

It was Josh's turn to stifle his amusement. He too wore a knitted jumper, only his was a colourful mix of Alaskan artwork. He popped the remainder of the sandwich he had made from the kitchen's contents and then chewed eagerly. Anna slapped him playfully on the arm.

"Enjoy it while you can. It's all watered down porridge and cold gruel from now on."

"Nah—I hear prison food isn't all that bad," Josh joked.

"And who told you that?"

"A little bird."

"Really?"

"Yeah—I also heard that you get conjugal visiting rights too." He offered her a mischievous wink.

Anna slapped his arm again. "Dumbass. We're not even married."

"Oh—right, they not include common-law wives then?"

"Not sure, maybe they allow common-outlaw wives?" Anna joked.

"Well, either way, we should be just fine."

They looked at each other. Then smiled. Josh leaned in to place a soft kiss onto her lips. "I love you," he whispered.

"Love you too," Anna breathed back.

They kissed again, only this time they lingered and it quickly became passionate. Josh took her face in his hands. Looked into her brown eyes. "If we get out of this, then maybe we should think about making our relationship official."

"You proposing to me, Mister Sawyer?" Anna asked.

"Would you like it if I were, Miss Privalova?"

Anna looked at him earnestly. "I come with baggage—you know that don't you?"

"What baggage?" Josh asked, playing along with her.

"About two thousand years worth," she said.

Josh twisted his face into an over-exaggerated thoughtful look. "We may have to talk about that, but I think we can work through it."

"You're a real catch, Josh Sawyer."

"Me?" he said. "What happened to being a dumbass?"

Anna laughed despite herself. "That too."

They held onto each other, and the insane world around them seemed somehow diminished. As if their love for each other would protect them from the insanity that had set them on this path together: a path that would either lead them to freedom or the total annihilation of mankind.

Finally, they pulled apart from each other. Josh turned suddenly serious. "What the hell are those things?"

Anna sat thoughtful for a moment. "Not sure."

"Take a guess," Josh said.

Anna shrugged. "Not what you think, anyways."

"What am I thinking?" quizzed Josh.

"Dawn of the Dead. Day of the Dead, that kind of thing."

Josh nodded. "Maybe. But then why didn't those initial two victims reanimate?"

"You mean the bank teller and middle-aged woman found at the park?"

"The very two," Josh said.

"I'm not sure."

"Take an educated guess."

Anna laughed quietly. "Who am I, offspring from the Van Helsing ancestry?"

"Guess not," Josh agreed, "but have you ever seen anything similar?"

Anna shook her head. "No – this is something new. At least

to me. I may be old in years, but nothing I'm familiar with. And as you know, I've been around a long time."

"So no insight then?"

"I didn't say that," Anna responded.

"Enlighten me, please," Josh said.

"You're not going to like it."

"Try me."

"Okay," Anna said. "This outbreak is not totally random. Not everyone becomes infected. Clearly. The two victims that originally brought Fernandez here proves that."

"How?"

"Because they didn't become infected."

"They didn't show any signs of bite marks either," Josh countered.

"True," Anna agreed.

"But why?"

Anna paused for a moment. "Because they didn't have the right character traits."

"Meaning?"

"You're not going to like it."

"Just tell me."

"Because—Josh, they were of purest of heart. Innocents. Untarnished. And whatever is spreading this infection, the source, is only interested in the sinful."

Josh looked back exasperated. "Same old Anna."

"What does that mean?"

"Means you always see things black or white. Right or wrong. Good or bad."

"What other way is there?"

"All the grey bits in-between."

Anna shook her head. "You're missing the point. This infection does not have the ability to determine one's moral status, if a person is repentant for their wrongdoings. It just fixes on the malignant part of the soul and locks onto that."

"So the two victims were saints then? Having never done anything wrong. Ever?"

Anna simply nodded. "You asked me for my opinion. I'm just giving it. There is something out there Josh, that is feeding on the human condition. Growing stronger by the minute. I don't know why, or to what purpose, but we need to understand it, if we stand any chance of stopping this spreading."

"Can it be done?" Josh asked.

"Find me the source, I will try," Anna replied.

"I'll do my best."

And he would too. Because he had the deepest dread that his actions back in Mexico would eventually seal his fate, if one of those infected things outside finally got its teeth into him.

Chapter Thirty-One

Police Precinct

Time had little meaning in this place. Night ruled absolute. Daylight was nothing but a short, tantalising glimmer of hope. In this place, the dark had rendered everything mute and inhospitable.

How anyone could live here was beyond Josh's comprehension. He was even beginning to think that Mexico, with all its fetidness, had been a better place to be. Hell, at least he'd only had his fellow human beings to worry about. In contrast this place was like being dropped into George A Romero's living nightmare.

Josh and Anna had hid out within the mall until the horde had finally dwindled, which had then given them the chance to slip back into the night and find solace here in the police precinct.

The precinct had become their base of operations now. It made sense. Communication lines were still in operation. Utilities were working, water and electricity available, and warmth radiated from the gas heaters that burned silently about them.

Josh and Anna were sat around one of the vacant desks found in the main office. Isabelle was sat between them, her small hands sketching out a drawing on the back of a blank crime report.

Josh chanced a look at the drawing and was relieved to find the theme had a happy nature about it: swings and children playing in the park. Not darkness and damnation like what they had recently found themselves in.

Josh looked towards the smaller office that Fernandez occupied. The agent was on the phone, speaking animatedly, this call one of many, his need for urgent assistance apparent. Detective Balooga was seated to the side of the agent. His face looked ashen and drawn. He looked tired. And Josh had a moment of pity for the Chicago lawman – the determined individual that had chased them halfway across America less than a year ago was no longer present. Josh sensed that Balooga was a spent force. And this worried him to the core. They needed the Balooga of old if they were going to make it through the next few hours.

"You okay?" Anna asked.

Josh sighed wearily. "Not your average day."

Anna laughed humourlessly. "It never is where we're concerned – is it."

"Anna – seriously, what are we looking for? Where do we begin?"

Anna looked at the little girl. Isabelle appeared engrossed in her drawing, and seemed distant enough for them to talk openly.

"In truth – Josh, I don't really know."

They sat silent for a moment, Fernandez's voice growing beyond a muffle. From what they could hear, he didn't seem to be getting the response he required. Balooga had found his feet and was currently trying to calm the seemingly irate FBI agent.

"You must know something? Anything?" Josh asked, desperate to understand what was happening here, in this desolate place, and more importantly, how to end it.

"Okay," Anna began. "This is not the same as Colorado. We're not dealing with someone like Jonus."

Anna's use of her adversary's name sent a shiver down Josh's spine.

"Then what?"

"I'm not sure. But there are similarities."

"Go on," Josh prompted.

"I think we're dealing with an entity that has a penchant for human flesh. Needs it in the same way I need the life that flows through human veins."

Josh felt uneasy about having to listen to Anna describing her need for human blood. It was a condition he had accepted, but he still didn't like the notion, nor condone such a thing. It was Anna's choice of victims that allowed Josh to cope with such knowledge – yet this understanding still carried with it a burden of responsibility, and that had stretched his moral values, even if the woman he loved only sought out the souls of sinners.

"Yet they don't die," Josh said, aware that there was no resurrection for Anna's victims. The dead stayed dead. Not like this place.

Anna said, "This thing we seek is not interested in collecting the souls of the dead. But in unleashing them upon this world."

"But for what purpose?"

"Anarchy? The demise of Man? Who knows what motivates such a thing. Or even if there needs to be a higher purpose for such a thing."

"Meaning?"

"Meaning – how many species has Man wiped off the face of the Earth? And for what, profit? Fun? A noble cause?"

Josh felt ashamed for what his predecessors had done. Anna was right, there didn't appear to be any legitimate reason for the destruction of a species. None whatsoever. So why was he trying to find a deeper meaning to what was happening here. People were dying, and then returning from the dead to claim others. Deal with it.

If only it was that simple.

Josh didn't have an affinity to any one person here in Fairbanks, but they were normal people with families, mostly hardworking families and simply struggling to get by in such a hostile environment. This could be happening anywhere in the US, even in his hometown of Chicago. How would he feel if his father and friends back there were enduring such a thing?

Anger flared in him then. He wasn't about to sit here and accept the fact that people were dying and then turning into things of unspeakable horror—just because they were. No, there had to be something deeper at work here. A purpose.

"We better figure out what's going on here. And more importantly—why?" Josh said.

Anna nodded. "I agree Josh, but in all honesty, I don't know where to begin?"

"What about the sawmill? You said you were initially drawn to that place. Why?"

Anna considered this for a moment. "Maybe it was where this all started. Out there on the outskirts of town, with no one to witness the events."

"But why the sawmill? What significance does it have?"

Anna flipped her hands upwards—she didn't know why.

"Come on—think. What did the place have that others had not?"

Anna closed her eyes and visualised the layout of the place. Her memory drew up dark pictures of rot and decay. She walked her mind's eye through the derelict building, seeing nothing of real interest, until reaching the place where the clothing had been found. There, she remembered the dull and metallic lines of the rail track.

The track had been present throughout the main building too but the twin rails had rusted into disuse. It was only when the rails stretched towards the surrounding woodland that they appeared to be in working condition.

"The rail track," Anna said. "There was a rail track leading from the sawmill. Still maintained. Usable. But I didn't see any trains."

"Okay," Josh said, "but where did the tracks lead to?"

Anna shrugged her shoulders. "We need to find out."

Josh stood. He looked towards the office. Agent Fernandez

was just getting off the phone. Josh moved towards the office
—his hope that together they could find a reason as to why this
was happening and, more crucially, to what end.

Chapter Thirty-Two

The Alaska House Art Museum

An audience of faces peered back at the security guard as he made his way through the dark corridor. Some of these faces looked angry, hostile expressions glaring accusingly as he walked past. Other stared out straight, unblinking, seemingly impassive towards the guard's passing. A few were hideous with features pulled into macabre shapes, eyes and mouths stretched unnaturally wide, and wax-like in their appearance.

The guard shone his light across the masks, and shuddered. He hated this part of his rounds. This subdued corridor with its haphazard faces pinned to the wall. A few of the tribal masks had spotlights positioned above them, with white light pointing downwards, which made the masks look even more bizarre and lifelike. Some of them watched him as he traversed from one end of the corridor to the next. It was a trick of the eye, yet unnerving nonetheless.

The guard moved the beam away from the last mask in line – the one he loathed the most. It gave him the creeps. And would continue to do so, even if he served out his remaining twenty years of work in this place.

Seal Hunter by Bobby Nashookpuk was the mask in question.

Bobby Nashookpuk could go fuck himself, thought the guard as he approached the mask. It was a three-faced affair, with a central face making up the majority, and two others cascading down either side to form a molten-looking monstrosity. The mask looked like it had actually come from the movie *The Thing*.

The guard shuddered as he neared it. He used every ounce of willpower to steer his eyes away from it, and focus his attention directly ahead. Beads of sweat popped on his forehead, and he used the back of his hand to wipe them clear, the flashlight bobbing about in his hand as he did so.

The end of the corridor branched off in a T-shape, one side leading to a collection of Native Alaskan paintings – more strange faces and weird illustrations, and the other opened out to a gallery of Native dolls, contained in glass cases and comical in their appearance.

The guard took to his right, favouring the dolls over the paintings. In truth, he didn't mind the dolls. Most were funny little representations of larger subjects: fishermen, hunters, bears and other wild animals indigenous to this part of the world.

He entered the gallery – his flashlight reflecting back at him in a white glare as the beam hit the glass cases dotted around the area.

A sudden movement caught his eye. Quick and furtive, the shadow danced from behind one display case to another.

"Hey!" called the guard. "We closed over an hour ago."

No one appeared, red-faced having been caught here at such unsociable an hour.

"Hello," the guard called out.

His heart-rate had already gone up by ten beats per minute. He had no real weapon to call upon, just a nightstick that had been handed to him from the previous night guard like it was some lost artefact, intended to be revered by its next holder.

The guard pulled the nightstick from his belt.

"Kids," he said, expecting the intruder to be a local juvenile sent here on some sort of prank, "I'll whip your hide if I get my hands on you."

The darkness mocked him with its silence.

"Little fuckers," he spat.

The flashlight played out over the display cases to reveal nothing. Deciding to head back and phone his superior, hell —he could come over and sort this shit out himself, the guard about turned, his intentions on returning to the front desk and contacting the museum's manager. Post-haste.

But no.

He turned to find the short figure of a little girl stood before him. The lights from the adjacent walls hid her features in a veil of harsh shadows.

"Kid – seriously, I'll use this on your hide," he warned, raising the nightstick.

The girl just stood silent.

"You a retard?" he asked.

No response was offered.

"Okay – that's it. Your ass is mine!" he said; ready to give the girl a good hiding with the stick.

He took a single step closer before the lights on the walls flickered and died. He had a moment of near-blindness, the flashlight bobbing about the floor uselessly, and then the wall lights burst back to life. The girl now gone. As if the gloom had swallowed her whole.

"What the fuck . . ." breathed the guard.

He spun full circle.

To find himself alone.

Quickly and with purpose, he headed towards the front of the building. There he would use the phone to contact the manager. And quit. Right here and now. Enough of this fucking place. He entered the main foyer, his feet quickening with every step. He reached the main desk and his hand sought out the telephone. His fingers closed around the hand piece.

The phone line was dead.

No dialling tone, crackle, beep, nothing.

"Shit," he snapped, his digit finger pressing down on the receiver. The phone just lay dead in his hand. He dropped the handset into the cradle.

Think for a moment.

To hell with contractual agreements. He was leaving now. What did he care if all the artwork found inside got stolen in his absence? It was mostly crap anyway.

He dropped his cap in the chair near him, and headed towards the door with keys in hand. Something clattered noisily from behind. He spun to find the phone had fallen from the desk, the handset free from its cradle and lying off to the side, at least ten feet away. The wire from handset to base had been severed – bare strands of copper visible as they poked from the insulation.

The guard panicked then, falling over his feet, as he rushed to get out of there. He landed heavily on his behind. The nightstick spun away, out of his grasp, before skidding and disappearing from view.

The little girl was beside him then. Her face only inches from his, her breath hot against his cheek. He jerked away from her. But she was not willing to let him go. Before he could move away, she sank her teeth into his throat. Blood burst forth in an arterial spray. He cried out. Tried to push her away, but she held on with supernatural strength. Now, she wrapped her arms around him, her teeth sinking deeper into warm flesh.

The guard started to kick uncontrollably and the heels of his booted feet slipped in the pool of gore which now surrounded him. His bladder and bowels had opened to mix with the red liquid that continued to pour from the open wound.

The guard's mind sent shock-waves of fear throughout his body. He could feel his life's fluid seeping away, taking with it the warmth of living breath, and replacing it instead with a freezing numbness that chilled him to the bone. The sensation of losing heat continued until he was left cold and hollow. The last of his breath slipped silently from blue-tinged lips, yet his guts continued to feel pain.

A hunger was growing there, in the pit of his stomach, which thrashed about like an infuriated and chained beast. It continued to grow. Heat now restored, to quickly rage out of control. A burning inferno of need had ignited, and this need was quickly spreading throughout the guard's veins.

He climbed to unsteady feet. His vision had blurred with a red tinge. Now, he looked about, his fear forgotten and this new hunger in its place. He staggered past the little girl, paying her no heed and then staggered towards the entrance.

The locked door blocked his escape. His fingers scratched frantically at the deadbolt, his hands scraping heavily against it, uselessly, to leave red smears as his palms cracked and split to weep blood.

A fleeting figure brushed past the window adjacent to the secure doorway. The guard's fevered mind focused on this. With a demented roar he launched himself through the window, exiting the museum in an explosion of shattering glass.

The night and its promise of freedom were waiting there to greet him.

Chapter Thirty-Three

Police Precinct

Agent Fernandez felt like the darkness outside had finally found its way into his soul. An almost total feeling of bleakness had saturated his thoughts, and he was now close to exhaustion. Not a physical exhaustion, he was well versed in long, drawn-out investigations, and he had learned to pace himself during the weeks that could follow, but a weariness to his spirit. He had not felt this uncertain or unsure about his own abilities, ever. Even as a fresh-faced cadet he'd had the fearlessness of youth, if none of the experience required, and an unlimited level of optimism, that most young adults had the privilege to draw from.

Now, though, Fernandez felt as if that once infinite well of self-belief had run dry.

Things had gone from the difficult to the realms of the insane. How the hell could he rationalise, as an intelligent individual, the events that he had seen? Human cadavers rising from the dead, attacking others, only for them to shrug off mortal wounds and they themselves seek out other victims, to satisfy a thirst that was shocking to think of.

The agent still had the original case files on his desk, but considering what had happened since, they seemed hardly significant, or important, now that they were dealing with a countless number of victims. As the agent looked at the profile photos, he actually thought that these first two victims, the ones that he had originally been sent to investigate, were the lucky ones. Neither had been torn to shreds. Nor were they currently running around seeking flesh to tear at. Both had died in what Fernandez now thought was a serene and civilised manner.

The agent looked up at his small audience. Balooga was still sat at the table. He appeared to have found a fresh level of energy, some colour had returned to his face and he was sprightlier in his manner. The agent felt a certain degree of relief at having the Chicago detective here with him. Once already the detective had saved his hide, and the agent now hoped that the Balooga of old would offer some sort of help in resolving the madness that had Fairbanks in its grip.

Both Josh and Anna stood just within the office. They were alternating between watching the girl sat in the main department and then looking expectantly at the FBI agent. The little girl seemed happy to be sat drawing at the desk. Occasionally, she would stop and look towards the couple, nod to herself, as if them being near her was okay, then return to her drawings.

Fernandez stood back from the case files. "Okay – anyone got any ideas as to what the hell is going on here?"

Balooga laughed humourlessly. "The end of days – I'd say." He looked towards Anna, expectantly, as if waiting for her to confirm such a theory.

She didn't disappoint. "The detective may be right."

"Meaning?" asked Fernandez.

Anna took a step further into the office. Her voice safely muffled from Isabelle's hearing. "What other explanation could there be, government experiment gone wrong, new virus about to spread across the entire world?"

Fernandez replied, "I'll take either of those as reasons. It's better than some sort of supernatural entity at work."

It was Anna's turn to laugh – a short brutal admonishment. "You still unwilling to believe in what you have seen with your own eyes?"

"Referring to yourself?" Fernandez asked.

"Perhaps. But you must maintain an open mind as to what's happening here," Anna said.

"Enlighten me."

"You mentioned witnessing a young girl at one of the earlier crime scenes. What do you think her role may be in all of this?"

The agent's face tensed slightly. He hadn't given the girl much thought since all this madness had started. The most recent events had overshadowed her involvement somewhat. Maybe they needed to revisit some of the earlier episodes in an attempt to gain understanding.

The agent replied, "She is the one factor in all of this that doesn't seem to fit. Not into any of it."

"Right," Anna agreed. "So, by logical analysis, she must be an integral part of what's going on."

"I'm listening," Fernandez said, expecting Anna to elaborate.

She did. "So far, she's the only non-infected that has been seen. Right? Is it not possible that she is therefore the one spreading this infection? At least the initial point of origin."

"If that were true, then how is she bringing the dead back from . . . well from death itself?"

Anna considered this for a moment. "Are you sure they're coming back from the dead – spiritually speaking? Have any of the infected shown signs of previous behaviour?"

Fernandez said, "It's too early to tell. Who knows what they're doing out there—right this minute."

"What if their actions are not random?" Anna said, adding another layer of intrigue to the conversation.

The agent and Josh waited for her to expand on this idea. Balooga sat silent; his face so far had remained impassive.

Anna continued. "What if the first two victims added nothing of value? Didn't fit in with this entity's MO? Maybe that's why they didn't rise after death? Maybe it was simply down to the wrong choice or selection."

Josh nodded in agreement. Their earlier conversation back at the mall was now starting to make some sense.

"Why though?" asked Fernandez.

Anna considered this. "What if they weren't the first two victims in all of this? But the first two that didn't fit a particular profile or purpose. And they simply stood out because it was early days."

The agent nodded. "Okay, even if I agreed with that in principle, then why hadn't we—the agency—been notified of other deaths?"

"Because they're not dead," Balooga announced.

The detective looked from one face to the next. His comment had rendered all three silent. And now they stood waiting for him to shed some light on its meaning.

Balooga grinned ruefully. "What if they're actually in a state between life and death? And after their initial frenzied behaviour they fall back into more coordinated pattern of behaviour."

It was the agent's turn to laugh bitterly—his willingness to accept any of this was unmistakably absent. "Really detective, so I guess we can expect everyone already infected in Fairbanks to simply sleep it off, and be back in work tomorrow? Fantastic! I can have my things packed and be out of here within the hour."

The detective shrugged off the agent's abruptness. "I don't mean going back to a fully functioning individual. Not capable of returning to their normal lives anyway, but still maintaining a small semblance of their identity to continue interacting on a cerebral level."

"Ridiculous!" Fernandez snapped. "Are we all forgetting that we recently witnessed a guy climb off a coroner's slab with his heart torn out!"

Anna said, "Haven't there been genuine recorded incidents where chickens have been beheaded, yet they've continued to run around – for days on end, some laying eggs, even?"

The agent threw his hands up in exasperation. "I give up."

A deep, unexpected voice came from the office doorway. The group turned to find Chief Zager and the native Alaskan standing there. Both looked wild-eyed, as if their recent ordeal out in the woodland had stripped them of their sanity.

"How the hell did you get in?" asked Fernandez.

The precinct had been locked down tight.

Chief Zager continued to look dazed for a second, as if the simple question had thrown his senses further out of kilter. Then he seemed to regain some of his composure as he tossed a set of keys onto the table.

"It's my precinct, remember," he said, simply. "Don't panic. I locked the main door back up. Nothing's coming in without first getting an invite."

Tonrar Kavik threw his bloodied axe onto the table, next to the set of keys. It landed with a hollow boom, scattering the paperwork from the crime reports to the floor. It was hard to tell if the head of the axe had originally been polished steel, due to the sheer amount of dried blood and gore encrusted on its blade.

"You need to listen to the young woman," Tonrar said, nodding in Anna's direction. "She speaks the truth. And the reason I know this for sure, is I used that very axe weeks ago to take the head from one of these *things*."

The agent looked shell-shocked. "Who?"

Tears sprung from the corners of the Alaskan's eyes. He shook his head as if trying to shake free the terrible images that resided there.

"My wife," he said, bringing a gasp of startled horror from the entire group.

Chapter Thirty-Four

Police Precinct

The big Alaskan had slouched in the corner of the room, unable to take the few steps required to find an unoccupied chair around the desk. His head was in his hands and he was weeping softly. His hands were soiled, nails chipped dry with the remnants of blood, and his fingers looked blackened with disease, so much life having been spilt by them. The tarnished axe was still laid across the table.

An unsettling moment dragged out as Tonrar continued to weep, his emotions pouring from his weary body.

"What is this he speaks of?" Fernandez asked now.

Chief Zager was at Tonrar's side, and he had one hand on the Alaskan's shoulder. It was clear that the police officer was trying his best to console the big man. A gesture that told the others, with no words spoken, that the lawman was not condemning Tonrar for his murderous actions.

"A terrible thing," Zager said, pityingly.

"What happened," Fernandez asked again.

Zager moved away from the grieving Alaskan. He stopped just short of the table and eyed the axe with a look close to reverence.

"Your suspicions are correct," Zager began. "Whatever these people are becoming, they do eventually slip back into known traits and patterns. Behaviour that is ingrained deeply into the human psyche."

"But how do you know that—for sure?" asked the agent.

"Because this has been happening in our town for some time. On a much smaller scale, initially."

The agent frowned. "And this you've known for how long?"

The officer looked back apologetically. "Not long enough. It was Kavik that brought this knowledge to me. He has witnessed this transformation, over time, with his own eyes."

"How?"

Zager lowered his tone and ran his hand over his face wearily. "Because Kavik's wife must have been one of the first. One of a few that had the time to go through the full transformation."

Anna asked, "Transformation into what?"

The police chief stood silent for a moment, his understanding of this given to him through the Alaskan's experience – and not his own. A difficult thing to articulate in words when not experienced first-hand.

"Okay," began Zager, "I think we have all seen what happens when first infected. They turn rabid, hungry for human flesh. But from what Tonrar has told me, that must pass given time."

"And then what?" Fernandez asked.

"Then they slip back into a more innate manner. Able to fit back into expected behavioural patterns."

"But they're dead for Christ's sakes . . ." Fernandez said. He picked up the one photo that hadn't been scattered by the axe and raised it out before him. "Are you telling me these people can one minute be running around tearing out throats, and the next returning to their lives—as normal people?" He threw the photo down. It fluttered wildly before coming to rest partially covering the bloodied axe head.

The group followed its progress to find the dismembered image of Jonny Tarver splayed out in high definition colour. It was a grisly sight, and it made these unbelievable circumstances even harder to comprehend. It was a sobering image which made the group question these early facts.

Fernandez said, "How can *that* return to any semblance of normality?"

"They don't."

The voice had come from the doorway. Kavik Tonrar had found his feet. His tears had dried. "Not normal at all," he said. "More an empty shell of what they once were. Able to pass as normal only to the outside world. Not to the ones that loved them. Knew them intimately."

Fernandez asked, "Like your wife?"

The Alaskan's head dropped and his big chest hitched with a silent sob. "Yes—like my wife."

"Take your time," Fernandez said.

Kavik cleared his throat, and then began his narrative.

He had been AWOL for at least three days, those 72 hours shrouded in an alcohol-induced fog, as the Alaskan had set about spending his entire monthly income in just one night's drinking session.

What had initially started out as just an evening's binge had quickly extended into a three-day affair with Tonrar's true love —Whisky.

Stinking of stale sweat and Whisky, Tonrar had finally found his way home, his pockets empty, and the last few days nothing more than a drunken haze.

His wife had not been there to meet him. Instead, Tonrar had been met with a freezing house, dark and empty.

She's finally left me—were his first thoughts.

And indeed she had, but not in the manner he had first thought.

He found his wife cowering in the basement, bloodied and soiled. She was mumbling incoherently—about a thirst that would, could not, be satisfied—during the time it had taken him to carry her to bed.

Tonrar had climbed wearily beside her once she had settled into a restless sleep. Perhaps he had been imagining her strange behaviour, over-exaggerating it, due to being near exhausted after his drinking exploits. Tomorrow he would awake, refreshed and these strange events would be nothing more than the workings of his tired mind.

Yet, the following morning had yielded no real change. His wife had still been making little sense, gibbering and repeatedly clawing at thin air, and speaking in a tone the large Alaskan had not heard. A tirade of obscenities had fallen from her greying lips in a vile cascade of words.

Now half sober, Tonrar had considered calling out the family doctor; however, his wife's continually odd behaviour had started to scare him.

He had taken the coward's route. Their medicine cabinet had a full array of tablets; pills for sleep, sedation, anti-depressants, and an entire collection of barbiturates. The prescriptions were all made out to his wife. She had fallen into the pattern of addiction having suffered with Tonrar's constant drunken absenteeism. His drinking had pushed her past her limits, and the dull cushioning that the pills offered were the only thing that had stopped her from leaving.

Tonrar had crushed an entire bottle's worth of unpronounceable pills into a glass and then filled it with water. He had then sat at the bed's edge forcing the clouded liquid down his wife's throat.

She had continually slipped in and out of consciousness, and only occasionally becoming lucid enough to communicate on an intellectual level. And in those rare moments she appeared bereft by her recent actions, speaking gravely about what she'd done.

What had she done? Tonrar wanted to know. But she was unable to convey, on a level that he understood, just that. She repeatedly spoke of doing unspeakable acts. Then the dark madness would descend and she would once again rant about the need to satisfy this unquenchable thirst that raged throughout her being.

Tonrar had wondered if the years of heavy self-medication had finally caught up with her, rendering her insane. Again, he had considered calling out the family doctor, but his shame for what she had become, what he had pushed her to, stopped him short.

Then on the second night, Tonrar had awoken to his wife standing over him, her silhouetted figure swaying from side to side, speaking in a tongue that the Alaskan had never heard.

She attacked him then. Teeth and nails snapping or clawing at exposed flesh. The large Alaskan barely managed to fend her off. Naturally a slight woman, she now possessed the strength of many. The confrontation spilled outside, as the two of them crashed noisily into the rear yard.

Tonrar had been begging her to come to her senses at this point. But something with darkest intentions had her in its grip. Her attack was relentless and, close to exhaustion, Tonrar reached out blindly to find a weapon—anything—to help fend her off. His hand closed around the rough handle of the axe.

A deep impenetrable blackness filled the Alaskan's memory now. He had the vaguest recollection of swinging the axe out in front of him, in an attempt to ward off his wife's crazed assault.

Then nothing.

Whatever he had done afterwards was buried deep within his subconscious.

Now, the group offered a collective sigh, rendered speechless, unable to find the words required to help console the large Alaskan.

Chief Zager was particularly troubled. He had the answer —damn, the killer—to his headless victim stood right before him. Not only that, he also had the murder weapon laid out in front of him. His natural instincts were to cuff the Alaskan and throw him into jail. Yet, considering Tonrar had saved his skin less than an hour ago, the lawman felt compelled into letting the Alaskan remain free.

Everything Zager believed in, had sworn an oath to do, now seemed foolhardy and mute. The world around him had tipped towards absolute madness, and his once rock-steady ideology seemed infantile, like the beliefs of a naïve child. To survive what Fairbanks was throwing at him, he would now have to adopt a new mentality and trust in the instincts of others.

The chief knew if they were to live another day then it would require the combined efforts of all those found within this room.

Whether they were of purest heart or of murderous intent, they would need to stand together and become as one. Only then would they stand any real hope of survival.

PART III

Dead Until Dawn

Chapter Thirty-Five

Police Precinct

A natural calm had fallen. The precinct had an almost serene manner about it now. The small group inside were taking turns to man the phones or grab snippets of rest. The ones sitting behind desks need not have bothered. The missing lawmen had not called in to give positions or updates, nor had any patrolling vehicles returned with their rear seats brimming with the recently arrested; likewise, the few holding cells in the basement of this building were not overflowing with unruly citizens.

It felt like the entire city had died over night.

Balooga yawned, and then rubbed at his eyes. It felt odd after his extended absence to be behind a desk with familiar objects laid out upon its surface. He almost laughed at the irony of his situation. He'd wanted desperately to return to duty, to feel like he was making a difference, and here he was at the first strike of Armageddon waiting for the phone to ring. What would he do anyway if it did? What could any of them do?

The Chicago detective surveyed the department. Most had gathered in this larger part of the police precinct. Agent Fernandez was back behind his desk. His usually neat side-parting now looked dishevelled, and his eyes were puffy and raw. He'd recently been on the phone talking animatedly. Now he just sat there somewhat deflated.

The Alaskan police chief lay stretched out on the floor with his head propped up by his folded coat. Mercifully, the heating still worked in this place and most had shrugged out of bothersome overcoats earlier. Not too far away from the chief, sat the large Native Alaskan. He had his knees pulled up into his chest with his head bowed forward and resting on them.

Balooga couldn't determine if the Alaskan slept or not. He also felt a certain amount of anxiety about a deadly weapon—the bloody axe—being within easy reach of the man. It lay just to the side; all the Alaskan had to do was reach out.

The young couple, Josh and Anna, had taken the little girl downstairs, so she could rest easily on one of the cots in the holding cell. In about half an hour, they would all swap, Balooga would rest, along with Fernandez, and the young couple would man the phones.

Balooga wasn't sure if he could sleep anyway. He didn't feel tired. Not one bit. Damn, he'd had his share of bed-rest these last few months.

He reached out to take a small stack of papers, deciding he would read through them, whatever they were, in an attempt to fill the time. The papers were instantly familiar to him. They were crime reports, similar to the ones he used back in Chicago. Most of the reports were for misdemeanour charges. The majority were pertaining to drunken behaviour, DUIs, the occasional brawl, and a raft of other minor discrepancies. These reports had been generated months ago when Fairbanks had been in the grip of normality. Had anyone generated a more recent crime report it would have read like a short story out of an Edger Allan Poe book.

Balooga shuffled the papers around, separating them into two piles.

One pile contained a group of unknowns, people of this town that had misbehaved or been the victims of small crimes: a purse stolen, personal property damaged, a drunken driver pulled over by a duty officer, a few juveniles apprehended for shoplifting, nothing major.

The second pile consisted of just one person: Jonny Tarver, the individual they had encountered at the city morgue. Tarver had a history of drunken behaviour in general. Again, nothing major, not initially anyway, but consistent enough for the Fairbanks Police Department to have an up-to-date dossier on the local inhabitant. Balooga flicked through the reports, starting from the earliest one available.

A young mug-shot of Tarver filled half the first page. His face looked bruised, the right eye blackened and his nose swollen and slightly out of shape. His jaw-line looked fixed but he was failing to hide his conceited amusement at having his photograph taken. Balooga scanned through the report. Tarver had been out celebrating a recent boxing win, his first, which had gotten out of hand and quickly lead to a drunken bar brawl. He had been let off with a caution.

The next report was for a DUI. Tarver stared out in black and white photography. Only now, his features were starting to show the damage taken from the ring. His nose had flattened, and his brow had thickened, and a thin scar ran through the left eyebrow—a permanent reminder of a clash of heads. This time Tarver had been given a fine and points added to his licence.

The third report was the most damning. Tarver now looked ravaged. His face had lost all its youthful exuberance, gone was the cocky self-assurance, and in its place a more cynical look of contempt had him gripped. His eyes had hardened, and lips that had once offered crooked amusement were now set in place. Tarver had beaten a man to within an inch of his life. Another bar fight, only this time the boxer had had an accomplice. A Native Alaskan named—Kavik Tonrar.

Balooga looked over towards where Tonrar was resting. The bloodied axe appeared even more menacing now.

"Shit," Balooga breathed, reading further on.

Both Tarver and Tonrar had been at the tail end of a two day drinking binge when a poor unsuspecting barman had refused them further service. Seeing that both men were on the verge of passing out, the barman had cut them off, citing that the bar had a responsibility to look after its patrons and customers alike.

The barman's over-enthusiasm to adhere to company rules had cost him his two front teeth. Both Tarver and Tonrar had spent 60 days in the comfort of the Fairbanks Correctional Facility.

The last report form surprised Balooga somewhat. Tarver had not been the wrongdoer, but rather the victim.

Now a reformed man, Tarver had found employment somewhere other than the boxing ring. It was a seasonal job, only called upon when the weather was at its worst, but a taxpaying job nonetheless. A group of mischievous youths had been playing near Tarver's place of work, and the ex-boxer had tried to run them off, only to be blasted by a rosary of expletives. Old habits die hard, and the ex-pro had chased them into the snow-packed fields, intent on delivering *his* method of punishment. Yet younger legs had carried the youths to safety, where they had continued to taunt the out-of-shape middle-aged worker.

Tarver returned to his place of work to find some of his tools had gone missing. Understanding that at least one of the kids must have backtracked whilst he was in pursuit, Tarver contacted the Fairbanks police department to file a crime report for stolen property.

Balooga finished reading the report. He sat for a moment as his mind started to work out this new information. He flicked back through the initial reports, looking to find previous data that could help. He found what he was looking for printed on the first sheet of each report: Tarver's occupation.

The first two stated him as being a Professional Boxer. The third had him down as being unemployed. Then this, the last report.

Balooga felt his heart race. Here in black and white was the reason for Tarver's reanimation. Why he had been selected to rise from the dead. It was plainly here for all to see. Only the dots had not been connected. Not only that, this new find gave Balooga a deeper understanding as to what would follow if this infestation reached beyond the bleached landscape of Fairbanks itself.

"Dear God," Balooga moaned, understanding these ramifications.

The Chicago detective jumped to his feet. "Tonrar," he yelled, rousting the Alaskan from his troubled slumber. "Get that axe of yours. We have work to do!"

Chapter Thirty-Six

Denali Park Train Station

Jonny Tarver felt empty and hollow. Literally. At some point during the night he had found a thick overcoat, yet the fur-lining and weather proof hood did little to warm his bones. A band of duct tape, wrapped multiple times around his torso, added another layer of thickness. Not only that, it also helped keep what innards he had remaining from falling out. The roll of tape had been found here in the abandoned workshop at Denali Park Train Station.

Some unaffected part of Tarver's brain lead him here, memories that were yet to be wiped clean, and he'd fumbled his way inside the workshop—a place that was familiar to him, by prising a rusty bar between the door and its frame. A gunshot crack had sounded, echoing eerily around him, but the remoteness of this place gave no suggestion of his passing.

The station was locked up for the winter season, and a wall of mountains separated it from the nearest inhabited city, Fairbanks. Vast, never-ending fields of snow covered the landscape in a seamless blanket. No one would be out here again until the thaws, brought here by spring, opening up the main highways.

Tarver coughed and a thin spray of blood dampened his lips. He felt his lungs hitch with the effort as they knocked against his ribcage. No pain flared within him. Pain had now been erased from his being. A thing of the past. Just like this place.

His hands moved about the work surfaces in a largely uncoordinated and lethargic way. Muscle memory. He was simply repeating an activity that his body had done countless times before. Bloodied fingers brushed against a bunch of keys and the sounds of heavy metal clunked noisily. He clutched the bunch against his chest, his fist pressing into the duct tape to leave a large imprint. What little sense he had screamed out in horror at the thought of what he was missing, but the voice in his head, the one guiding him through the darkness, silenced these feelings and sent them scurrying to a more distant place.

Tarver knew he was dead—in the normal sense of the word anyway. Yet here he was, heartless and all, eagerly trying to satisfy the whispers that plagued him. It was the soft, gentle voice of a child that filled his head with instructions, offering help when he faltered, and the promise of warmth returned if he obeyed and did the tasks that were given. Just like a child, and eager to please, Tarver did exactly that.

The keys dropped to his side in a loud jangle. He walked clumsily around the workshop, his bare feet leaving footsteps on the greasy floor, until he stopped before a large roller shutter doorway. A finger reached out to poke at the OPEN button. Nothing happened. The finger jabbed at the button again. A groan of annoyance slipped from between bloodied lips.

Backtracking, Tarver stumbled and shuffled his way outside, leaving the workshop in the same manner that he had entered. The busted door led him outside. There, he felt none of the wind's bite, or the chill of the ice at his feet. Just his empty chest aching with a cold suffering, and he wrapped his arms about his torso in an attempt to gain warmth.

Tarver sank shin deep into the snow. Even here, with the buildings offering some protection, the snow was almost a foot in depth. Further out, the drift would be impassable. Deeper than a man at its thickest. Impossible to cross. A perfect natural barrier.

The station's platform ended and Tarver was eventually forced into crossing the openness of the station. His bare feet sank even further. Half-crawling his way forwards he arrived at a building on the opposite side on his hands and knees.

His hands trembled as they worked the keys into the large padlock that held the door shut. The first key slipped inside the housing but it failed to unlock the mechanism. For someone else, it would have been a simple task of trying one of the others, but Tarver's brain struggled to come to terms with this, and he stayed on his knees for quite some time, twisting the key uselessly from left to right. His attempts became more erratic, to the point were his skin started to crack open, bloodless and fish-belly white, and the bones of his fingertips broke through rotten flesh.

Finally, his hand stopped working the key. He pulled it clear from the lock, nodded to himself, the voice in his head offering its guidance, and then he slipped another key into place. This time he was rewarded with a satisfying click as the lock disengaged. The clasp sprung open and the lock fell heavily into the snow.

Climbing to unsteady feet, Tarver gripped onto the door before placing his hands on either side of the entrance. With a squeal of resistance the door opened, casters rolling the doorway to one side. The effort to open the door had pulled some of the duct tape open and a ghastly vapour of putrefied flesh wafted outwards in a noxious cloud. Tarver laughed hysterically. This was turning into a really bad day. Fucking awful, if he was being truly honest with himself.

He tried to force his mind into remembering what had preceded this. *This!* A vague recollection of sharing a beer at his local bar formed in his mind, faces known to him, now twisted and warped and leering out at him from memories past. He left all that behind him. All that consumed his thoughts now were the insistent whisperings that ordered him to keep moving, do as he was told, and the cold agony would end.

So Tarver did exactly that. He shuffled and stumbled his way around the gloom until his hand fell against a protrusion in the wall. His cracked fingertips pressed down on the switch, leaving behind a trail of yellowing pus, which ran towards the floor in slow, lazy globules.

The sudden buzz of electricity sounded. And the smell of ozone filled the air. Lights flickered above, the electronic starters inside the fittings bringing them to life, and they burst brightly to reveal the contents within.

It was a huge depot, with trains filling the floor space with their enormous engines, lined up side by side, and dark cabins hidden under a layer of ice; windows stark white and frozen. There were only a few carriages to be found, as most of the locomotives found here were only for the maintenance of the rail network.

Tarver's eyes focused in on the colossal shape found dominating the main space of the depot.

It was a monstrosity of blood-red and deepest black. A 12ft box with rotary blades fixed inside, each the length of an average man, for cutting through packed snow, and something that looked more akin to a jet engine than that of a typical snowplow. Designed and built in 1966 by Union Pacific Railroad, the rotary snowplow was the heaviest ever made, weighing in at 367,400 lbs. When at maximum power the blades were capable of 130 rpm, chopping through snow and drawing it inwards before two side ports ejected the snow outwards in a billowing exhaust. A massive cabin sat directly behind the rotary blades, painted black, with windows and doors splashed crimson in colour. It was a sight to behold. Like a machine from out of Dante's Inferno.

Tarver looked longingly at the monstrous snowplow. He closed his eyes for a second, and happier memories fought their way to the surface of his fevered mind. He reached out with his hands, his broken fingertips stroking lovingly at the blades, and his exposed bones scraped eerily along sharpened edges.

He moved along the snowplow until he reached the access ladder that ran to the cabin. His fingers hooked themselves around the rungs. He grinned then. Pleased to be back where he belonged. Ready to get this beast started. Eager to do as he was ordered.

Yet, more importantly, willing to do whatever it took to fill the emptiness that had spread throughout his soul.

Chapter Thirty-Seven

Richardson Highway

A party of five misfits was what Fernandez could see, heading into the unknown with nothing less than the survival of mankind at heart. How would they achieve such a thing?

Tonrar, the Native Alaskan was behind the steering wheel, using his intimate knowledge of this place to his advantage, as he drove the state cruiser along the deserted highway. Occasionally, he was forced to slow to a crawl as he negotiated his way around a stationary vehicle. All five tensed at such points, readying what weaponry they had, expecting a ravenous horde to spill from doors left ajar or smashed windows, and rush at them with open jaws. It never happened. The vehicles were abandoned; their occupants either pulled into the surrounding woodland and set upon, or worse, added to the legions of the infected.

At Tonrar's side sat detective Balooga. He was using one hand to grip onto the handle above his head, to hold him steady, and the other to point out the larger obstacles that stood in their way, forcing the Alaskan to throw the vehicle around violently.

In the back, were Josh and Anna, and the FBI agent. Fernandez was struggling with his cell phone, in an attempt to get a connection.

"It's no use," he moaned, unable to see even one bar of signal strength. The agent tried the cell again, irrespective of signal strength or not. The phone beeped once in his ear before the connection faltered.

"This is useless," Fernandez said, finally giving up on the cell. "We're on our own from here onwards. Help isn't coming."

"Yet here we are," Balooga said.

"And where is that exactly?" asked the agent.

Tonrar scanned the dark horizon before replying. "We are a few miles out. Almost there."

"And then what?" Fernandez demanded.

Balooga twisted in his seat, leaving the Alaskan to deal with the dangers up ahead. "And then we stop this."

"Stop them all?" Fernandez asked.

"If possible," Balooga replied.

The agent looked irritated. "This 'infection' as you call it, may have already spread. Even with the help that I've managed to coordinate, it's probably too little too late."

The agent had done his best in coordinating a plan to halt the spread already. He would attempt to stop them here – in Fairbanks. Or, more precisely, the help he had managed to organize with the US Army would hopefully stop it. This is how he had spent his time, making those countless phone calls from the small office.

A company of Army infantry had been posted at the local Air Force base here weeks ago, in wait of transport, their original mission to fly out to an undisclosed location and engage in a training operation. Only bad weather had halted that manoeuvre. Now, after the agent's dogged determination and numerous phone calls, working his way further up the chain of command, he had been able to reassign the company of soldiers and throw a cordon around the city of Fairbanks. He had remained somewhat sketchy about why he needed such help, only stating it was a matter of national security. He just hoped that the additional three hundred soldiers defending the perimeter would recognise the danger the infected offered, if encountered. Had he told the truth and said that a suspected plague of the undead was roaming free, then he would have probably been dragged off to the nearest lunatic asylum. And rightly so.

Therefore, with luck, nothing would be getting out from the main roads. And the hundreds of miles of frozen wasteland which surrounded them would lay claim to any that tried to escape cross-country.

Fernandez said, "Why would they attempt an escape from such a remote place?"

Balooga replied with a question of his own. "Why the need for Jonny Tarver – and the skills he possesses?"

Irritation turned to anger. "What skills? The guy's a thug. You could be wrong about his involvement altogether. Purely coincidental."

Balooga glanced towards Tonrar. Had Fernandez insulted him by openly condemning his friend? The Alaskan simply nodded in agreement.

"Okay," Balooga said, "maybe you're right, but he also has the technical know-how on how to drive the one thing that can clear a path out of Fairbanks."

The agent groaned. The detective's notion that the ex-boxer had been resurrected to simply drive a train was somewhat preposterous. If the infected did want to walk out of here, then they could do exactly that – walk.

This left just one getaway route. The network of rail tracks which snaked out from the city.

Agent Fernandez had tried to get them to see the sense in checking the main lines, or the few stations that were still operating in such weather, rather than heading out to the middle of nowhere in the hope of catching an alleged escape plan.

But Balooga had thrust the crime report in his face and jabbed at the information printed there. Yes, Agent Fernandez had said, I can see that Mister Tarver worked as an Engine Operator for a few seasons over at Denali Park, clearing the winter snow drifts, but how did that equate to an out and out attempt at fleeing the city via that route?

Balooga had simply thrown his hands up in exasperation. Stating that the agent needed to pull his head from out his arse and get with the programme.

***

Josh sat across the opposite side from the agent, with Anna in the middle. The agent looked uncomfortable. Whether it was from being so close to the fugitive he sought, or with their imminent destination drawing close, Josh was not sure.

Josh remembered Anna's look of amusement when Balooga had openly proposed this idea. She had laughed and then stood by the detective. "I'm in," she had said, simply, ready to believe in the detective's notion and embark on a mission to intercept.

Josh had not agreed so willingly. Isabelle had been his worry. The little girl was grasping tightly onto his hand, and he could feel the knock of her heart through her grip.

"We need to slay some dragons – like back in Mexico," he said.

Isabelle had nodded, and then swallowed her fear. "Will that help the children here?"

"Yes," Josh replied. "It will."

The little girl surprised Josh then by saying, "Then go, Sir Josh, but promise to come back, please."

Josh had knelt. He offered his hand with a bent little finger. "Pinkie promise."

Isabelle had hooked her little finger around his. "Pinkie promise," she echoed.

With the deal done, Josh stepped back. Chief Zager moved forward and placed his hands gently on the little girl's shoulders. "Go – I will take good care of her," he said. Josh had nodded. He'd felt both relief at the chief's offer to keep the girl safe, and fear at the thought that they would be without the help of one of Fairbanks' most trusted people.

Zager had wished them God speed. He had made the decision to stay behind and help those that were in need by maintaining communications at the precinct.

"We're almost there," Tonrar said, forcing Josh back into the moment.

Josh felt Anna's hand tighten around his. "You okay?" she asked.

Josh kissed her gently on her cheek. "Ask me again when this is over."

The state cruiser navigated around a tight bend, its headlights cutting twin beams of white light to reveal the dark outline of Denali Park.

Josh's first thought was that the detective had been wrong. The place looked deserted. He didn't see any trains or carriages. Nor people for that matter. Just an abandoned train station.

He was about to voice his concerns when an almighty wail of a noise sounded. The disturbance continued to grow in amplitude, quickly rising to a deafening pitch. Then the noise changed and it became a great tearing sound. Josh felt the thud of earth being torn away even through the floor of the cruiser.

In the next second, he spotted the gigantic snowplow – dark and threatening, and tearing a channel of cleared snow from the rail tracks.

A moment later a second shriek of noise sounded. But this one came from all about them. The hordes of infected broke from the surrounding woodland then. Their eyes filled with hatred and hunger as they began to slowly close in around the state cruiser and those trapped within.

Chapter Thirty-Eight

Denali Park Train Station

It was as if the apocalypse had happened overnight, driving the masses to madness, and leaving but a few clinging to the recollections of old. The swell of bodies staggered and crawled towards the state cruiser, with abhorrent desire twisting their features into ghastly masks, and the sounds of longing echoing eerily from open jaws.

Anna watched as they drew near. Her heart was racing. And, not dissimilar to the beasts outside, she felt her skin tingle with the thought of bloodshed. Fear for herself was the furthest thing from her mind. Her only concern was for Josh. She would burn the world down if anything happened to him.

"Dammit to hell," Tonrar was saying, pulling Anna's attention away from the advancing mob.

She realised then that the cruiser had come to a halt. The Alaskan was revving the engine crazily, but the vehicle's wheels were just churning mud and slush. The state cruiser had bottomed out in a drift of snow.

"No time to waste," Anna said, reaching out for the door handle.

"Wait," Josh said, grabbing her arm. He looked into her eyes imploringly. Anna had already made her decision. She had reached the point where it was time to do what was needed.

In essence this is what Anna was, a thing of the night. Not unlike the horrors outside. There would be no discussions or debates this time. Anna was ready to act. Had been waiting for this moment to come, and relishing the thought with eager anticipation.

"I love you," Josh said.

"I love you too," Anna replied.

She embraced him quickly, placing a kiss onto his lips. "Stick with them. Run when it's clear to do so," she said.

Josh nodded. "Be careful."

Anna flashed him a mischievous smile. "Time to go."

She cracked open the door, pushing against a drift of snow to clear her exit. In the next second she was gone.

"What the hell!" snapped Fernandez. "What is she doing?"

"Buying us time," Josh said. "Be ready."

Josh scanned the immediate area. The night had already embraced her and she was nowhere to be seen.

***

Anna felt as if a suit of chains had slipped from her body, finally releasing her from its restrictions and allowing her to run free. She was cutting a path in the direction of the horde, yelling wildly at them, drawing their attention away from the stricken state cruiser and towards her.

The fevered mob changed their direction. They stopped in the snow, some up to their waists, before clawing at the frozen earth to get at her.

Anna chanced a look behind her. She could see the interior light of the state cruiser. The vehicle was empty. The rest of the group, Josh included, were making a run for it.

A maddening wail sounded to her left. Anna turned to find a woman dressed in business attire stalking her. The woman's white blouse was soiled with a mixture of blood and grime. A blossoming stain, like a neck tie, had formed down the front of her work shirt. Her lower lip was missing and a dried crust of blood had formed into a thick scab on her chin. Anna could see the indentation of teeth marks where the flesh had been torn away. The woman shrieked, her deformed mouth twisting grotesquely.

"Come on then, bitch," Anna said, readying herself.

***

The ground at Josh's feet trembled. He could feel the effects of the gigantic snowplow as it cleared the tracks, leaving a deep channel in its wake. The party were almost at the platform, having encountered little resistance on their way. A few of the infected had leered out at them, but the Alaskan's axe had made short work of them. Tonrar was breathing heavily from his exertions. Josh was doing his best to keep the imposing native as close to him as possible.

Balooga and agent Fernandez had taken up position at the rear of the group. A couple of pistol shots rang out as the lawmen fired short volleys into any that followed.

The deep powder at Josh's feet gave way to a harder surface as he stepped onto the platform. The small group came together with laboured breaths.

"What are we waiting for?" Josh asked.

Balooga was clutching at his side. "I can't go any further. "You go. I'll hold them off. Go now!"

Josh turned towards the other two men. Tonrar was already focused on the track ahead. He had the bloodied axe firmly fixed in his hands. It seemed he'd made the decision to see this through to the end. No matter what.

Agent Fernandez looked torn and indecisive. Then a cry of insanity, from a mass of voices, came to them. The gloom parted and shadows formed themselves into macabre shapes.

"We'll do our best to buy you time," he said, his decision made. He reached down to pull a secondary weapon from his ankle holster. "Here—take this."

Josh accepted the gun. Moments later he was following

208

the Alaskan into the tunnel of plowed snow, racing headlong towards the roaring engine, and wondering what horrors would be waiting for him when—*if*—he got there.

***

The business woman's head lay looking up at the dark sky. Her feverish eyes were now glazed over, and her crooked mouth had fallen open. The rest of her lay yards away, the headless torso slumped in the packed snow, arms spread out, palms upward, as if in rapturous acceptance.

Anna left the mutilated body behind her. More of the infected had been drawn towards the noise of the confrontation. They were closing in fast. Too many to fend off alone, which forced Anna to change her tack. She had to find away of slowing them down, or incapacitating them, and quickly.

She crashed through a tangle of trees, to feel the sting of bare branches against her face. A sudden drop in ground level presented itself. And Anna grinned with devilish delight. Here, now, was the answer to her problem.

She paused, halting her descent into the natural basin, until she had located an item of interest. Finally finding what was required, she then bounded through the snow, to arrive at the edges of the clearing.

Spectral figures appeared all around her then. They seemed to sprout from the very earth, as if awakened from their graves, and given purpose to rise again. The first few started to work their way down the embankment. Some of them fell head first into the white drifts, and there they thrashed about like speared fish. Yet others made it onto the flattened earth with ease and dexterity.

"Come on!" Anna taunted, trying to get them all to their feet.

She took a few steps forward. The soft snow at her feet turned instantly hard, and her next step took her away from the safety of the solid embankment and onto the frozen waters of the lake.

***

Josh was struggling to keep up with the Alaskan. Tonrar had gained a significant lead on him. They had encountered few of the infected whilst caught in this excavated channel. The crunch of rotary blades chopping into packed snow was fast becoming deafening. The snowplow, although massive in design, was restricted in speed, and the two men were quickly gaining on it.

Josh redoubled his efforts. The agony of old wounds forced from his mind as he closed the gap between him and the engine.

A body toppled over from the wall of snow to land just in front of him. Josh had a second to see the dark blue uniform of a security guard. One of its clawed hands made a grab for his ankle. Josh vaulted over it, feeling a moment of triumph at dodging danger, before he tumbled heavily onto the tracks. The guard was up in an instant. Half his throat was missing. The guard lunged forward with arms raised and hands bent into claws.

Josh fired at point-blank range. The bullet ripped through the guard's jaw, almost taking his head with it. A huge, ragged hole sent a river of blood cascading down the blue uniform. The guard dropped to one knee, his hand reaching up to stem the blood-flow. He bared his upper teeth then, which had turned the colour of deepest red. His free hand clawed at Josh's face.

The images of the guy climbing off the coroner's table flashed through Josh's mind, with his heart ripped out and lungs visible through the gaping cavity. These things could not be stopped by normal means.

Raising the weapon higher, Josh fired again, splitting the guard's skull in two. The body collapsed to the tracks instantly. Shuddered once. And then lay still.

Josh got to his feet. The Alaskan had disappeared ahead of him. Josh followed with the knowledge that these things could be stopped.

"Aim for the head!" Balooga was yelling. He fired again and another body fell to the earth. He changed position to cover the agent's flank. Something came screaming at them, and the bullets from both the agent and lawman's weapons caused its head to explode in a pink mist.

"We're losing ground," Fernandez cried, seeing more of the mob swell towards them.

"We need to hold them off. No matter what," Balooga replied.

Fernandez looked haplessly at the gathering numbers. "What can we do?"

"Keep firing," Balooga said. "We need to buy them more time. Buy *her* more time."

"Who?"

"Anna Privalova."

"To do what?"

Balooga took his eyes off the horde for a second. Glanced into the agent's eyes, and replied, "To do what she does best."

"Which is?"

"*To KILL*"

Chapter Thirty-Nine

Iniakuk Lake

At its deepest, the lake was a staggering 261 feet in depth. Almost a mile wide, it was not the biggest body of water to be found on the perimeter of Fairbanks, but a significant one at that. In summer it would offer the locals an abundance of fishing opportunities, once the surface temperature reached higher than freezing. Now, in the grip of winter, the lake was little more than a frozen slab of dark ice.

Anna was a hundred yards from the lake's edge and the point at where the ice was at its thinnest. Some of the infected had started to make their way across the ice towards her. They were coming slowly, their uncoordinated minds struggling to keep their footing steady. The rest had finally reached the water's frozen edge. Anna needed them all to gather – and quickly.

A large rock, more a boulder, was laid at her feet. It was the item she had taken from the embankment. Now, all she needed to do was wait for them to come.

Some of the more able bodies were drawing near. Faces that had lost all humanity leered and snapped bloodied jaws at the figure before them.

"What are you waiting for?!" Anna yelled at them. "Come on!"

Her taunts seemed to ignite the bloodlust of the rest, as the ones at the lake's edge quickly gathered onto the ice.

They were coming fast then. The first few having already reached striking distance. One launched itself towards Anna with arms stretched out and teeth bared. Anna sidestepped easily to send the thing sliding across the frozen water. It was up again in an instant. Two more dark figures filled Anna's periphery.

She could smell the fresh blood on their skin. Clothes had been dyed from bright patterns and colours to dark reds and bloodied stains. The smell, now so close, was intoxicating. Anna's nostrils flared. And her head swooned for a moment at the rich scent.

Something spectacular happened then. Anna's body seemed to swell, her lithe figure hardened and muscles bunched into solid slabs of tissue. Hands became claws as her fingers stretched in length and nails grew into hooked points. Her face burst forwards as lips and nose reformed into the shape of a muzzle. Jaws opened and two rows of sharp canine teeth glinted in the moonlight. Her hair retracted, gathering around her scalp in a thick hide, and the two elongated tips of her ears burst through this veil like fins cutting through dark water.

She spun to face her nearest attacker. Some uninfected part of its intelligence caused it to pause, aware that what stood before it now was not a figment of its diseased mind. But then the bloodlust that drove it shattered all reasoning, and in the next instant, it launched itself towards the wolf-like creature that stood before it.

Anna released a baleful hiss as the infected reached out. She ducked as it grabbed for her, and then gripped a handful of its tattered jacket. Using her attacker's momentum she lifted it up off its feet, her arms locked out straight as the thing sailed over her head, to bring it down face-first into the ice.

The frozen surface exploded in a bright red bubble of blood, as facial features disintegrated under the impact. Anna tossed the body away.

The next two rushed towards her. She bent forwards and

simultaneously rammed her hip into the nearest one. It flew over her before skidding across the ice. Already bent, Anna reached out to take the rock. Using the heavy object to gain momentum, she brought it up in an arc, catching the next attacker before it could strike. The weight of the rock crushed in the side of its skull, dropping it to the ground in a twisted heap.

Anna readied herself for the next assault.

The blood-thirsty masses had now found purchase on the lake's surface. They were gathering in groups – their grotesque faces brightly lit by the moon above. More and more came. Anna held her nerve. And waited until the first mass gathering was almost upon her.

Then, with her periphery filled by the shadows of writhing shapes, she brought the rock high above her head.

The rock hit the frozen surface with an almighty crack. Ice split instantly as deep fissures appeared, snaking out in a zigzag pattern, spreading from the point of impact to the furthest edges of the lake.

Anna stood back as freezing water gushed upwards to cover her feet. The small platform of ice she stood on tilted forwards and she almost slipped and fell into the black depths. Dropping into a crouch, she managed to redistribute her weight and the ice steadied.

The mass of infected were not so lucky. Unable to rebalance themselves, their rotten brains no longer capable of such dexterity, they began to slide into the water one by one. For a few seconds they splashed about, before the combination of sodden clothes and freezing temperatures rendered them immobile. The first head disappeared underneath in a silent scream. More followed as large chunks of ice tilted sideways, dropping bodies into the lake, where they were quickly claimed by the icy waters.

One soul tried to climb back onto the ice that had just dumped him in. His hands were frantically clawing at the frozen surface and he was whimpering like a child. The bright orange jumpsuit that he wore, the common garb of a prisoner, was stuck tightly to his flesh like an additional layer of skin. He managed to gain some purchase by digging his elbows into the ice. For a second it looked like he would pull himself to safety. But the frozen mass of another chunk of ice, two feet in thickness, and recently tipped upwards by the weight of sliding bodies, came down on top of him. The jagged edge smashed down, severing the prisoner in half, which sent his kicking legs down into the abyss. His upper half continued to pull itself forward with gushing entrails following it. It tried to roll onto its back but only succeeded in tipping the floating ice sideways. And with one last gasping breath, the disembowelled thing slipped from out of view.

Anna watched as they continued to disappear under the dark surface. It was a horrible sight to witness. Some of them – those with some humanity remaining, screamed out for help or mercy, or the names of loved ones, but the lake was without compassion and it took these few individuals with the same conviction as the others.

In just a matter of minutes the lake had claimed the entire mass of the infected, dragging them into its deepest depths and keeping them there.

Anna stood balanced on the floating ice. Other chunks drifted and bobbed about. She readied herself as the largest one closest to her drifted within range.

Then she launched herself into the air, hopeful that the lake was not yet ready to claim another soul.

Chapter Forty

Police Precinct

Chief Zager was not sure if he was more terrified by the person inside the police precinct, situated just to the side of him, or the horrors that roamed freely round Fairbanks, looking for human flesh.

The little girl was looking at him intently; blue eyes fixed to his, and face quizzical.

Isabelle had grown tired of her drawings, and was now seemingly preoccupied by studying what the lawman was up to.

Not a lot.

The phones hadn't exactly been too hot to handle. No incoming calls had yet to break the silence with an urgent ring for help.

Zager had taken a while to try and contact some of his men, friends, professional associates, his doctor for one, yet none of his attempts to break the silent deadlock had yielded any results. Fairbanks had gone to shit.

Which now left him simply sitting here under the girl's continued scrutiny.

Zager didn't have a clue how to react. Children scared the bejeebers out of him. He didn't have any of his own and, in truth, had never really felt the desire to. His job was his baby.

The thing he cherished most. What he'd dedicated his life to.

Zager almost laughed at the absurdity of it all.

He was top dog in the department, a respected man of the community, liked, easy to get on with, with good friends – if any remained, and yet, here he was sweating profusely as a result of a little girl's presence.

He glanced up from the crime report – blank – and momentarily made eye-contact with Isabelle. His heart quivered for a second. Looking down, he continued to study the otherwise clear sheet of paper.

Zager could see the girl's little feet swinging continually underneath her chair; red flashes of movement blinking on and off at the side of his periphery.

He had a few more moments of studying the report, when the movement at his side stopped.

Zager's heart almost stopped, too, when those little red shoes squeaked their way across the precinct to stop at his table.

The chief looked up, his head slowly tilting higher, anxiously, with the same trepidation as a guilty man awaiting the verdict of a jury.

Isabelle just stood there.

It took all of the chief's will to manage a weak, "Hey."

Isabelle tilted her head slightly.

Zager almost fell out of his seat.

The little girl stood on her tiptoes to get a better look at what he'd been doing for the last ten minutes. Nothing. She let out a gentle laugh then, finding the lawman's behaviour somewhat funny.

Zager cleared his throat. He didn't have a clue as to what to say.

"Writer's block?" asked Isabelle.

Zager's face flushed red. "What?"

"Writer's block," Isabelle echoed. "When you can't think what to say."

Kids Block was what Zager suffered from.

Isabelle must have misunderstood his silence for confusion.

She reached out to take the pen from Zager's hand. Then pulled herself up into a chair at his side. Reaching out, she turned the blank crime sheet so she could read it, then studied it for a moment.

The top half of the report required a list of basic information. Isabelle put pen to paper.

NAME: Isabelle

DATE OF BIRTH:

She struggled with that one. Her little face bent quizzically.

Now, here was Zager's chance to speak. He'd filled hundreds, if not thousands, of these reports over his long career, having to often help guide those that were unable to either read or write.

"The day you were born," Zager said.

Isabelle looked at him. Shrugged her shoulders.

Zager thought for a moment. "When your parents gave you presents and cards, what day would that be?"

For the first time since they'd been left together, Isabelle's eyes lost focus. Her gaze seemed to drift off and those startlingly blue eyes lost some of their intensity.

Zager silently rebuked himself for being so stupid.

On their first arrival it was clear to the chief that this kid was not the natural offspring to the two adults she was travelling with. It didn't take over two decades of policing to figure that out either. The kid was clearly a newcomer to the strange couple. The little girl didn't appear scared or uncomfortable around the two – just somewhat apprehensive.

Sat there now, Zager was surprised to realise that some hidden parental instinct told him that the girl's obvious caution towards the young man and woman was more akin to rejection than anything else.

The girl was simply playing it safe. Not giving too much of herself too soon.

The agent had not filled in the blanks either. Fernandez had not offered any kind of explanation as to why the child was here—hell, he hadn't really hinted as to why any of the newcomers had suddenly arrived. But they had. And that had somehow brought things closer to an end.

What end, Zager was unsure.

Admittedly, he had seen with his own eyes what was roaming free out there—but could not rationalise it. Not unless he dismissed all sense whatsoever.

Therefore, he had agreed to stay here, in the hope that some of his deputies would return with something—anything—resembling an answer.

Now, though, the lawman understood that this girl had been plucked from her present predicament, with good intentions at heart, and maybe her past was one that didn't warrant too much investigation. Not now anyway.

"Maybe we should write Christmas down for that one?" Zager quizzed.

Isabelle refocused on the police chief. Nodded her head slightly.

"Good," Zager replied. He shuffled his chair closer. Reached out to take another pen from the desk.

DATE OF BIRTH: Christmas Day.

Zager moved his hand clear so Isabelle could see what he'd written.

She clapped her hands excitedly.

"Every child gets a present on Christmas – right? From Santa Claus."

Now, Isabelle's eyes lit up spectacularly. "Yes," she replied wistfully.

Zager felt his heart steady slightly and his nerves seemed to be lessening to a degree.

"Okay," Zager began, "next question."

OCCUPATION:

In truth, the next few questions had all been related to place of origin, current address and such. Yet, Zager had tactfully skipped those.

He looked at Isabelle to see if she had understood the next bit.

She had. And this seemed to have tickled her a bit.

"I'm just a kid. I don't have one of those," she said, eyes now filled with mischievousness.

"Really?" asked Zager, as if surprised.

"Really," Isabelle echoed.

"You don't even have a job? Jeez – what can I write in here then?"

Isabelle sat thoughtful for a moment. "I like the circus. A lot."

"Then what about – clown?"

The little girl gave the larger man a frown.

"Okay – okay. Forget clown then." The chief considered his options for a moment. "Which part of the circus do you like best?"

Isabelle's hands became a sudden blur of motion. She had two fingers pointed outwards on both hands, and was bringing them together – backwards and forwards – repeatedly.

"The trapeze?" Zager said.

The fingers stopped in mid-flight. Isabelle nodded animatedly.

OCCUPATION: Acrobat.

For the next few minutes, they went through the crime report, playfully, filling in various bits as they went along.

And in those few minutes of fun, Zager forgot about his fears of children, or the horrors of what was happening to his town, and simply enjoyed the girl's company.

They had reached about midway down the first page when Zager spoke out the next line. Without thinking.

"CRIME."

Instantly, the child's demeanour changed. Her face flipped from enjoyment to trepidation in a heartbeat. Her eyes moved away from his, just past his left shoulder, and they widened into two bright blue orbs.

Zager sensed, more than visualised, movement at the periphery of his vision. He was hit then without warning. Hard. His head rocked back, eyes swimming in a hazy fog, and his large bulk tipped sideways, off his chair.

He had a fraction of a second to wonder what the hell he had said to anger her so much, before he was heading towards the floor.

His head bounced once.

And then the lights went out.

Chapter Forty-One

Train Tracks

Frost as caustic as acid burnt at the palms of Josh's hands, and the smack of compact snow being chopped to pieces filled his head with a dizzying thump. He gritted his teeth and continued to climb aboard the train engine. The access ladder gave way to a narrow platform which ran the length of the engine. Now this close, Josh could see the billowing trail of steam as it trailed out behind him.

Although the engine was not moving at such high speeds the close proximity of the vertically cut walls of ice made Josh feel disorientated and dizzy. He hugged the sides of the metalwork as he inched his way along the platform. A doorway, found ajar, gave him entrance into the main body of the machine.

Stifling heat almost sucked the air from his lungs. A furnace glowed brightly, waves of intense heat radiating outwards, which made the air shimmer. Surrounding the furnace were pulleys and levers that looked ancient in their design.

The confined space was filled by the imposing figures of Kavik Tonrar and Jonny Tarver. They stood facing each other in silent regard. Tonrar had the bloodied axe pressed against his chest. While Tarver's fleshless hands curled onto the shaft of a shovel. A pile of discarded coal lay at the dead man's feet.

"Do not linger," Tonrar spoke, raising his voice over the hiss of steam. He maintained eye contact with what had once been his friend, yet repeated his warning.

Josh understood. He backed out of the cabin, the heat almost pushing him as he went, to find himself back on the platform. He was still only halfway to the front of the snowplow—the business end that cut its way through the wall of snow and ice.

He realised then that the plow was being pushed forwards by the steam engine, and the actual controls of the rotary blades would be somewhere up ahead in the other cabin. If he could stop the machinery somehow, then he could end this escape.

With no connecting passage, he was forced to climb upwards, in the hope of finding a way onto the control carriage. His fingers found purchase on a protrusion of metalwork, and he used this advantage to climb quickly higher. The raging wind howled wildly and its frozen bite sought out exposed flesh. Josh used the guardrail to push himself higher.

In a half crouch, he staggered towards the connecting carriage. Looking down, he saw huge buffers pushing the snowplow forwards. Below them rail tracks flashed by in a dizzying blur.

Josh tensed for a second before making the jump for the other side.

***

The Native Alaskan could feel his strength abandoning him. The heat in this small place was sapping his energy as it drew sweat from his soiled pores. A bead of perspiration dripped into one eye, and he blinked it away quickly in an attempt to keep focus.

The thing that had once been his friend stared back with unblinking, glazed eyes. Gone had the spirit that had once driven the imposing man. What had replaced his verve now was of deepest dread. And not of this place. The dead man's hands tightened around the shovel. Exposed bones cracking under the tension.

It lashed out then, aiming the flat of the shovel at Tonrar's head. The Alaskan read the attack, and he brought the axe up to defend himself. The metal shovel, still hot from the furnace, clanged noisily off the axe.

Tonrar dropped his shoulder and barrelled forwards in an attempt to knock the fiend from its feet. He felt the air explode from Tarver's lungs and the stench of decay and rot was overpowering. He reared back to get a lungful of clearer air. But the heat robbed him of such a thing. Gasping for breath, he staggered away.

Tarver was coming at him again with the shovel's blade now aimed towards his throat. The Alaskan tried to duck in time, but the sharp end caught him across his forehead. He felt searing pain as his skin was peeled back. A rush of blood cascaded down one side of his face, blinding him for a second.

Jonny Tarver raised the shovel high, ready to bring the weapon down across the back of the Alaskan's head. However, Tonrar was not yet a spent force. He witnessed the danger with his good eye and he managed to bring the axe up in defence. The flat head of the axe connected with the thing's jaw. Bones shattered and broken teeth flew from torn lips.

The force of the blow sent Jonny Tarver flying backwards until his head connected with the dense metalwork of the furnace. Dazed, he stood shaking his head, giving the Alaskan the advantage needed.

Tonrar dove forwards thrusting the axe out in front of him lengthways; his hands gripped on either side of the wooden handle, and he smashed it into Tarver's throat. The thing thrashed about under the force of the handle. Tonrar dug his feet into the floor, pushing with enough effort to make his shoulders pop. They collapsed to the floor, the Alaskan still on top and the axe holding snapping jaws at bay.

Heat seared the skin off Tonrar's knuckles. And the smell of burning hair filled the compartment. The furnace door was only inches away—red-hot coals burning intensely.

Seeing this, Tonrar knew what had to be done. He dropped

the axe and grabbed a handful of Tarver's coat. The garment opened and he got a picture of rotting innards. Fighting back revulsion he yanked it off the floor and then rammed it head first into the open maw of the furnace. An agonising scream sounded. Jonny Tarver's hands clawed blindly at the Alaskan's face and his feet kicked wildly.

Kavik Tonrar felt a rage unmatched then. He hated what this thing was. What it represented. More so, what actions he had been forced to do when his wife had befallen a similar fate. He reached out to grab two wooden levers to hold firm. His knee pushed itself into the open cavity of the hideous thing's chest, only stopping when it reached the exposed backbone, and he used all his might to remain positioned there.

Jonny Tarver continued to thrash and scream until the searing heat of the furnace silenced him with its purging flames.

***

The effects of the wind were brutal. Exposed skin felt like it was burning, and eyes smarted with hot tears. Josh was fighting to stay upright. His feet were sliding around as he tried to make his way to the front of the snowplow. Now almost there, he could see the twin exhausts venting excavated snow in a powerful rage. Some of it was blowing back over him, making his progress dangerous and difficult, and chilling him to the bone.

Only a few yards to go. He chanced a look to one side to see if there was a safe way down. There wasn't. No ladders or handrails or platforms on this part of the machine, just straight sides leading to the track below. The channel created was only marginally wider than the engine itself, and Josh knew that trying to gain access by entering the sides would be tantamount to suicide. If he didn't slip, then the icy wall would drag him clear, dropping him below, where he would surely be crushed by the iron wheels.

With no other option he headed to the front of the engine.

The sound of the snow being torn away was deafening at such close range. Suddenly the carriage swayed to one side as a violent gust of wind funnelled into the channel, forming a demented vortex, which battered the carriage about with violent disregard.

Josh staggered forwards before falling to his knees. Reaching out quickly he stopped himself from landing spread-eagled. His hand rested on a raised seam that protruded from the roof of the carriage. Realising that this was an access – an opening for a maintenance crew maybe, he ran his fingers around until finding a handle. It was just within reach, almost hidden in a recess. Numb fingers worked at the release mechanism. He felt the catch disengage and then he pulled at the access panel.

The panel burst unexpectedly open as if the cabin below had lost instant pressure. Josh felt the full force of impact and he was knocked violently backwards. He felt himself skidding towards the edge of the carriage. Throwing his hands out, he managed to halt his progress, finishing with his head almost hanging over the side. The ice-packed wall rushed past with the noise of thunder.

After pulling himself clear he looked towards the dark hole where the panel had burst open. Small hands hooked themselves onto the edges of the opening. Hair, long and dark, flapped wildly as the figure's head appeared. Then it was climbing free, to join Josh on the roof of the cabin. The raging wind stopped for a second, and the newcomer's face revealed itself.

Isabelle!

Chapter Forty-Two

Police Precinct

Zager found himself sprawled out on the precinct floor. His head felt like it had been split in two. He panicked then, unsteady hands seeking out torn flesh and broken bones, worriedly probing for an open wound, leading to exposed brain matter.

His fingers found nothing but a rapidly growing lump. He sat up. A bout of nausea forced hot bile up the back of his throat. He steadied himself by bringing his hands down flat against the floor, and rode the wave of sickness until it had petered out.

In the next moment, his mind cleared. He had not been bitten or mauled at by one of the infected. Therefore, he was not about to go on the immediate rampage seeking out human flesh. The internal clock inside his head told him that only a few seconds had passed since being knocked to the floor.

He looked quickly about him then for signs of the little girl. Isabelle had vanished.

Using the chair – the one he had been so forcibly tipped from – he climbed to his feet. The office swayed first one way, and then the next. The moment of disorientation lasted for just a second. Then Zager was heading for the doorway, simultaneously seeking out his weapon with one hand. The firearm was free from its holster by the time he had reached the opening.

Footsteps came from below.

The sounds belonged to more than one, and were too heavy in nature to be that of a single fleeing child.

Zager took the stairs three at a time in hot pursuit. He hit the exit doorway with his shoulder as he barrelled his way outside. The raging winds and snow tore at his bare skin. Narrowing his eyes, he brought a hand up to help shield against the raging turmoil.

Footprints, two pairs, side by side, led away from the precinct.

Zager set about following them. He dug his chin into his chest and pushed against the harsh conditions. The fact that he was focusing downward helped a little, and he quickly traced the footprints to the end of the police compound.

There, the trail got harder to follow. The footprints ended at the sidewalk, as they were quickly replaced by a combination of black slush and fresher snow. It was impossible to pick the tracks out amongst the churning mess of vehicles and other earlier pedestrians.

Zager looked about him, trying to spot a mark or print that would help him in his pursuit. Anything to get him back onto the right track. Just empty and blank store front windows stared back at him.

He crossed to the opposite side of the street, his feet and pants sodden as he pushed his way through the deep slush. More footprints could be found on this side, which led him away from the main street and into an adjoining avenue.

Zager stopped. Looked through the falling snow. And could just about make out the faint outline of a building. Or could he? Was it his imagination – memories of years past – that was offering up some sort of manifestation?

Zager knew the building that this avenue led to.

Knew it implicitly.

Zager took a breath – a deep one, and then readied himself for what was to come.

***

The shattering of glass did little to test the rage of wind. The noise was barely distinguishable – even this close, as Zager used the butt of his firearm to break open the window. The majority of glass dropped in a single sheet to shatter into smaller pieces on the inside. Zager tapped out the remaining shards until he had cleared the framework of any sharp slivers.

He ducked down to take a glance inside. An empty room beckoned.

The room was familiar in design and layout. It was a universal layout, copied throughout the entire world, from the furthest tips in the north, to the lowest reaches of the south.

Zager planted one foot firmly into the snow before hitching his other inside. Beguiling his size and bulk, the chief slipped effortlessly inside the classroom.

There were no lights illuminated inside, yet the murky glow of streetlights filtered through inside the room. Everything inside was tarnished in a sickly yellow.

The police chief navigated easily around the rows of desks. The door to the hallway opened with barely a whisper. A long stretch of gloomy corridor branched off in opposite directions.

Zager waited as he mentally worked out his present location in respect to the entirety of this place. He had come in from the east side, the block that housed the 7th Graders – if memory served him well, which meant the assembly hall would be to his right. The sports hall would be at the other side.

Left or right then.

A simple choice.

One would take him the correct way, the other not. What was it that his favourite fictional character would say? Jack Reacher, an ex-military police officer, loner, troublemaker, helper, hero, and the main protagonist to many a novel, followed a simple rule of thumb:

If in doubt, turn left.

Zager took the right. Fuck Jack Reacher, what did he really

know anyways.

The police chief worked his way down the hallway, ducking lower as he passed the doorways to connecting classrooms. He didn't waste too much time checking each and every one of them. They would be too small. Not fit for purpose.

Zager now knew what he was looking for. And rebuked himself for a second time within the same hour.

He was surprised that the others, the agent and his strange entourage had not picked up on such a thing, especially the woman. Still, his thoughts were not of a critical nature. They'd had their hands full, and the obvious had simply eluded them. Him too. Until now.

It was the children.

Or lack of them.

They had yet to encounter an infant or young child that was infected. Or anyone beyond the early-to-mid teens come to think about it. He hadn't encountered any. Nor could he recall having heard the group say that they had. None whatsoever. The thought had not even crossed Zager's mind until now. Stupid of him really.

So where the hell were all the children?

Here.

That's what Zager believed.

Isabelle included.

But what purpose could they possibly serve?

Chapter Forty-Three

Denali Park Train Station

Agent Fernandez was trying to keep it together. Trying to keep his irrational fear of the darkness from blurring his capacity to fend off this mass of infected, that rushed at him from every corner of the night.

A rare, fleeting moment of bitter amusement – perhaps hysterical in nature – prompted the agent into thinking that this fear was actually far from irrational. Not now. Not with these hideous things rushing at them with madness and bloodlust present in each and every one of them.

Yet, Fernandez felt as if the ever-present gloom that seemed to reside here was doing its best to suffocate him, forcing his lungs to the point of hyperventilation, with his breaths coming quick and short.

His anxieties were throwing off his ability to aim with any real hope of accuracy. Some of his shots were tearing off into the dark, disappearing without trace, allowing the infected to gather closer.

The large Chicago detective was faring better. He seemed to have accepted their predicament, and was picking off the masses with more success than that of the agent. His handgun was booming with successive hits, the infected dropping heavily to the ground; some disappearing in the drifts of snow, while others simply stopped where they stood, their legs too deeply embedded in the white powder.

The detective's weapon fell silent.

"Cover me," Balooga said, pulling a new clip from his belt.

Fernandez shook his head, cleared his mind and did his best to focus on the task at hand. He sidestepped to take up position in front of the detective. And then channelled all of his efforts into pushing back the dark veil that had started to blank off the periphery of his vision.

A young infected male in his late teens rushed at them, kicking up snow as he came.

Fernandez levelled his weapon towards the teen's head, and then applied force to the trigger. Then froze; his finger was unable to squeeze out those last few ounces of pressure required to fire.

The kid looked more fearful than enraged, as if he was being driven by the needs or direction of something other than his own bloodlust. His eyes were large and scared. The clothes he wore, although sodden, were somewhat smart, and not like the bedraggled garb of the masses.

The agent remembered what the Alaskan – Tonrar, had shared with them back at the precinct. How his wife, by her own admission, had initially been beyond restraint during his absence, only to gain some measure of control once the infection had entered its second phase.

A sudden understanding crossed the agent's mind then. The kid's actions were similar to that of young infantrymen from recent conflicts. Driving forwards, towards their certain doom, yet compelled to do so by the orders of others. They too must have been terrified – yet had sacrificed their lives to achieve some pointless or unknown – political – purpose.

Fernandez locked onto the young man's eyes, imploringly, trying to halt his crazed attack by look alone. It almost worked. To some degree. The kid halted. His legs half-buried in the snow.

Some level of recognition appeared to clear the teen's mind.

He stood there for a moment, horror present in his features as he watched on as the rest of the horde rushed past, their faces twisted and demented with rage.

The kid and Fernandez maintained eye contact for the briefest second. Then one of the infected barrelled into the kid, knocking him forwards and into the snow. When he raised his head again the look of sanity had gone, wiped clean, as if the ice had burnt away what sensibilities he had remaining.

Now, the kid was tearing his way through the snow, with the same blind fury as his counterparts.

Fernandez waited in the hope that the kid's moment of sanity would return. But it was a senseless longing. Because madness had gripped the kid again. The teen's face mirrored the rest of those that gathered, his eyes wild and hungry, and far beyond any reasoning.

The agent fired.

The kid's look of yearning disappeared instantly along with the rest of his features. His body tipped over, half burying itself into the snow. The trampling of feet pushed the rest of him underneath the white powder, where he disappeared, as if having never existed.

The agent focused on the next figure. Made a point not to delve too deeply into this individual's eyes, and fired without pause. More rushed towards him.

Now, Balooga had reloaded and he too continued to bring down the infected, brutally halting them in their tracks.

The agent had a second of sickening self-doubt. Had he consigned the company of army servicemen and women to their deaths, having not disclosed the dangers that the infected possessed. Were they now being besieged by those trying to escape the city's boundaries? Only to join them, as teeth and nails ripped at exposed flesh.

Even more terrifying to think, was he no better than the politicians of past or present, who had so needlessly surrendered the lives of the young; with little or no consideration for the ultimate sacrifice that they had given?

Chapter Forty-Four

Snowplow

No, not Isabelle, Josh realised, but a girl similar in size and age. He was rendered speechless for a second, his mind unable to compute why such a child would be found here. He panicked then, thinking she must have been one of the infected. But her eyes did not contain any hunger within them. Rather, they looked upon Josh with curious regard.

"Hey – you okay?" Josh called to her. "Don't move."

The girl's small face did not register any alarm. She appeared unfazed by the events surrounding her. As if this was a natural occurrence – mundane, and nothing to be feared.

Then her face turned suddenly dark. The serenity there slipped away, hatred and anger forming her small face into a ghastly mask. Her narrow lips parted and a black and wet tongue uncoiled itself.

Josh felt his heart knocking against his chest. His mortal soul was screaming out in warning. He reached into his waistband to pull the small revolver free. He had no idea how many bullets he had fired on reaching the first carriage – but prayed the cylinder had not been spent.

The girl hissed in his direction—a baleful sound of contempt. She took a step closer, her body shaking now as if her rage had grown immeasurably and was fighting to break free.

Something exploded in front of Josh. A sudden flash of movement, and Josh lay there in startled amazement as a pair of leathery wings spread outwards across her back. Her face twisted to one side in a grotesque manner, and then her neck split open as skin became overstretched. Flesh opened up in hideous tears, blood pouring freely from them, and wet and glistening scales moved directly underneath.

Josh watched mesmerised by what stood before him. His arm had frozen in position. The gun levelled at the ghastly sight, yet unable to find the strength required to pull the trigger.

The girl's head was now growing away from her body. Her neck had split entirely open and black scaly skin had taken its place. The head continued to reach out, and it bobbed in the darkness like something serpentine. Her mouth opened impossibly wide then, the dark tongue lolling out and fangs burst from bloodied gums as they grew into needle-like points. What remained of her human form disappeared as it shed its skin to reveal a nightmare of living terror.

It snapped its jaws and the noise created sounded like the crack of broken bones. It flexed its claws and then dropped onto all fours.

Josh could see that it had hideous tentacles growing from its back. They rose above its body and then twisted and turned like dancing snakes. But it was those wings that turned his blood cold.

They stretched outwards to reach their full span, and then locked out as the flow of air brushed against them. Yet unable to attain buoyancy, they fell to the thing's sides uselessly. The wings looked like torn banners. Thin strips of membrane flapped wildly about. Yet some of these strips of translucent flesh had knitted themselves together, with patches of newer tissue, binding them as one.

It was these newly formed scraps of flesh that almost drove Josh to insanity. He could see what they were made from, and it was the stuff of deepest dread.

Twisted faces screamed out at him in silent tongues. Hundreds of them, tiny and tortured, were what held the wings together, connecting each new piece with the faces of the damned. Josh thought he recognised some of them. Had he seen these people on first arriving in Fairbanks? Were they the victims of the infection? It was impossible to be certain. But deep down in his being, he thought that these poor things were the souls of the individuals taken.

Josh understood it then. Why this thing had come here. And why it now needed to reach a more densely populated area. Only more souls would give it the power to break the bounds that the earth had put upon it. And if that happened nothing would be able to stop it.

Not him.

Not Anna.

Nothing.

Josh fired.

And missed by a mile.

Eyes that glowed like hot coals bore into him, and he felt its hatred towards him – towards all of mankind – reach deep within his being. It tensed then as it readied itself to strike.

Its jaws opened wide and its neck snapped forwards with the speed of a snake. Teeth sharp as needles sought out flesh. Then, inexplicably, they stopped less then an inch from his throat. The hideous head reared back slightly, eyes burning brightly fixed themselves to Josh's. Like flickering red flames, the eyes blinked —once, twice—then held their gaze.

Josh tried to break away from the intense stare, yet a curiosity within him wanted to look deeper, seek out what drove this thing, look further into its very core, and understand it.

The fiery eyes fixed themselves to his, unblinking, unwavering, hypnotic and tantalisingly mysterious.

Movement shifted then, at the periphery of his vision. Two of its tentacles whipped around to wrap themselves around his torso. They tightened, which forced his breath outwards in an explosion of air. Its nostrils flared. Breathed deeply. It paused momentarily, as if savouring his living breath, and then the tentacles unexpectedly released him.

It reared back then, shaking its head from side to side. Those two devilish eyes blinked repeatedly.

Josh understood it was in a state of confusion.

Then he understood.

It.

Why it had not attacked him with its teeth. Why it had spared him from the infection. And more so why it appeared puzzled.

His soul.

It wanted his soul. Needed it. Relished it. *Deserved* it.

Yet it could not take it. For Josh had not given his spirit over to the darker side of the human condition. He was pure of heart.

Yes, he had taken a life, and had done so willingly, but not with any malice. The killing had been justified. The leader back in Mexico, the one responsible for child trafficking, and worse, had deserved nothing less. Justice had been bestowed and Josh had been its helping hand. Nothing more. Nothing less.

And it was this fact that had thrown the beast into confusion. It could sense his involvement in having taken a life, murdered a man even, and yet was unable to fully comprehend why he did not possess even the slightest amount of malignancy within his soul.

To understand this, it would have had to have a soul of its own.

Josh knew this as a certainty. This thing was older than Man. Older than anything capable of compassion, or understanding, or love, or sympathy. Maybe even older than life itself; not of this plane or dimension, but from a darker realm. Brought here before sentient beings had walked upon the Earth.

The beast shrieked with immeasurable rage then. The noise was even more deafening than the blades at the fore of the machine. Its jaws snapped together like a pistol shot.

Josh watched in horror as the tentacles on its back rose upwards; their tips opening out, and sharp barbs, thinner than human hair, spread out like the blossoming of some hideous flower.

He tried to back away, but there was nowhere for him to go. He knew then that this thing would take his life, out of nothing more than spite. If it could not take his soul, then it would end it. Erase it. Snuff out the light of his very being. Maybe it was only the one light, out of billions, but this monstrosity would extinguish it nonetheless, and continue to do so indefinitely, until it had decimated the human race completely.

The faces of the two women from Fernandez's initial investigation burst into his mind. Just for a millisecond. Yet it was enough time for Josh to understand that this is what had happened to them. They, too, had been purest of heart, and the beast had simply wiped them from existence.

The tentacles wavered for just a second longer and then struck out.

Then, suddenly, a dark apparition appeared from the shadows. It landed directly in front of Josh, solid and immobile, to block the beast's attack.

The tentacles stopped short, the needles retracting instantly, closing up into their original shape.

The thing's eyes lit up spectacularly, twin coals burning brightly with devilish delight. Its jaws parted and the serpentine head twisted itself towards the obstruction.

Here, now, stood what it desired.

Tarnished; a mysterious soul.

One stained by a spiritual darkness that could not be altogether cleansed.

Chapter Forty-Five

Fairbanks Elementary School

A pinpoint of light could be seen at the end of the hallway. It blinked out occasionally, sometimes for just a second, at other times, longer.

Zager inched his way along the dark stretch of corridor. He knew what was making the light blink intermittently.

Someone was moving around, momentarily blocking out the light source. From the two sets of prints that had initially led him here, Zager guessed that it was more than feasible to assume he was dealing with more than just the one.

The light stayed steady for the duration it took him to reach the end of the hallway. He stopped there, crouching low, making as little a target as possible.

From what he'd witnessed back at the woods, he didn't think what he'd find inside would have the mental dexterity to use a firearm, but he wasn't taking any chances.

He checked the safety to his weapon was off.

Then moved swiftly to the open doorway.

The sounds of movement could be heard from this side. A continuous shuffling of bodies. The odd broken whisper found its way beyond the doorway, but these short breaks of near-silence were quickly dispelled by a hiss of annoyance.

Zager's senses were working overtime. The closer he inched

towards the opening, the more he could smell the rank odour of fear. And something else too – something rotten and diseased. All this helped him to build up a mental picture of what he would find inside. The picture that formed almost threatened to buckle the chief's knees.

He took a breath – perhaps his last, readied himself, and then simply stepped through the doorway.

The image inside his head became an instant reality.

The sports hall was a flood of bodies, huddled together, in large and small groups, with just the odd one, the older ones, sitting alone. A blaze of colour filled Zager's vision. Bright pastel colours, with embroidered faces, most of cute-face animals, and an array of clothing that displayed similarly looking optimism, woven into a blanket across the entire floor.

Hundreds of eyes, most tear-filled and fearful, turned as one as the police chief entered the sports hall.

Zager brought his weapon up. Looked away from all those expectant little faces, and instead sought out those few that were not.

The first presented itself immediately.

A bearded man stepped forth. Once, the beard may have been blond, but now, it looked matted with dried crusts of blood and gore.

Zager recognised the face immediately. It was older than he remembered. And that look of hunger and hatred had not been present the last time either.

The man stumbled towards Zager, having to navigate his way through the sea of tiny bodies. Yet, like Moses had, he appeared to part the waves, as the children scurried away in opposite directions.

Zager had a fraction of a second to make his mind up. He decided that his actions would not add additional horror to what the children had already witnessed.

A shot to the head brought down Zager's old geography teacher with a single bullet. His head exploded in a pink mist.

The children were screaming then, throwing off Zager's

senses. Another adult came rushing towards him, teeth visible, and fingers hooked into bloodied claws.

The police chief fired again. The first bullet missed, the shot too high. A group of kids were sat on the first row of the bleachers directly behind the oncoming attacker. If he aimed too low, then one of them could be hit. Zager had to side step to get a better aim.

His next shot disintegrated its face. The lead projectile entered through the left cheek, then exited in a spray of bone fragments and red tissue. Zager fired again. Point-blank. The body fell to the floor.

Two of the infected came at him then. One from each side. A woman leapt out from the right, while a stocky individual rushed him from the left.

Only the bravery of another saved Zager. A boy, perhaps thirteen or fourteen, a black kid who was already replacing ropey adolescent muscle with greater bulk, jumped forwards to catch the woman in mid-flight. They tumbled to the floor in a heap of arms and legs.

This gave Zager chance to lock onto the stocky guy and take aim. He brought the infected thing down with three quick shots: one to the throat, two to the head. Zager was already turning his back on it before it had even fallen to its knees.

The young black kid was wrestling with the woman. Her teeth were bared and she was snapping and snarling. Yet she did not sink her teeth into exposed flesh.

Zager didn't waste any time trying to understand why. He simply stepped over them both. Yanked the kid clear, grabbing a handful of his T-shirt and then fired into the woman. Her eyes flashed with surprise. The chief stepped back from the corpse. He recognised her, too. She had once taught art; now, her brain matter and fluids were leaking out to decorate the floor in a red and grey collage.

Zager brought the boy up to his feet.

"Thanks—kid," he said.

The teenager looked a bit rattled.

"You okay?" Zager asked.

The kid shook his head and blinked twice. His eyes cleared. Then they opened wide. "Look out," he yelled.

Both turned to face a wild-eyed old woman. Her face had collapsed in around her cheeks, cutting dark shadows down the rough plain of her face, and the wrinkles around her mouth were deep and many.

Zager knew her instantly.

Mrs Reid.

The old headmistress.

His old headmistress.

Long retired.

Wait – more than retired, dead.

Zager had read about her passing only a couple of weeks earlier, in the local newspaper. He had not been overly upset either. Reid had been an unpleasant individual, abrasive and short-tempered. The old hag had passed away at the ripe old age of eighty-three. She had spent almost fifty of those years terrorising the young kids of Fairbanks in this school.

A flash of recent memory burst to his mind. Her body had gone missing—stolen, possibly, and a report had been made. Zager had laughed whilst handing the report over to one of his deputies, stating that maybe an ex-pupil of hers had been dared to steal her body in some sort of prank, and she was now currently residing in someone's basement or attic.

If only such a thing were true.

Because Mrs Reid stood before them now, her bony arms wrapped tightly around a child.

Zager looked earnestly into the child's eyes.

"Don't worry, Isabelle. She's not going to harm you."

Isabelle just stared back, unblinking.

"Put her down," ordered Zager.

Reid hissed towards the police chief and teenager. Her arms tightened around the girl, and Isabelle let out a startled cry.

"Put her down – NOW," Zager said.

The old hag didn't seem to know what to do. Some uninfected

part of her mind must have given her the understanding that the child was a bargaining tool, yet the insanity of her rotten brain couldn't find the reasoning to act appropriately.

The reanimated headmistress just stood there snapping her few blackened teeth together.

With the gun aimed towards the thing, Zager drew the teenager's attention to him.

"Kid—I need your help."

"What."

"Can you get them all out? The kids."

The teenager paused momentarily. Then answered, "Yes."

"Good," Zager said. "You're officially deputised. Get them all back to the precinct."

Zager heard the kid take a deep breath. "Okay."

In the next moment, the teenager was rounding up the kids, quickly ordering them to get to their feet. The oldest were the first to rise. They stood one by one, before helping the next to their feet. A young teenage girl bent to pick one of the infants up. The toddler practically leaped into her arms.

It was like watching wildfire then.

The older kids were snatching up the smaller ones, and together they made their way towards the hall's exit. The black kid stood guard at the entrance, leading them out, offering encouragement and help.

Then a spectacular thing happened. A boy, seven if that, broke away from the main group. His little legs carried him to the police chief.

"Boy—what are you doing?" Zager demanded. "Go."

But the boy did not turn or stop. He instead took up position on the chief's right side. His little hands balled themselves into two pebble-sized fists.

"Kid! Seriously now—go!"

Zager's command went ignored. And then a second figure arrived at the chief's other side. A chubby girl, maybe ten years old. She stood at his side as well. And then, it was as if Zager had become some sort of child magnet. They were surrounding him, deviating away from safety and returning to his side. They gathered about him in a large group. He felt their presence, and was surprised when his resolve, his soul, call it what you will, seemed to gain strength.

One of the kids pushed his way to the front. It was the black teenager. He managed to squeeze himself in-between the chubby ten-year-old and the lawman.

The teenager flashed Zager a mischievous smile. "'Sup —Chief."

"Told you to get them to safety."

The kid shrugged his shoulders. "Thing is—this is our school, not hers."

Some of the older kids rattled out an agreement.

The black teenager said, "She doesn't belong here. Not now. Time we kicked her skinny white ass back into the afterlife."

Zager's eyes bore into the teenager.

Understanding he may have crossed the line, placed his toe just on it a little, the teenager nodded a slight apology, then said, "Sorry Chief, but you get my meaning."

Zager did.

"You ready then?" Zager asked.

"Hell yeah," came the reply.

Both Zager and the teenager broke away from the main group to take the few steps closer to the infected woman.

Then, as if simply taking a gift from someone's arms, the teenager pulled Isabelle free from the old woman's grasp.

What had once been Mrs Reid snapped and snarled but did little else.

The teenager grinned ruefully at Zager. "Funny as shit, but they can't really hurt us kids."

"No," agreed Zager. "Nor can they hurt a 9mm projectile travelling at supersonic speeds."

The trigger clicked.

Followed by a flash of gunfire.

A cleansing fire that brought about it the end to an oppressive regime.

Chapter Forty-Six

Snowplow

Anna pushed her shoulders back, stood her ground, and waited. She had the axe, the one that Tonrar had discarded, in her hand. It glinted faintly in the moonlight—a crimson sheen against the night.

"Come on, bitch! What are you waiting for?" Anna yelled.

The monstrosity reared upwards, to its fullest height, with its tattered and torn wings stretched wide. Like some Babylonian devil, it stood there for a second, hideously majestic, before lunging quickly towards Anna with snapping jaws.

Anna skipped back, simultaneously bringing the axe up in a wide arc. The blade whistled noisily as it cut through the air. It embedded itself in the beast's chest; the blade hilt deep, and blood dark with decay burst forth from the wound.

Some of this blood splashed across Anna's face. It felt like searing heat, acid-like as it ran down the side of her face. A picture burst before Anna's eyes. Moving imagery, akin to that of early black and white motion pictures, distorted and running at the wrong speed.

Landscapes filled her vision. Laid out exactly like the one she was in. Yet she wasn't seeing it through her own eyes. The mountains and snow-covered fields had none of their clarity, more monochrome than their reality, and twisted and warped.

She was seeing what her adversary saw. The landscape disappeared, replaced now by the channel of excavated snow. The actual snowplow was nowhere to be seen. Instead, the rails were filled with the slow and lethargic movements of the infected.

Anna shook her head. Cleared her mind and chanced a look behind her. Josh was still laid out on his back, his face a mixture of fear and relief. She looked beyond him, further back towards the way she had come.

The steam was still billowing up from the engine behind, maybe lessening slightly, but driving the snowplow onwards nonetheless. Out beyond the engine, the channel appeared clear, apart from a few downed bodies.

She turned back quickly.

Refocused on the beast before her.

Anna pulled the axe free.

Another spurt of blood covered her hands in a sickly black tar.

More pictures flared inside her head. A cityscape with moonlit buildings and thousands upon thousands of people milling around the bases of them, busying themselves like ants. Anna recognised the city. It was iconic with the Empire State Building in its fore. The buildings rushed towards her as if she were gliding quickly towards them.

Some of the tiny faces below looked up and screamed in horror as the winged serpent dropped towards them. The images fast-forwarded and Anna was now looking out beyond the ravaged city of New York. The streets were littered with the dead and undead alike.

Anna took a step back, now clearing her head of the beast's thoughts – its dreams, if such a word was appropriate.

That's what this thing wanted. What it had set out to achieve. It would move from city to city, each one growing in population, until it had succeeded in infecting the entire country. And then perhaps the entire world.

The burning cityscape faded out then. And the face of an

innocent child surfaced. Terrified looking and tears flowing freely down both cheeks. The vision opened to reveal two of the infected holding down the child. A rush of eager excitement filled Anna then, not hers, but the beast's, as two barbed tentacles appeared to open up and reveal a nest of fibre-like hairs. They wavered slightly, and then the fine needles all rushed towards the child.

Anna forced her mind clear. Not willing to witness what was to follow. But she had seen enough to understand that this hideous thing considered the young to be nothing more than a delicacy.

"Like hell," Anna stated.

She drew the axe above her head.

The beast's head bobbed and weaved like a dancing cobra, ready to avoid any sudden attacks.

Anna lashed out anyway in an attempt to catch it. The beast reared upwards, backing away at the same time, and the axe sailed past its mark.

One of the tentacles snapped out straight with a whip-crack of noise as it lashed across the plain of Anna's back. The pain was excruciating, forcing her to her knees. A second tentacle moved in a blur, sending Anna heavily to the floor. A foot, clawed like an eagle's talon, gripped onto her shoulder, pinning her hopelessly to the roof of the snowplow.

Its head lowered and jaws opened wide.

Anna felt the axe ripped from her grasp. She heard it bounce heavily as it landed somewhere out of reach. Her vision filled with the ghastly sight of a second talon. This one flexed open and closed, powerfully, as it descended towards her head.

"Josh!" Anna screamed, unable to move.

***

Josh was there in an instant. He had the small revolver still in his hands. He jabbed the weapon into its eye and pulled the trigger.

One of those hate-filled eyes exploded—the once burning red now just an empty void. The monstrosity screamed in agony, its jaws opening wide as its pain echoed in a nerve-shattering shriek.

Josh was not yet finished. He emptied the remaining bullets into its body. Some of them tore chunks away, while others seemed to skim harmlessly off its armoured scales.

Josh was still pulling the trigger even though the hammer was clicking uselessly against an empty chamber.

"Josh – the axe," Anna yelled to him.

Josh threw the firearm away, seeking out the fallen axe instead. He found the weapon just to the side of him, and bent instinctively to take it. That reflex saved his life. Two of the beast's tentacles came together with a crack of thunder, where a moment earlier his head had been.

Josh righted himself with the axe now in hand.

Its one remaining eye held him with its burning hatred and loathing.

"Right back at you," Josh said, the feelings mutual.

He rushed at it then.

The beast swelled larger—its leather torn wings spreading out in an intimidating gesture.

Josh was no longer frightened. Determination to end this had him gripped. He propelled himself forwards, waiting for the exact moment to strike.

It did exactly as he thought it would.

It leapt forwards onto all fours, crouching into its attack position, seemingly forgetting about the danger at its feet. The tentacles bobbed and weaved at its back, and those awful fibres reappeared as the tips spread open once again.

Josh threw himself to the floor just in time. The beast's tentacles came together an inch above his head; the fibres weaving themselves together right where brain matter should have been. Josh released his grip on the axe, spreading his fingers wide, and watched as the weapon spun wildly away, gliding effortlessly between the thing's legs.

Anna caught it on the other side.

"Hey—dumbass!" she yelled.

The beast tried to spin quickly, but those extended wings slowed it, as the raging wind caught underneath them. The resultant draught lifted it off its feet. It flapped its wings in an attempt to rebalance itself, but it was already too late.

Anna swung the axe around with what seemed like all of her might. The blade buried itself into one of its shoulders, and the wing on that side dropped like a dead-weight. The loss of air resistance forced the monstrosity back onto all fours.

It staggered and lost its footing. First one rear leg slipped free. Then another. Its front talons dug frantically for purchase. But the slick ice that had gathered at the front of the snowplow offered no such help. Claws scraped uselessly across the black mirror-like surface.

It seemed to hang in motion for just a fraction of a second, and, in the next, it slipped out of view as it toppled over the front of the snowplow.

The rotary blades pulled it in. And in the next moment, in less than a blink of the eye, the beast was reduced to nothing. The vents at the sides of the snowplow exploded in a black liquidised mess, expelling the creature in one quick burst, and what remained of its passing fell slowly to earth in a dark and sticky drizzle.

Chapter Forty-Seven

Denali Park Train Station

A carpeting of spent casings littered the ground, one or two of them releasing wisps of gun smoke, as they quickly cooled in the frost. Bodies lay scattered there too, bloodied and broken, some half-buried in the red-stained snow.

Now, as an unexpected silence filled the air, Harry Balooga looked from one fallen body to the next. He sighed wearily. He hoped that the dead, especially the ones that he had slain, would somehow find peace now that they lay in rest.

"What happened?" Fernandez asked, he too scanning from one individual to the next.

"They just stopped coming," Balooga replied.

"But how?"

The Chicago detective shrugged. "I guess she finally brought them down."

"You mean, Privalova?"

"Who else?"

Many of the fallen had died with gunshots to their heads, horrific wounds that had finally found the power to stop them in their tracks. Yet others had simply dropped to the ground, en masse, without the feel of hot lead searing their skin and bones.

It was as if they had all suddenly realised their mortality, come to understand that this was not the place or time now for them to be. And with one final collective breath, they had left this place and gone to the next.

Balooga thought otherwise. Anna Privalova had done this. Stopped them somehow. Some way.

Balooga said, "It's over. Done."

"How?" asked Fernandez.

"Maybe you should ask them," Balooga replied, pointing towards the rail tracks.

Three figures were walking towards them. Josh and Anna led the way, with the large figure of Kavik Tonrar looming close behind. They stepped onto the platform to join the two lawmen.

"Is it done?" asked Balooga.

Anna nodded. "Yes. It's done."

The detective simply accepted that. He felt no desire to know what had happened, no desperate hunger to understand everything. Once already, he had seen the incredible and unexplainable events that the world could offer. Things that no mortal man should have paid witness to. Balooga had come to understand that Anna Privalova was beyond this world. And could not be explained—not by any rational thought anyway. Yet, he knew implicitly that she was here to do good, and his trust in her, and in her actions, could not be wavered.

"Thank you," Balooga breathed.

Anna simply nodded.

Agent Fernandez was not so easily pacified. "Is that it? No explanation. We just accept that you somehow brought this to an end?"

"Let it go," Balooga tried to say.

But the agent did not listen. "I need an explanation. Something to tell my superiors! And an answer *I* can understand."

Anna said, "Not everything can be explained. Some things just are."

"Really?" Fernandez said. "And that's it."

"Yes, Agent Fernandez, that's it. We're done here."

Anna turned to Josh before taking his hand in hers. She was about to ask if he was okay, when the click of a gun stopped her short.

"What are you going to do—shoot me in the back?" Anna asked, looking over her shoulder.

The agent had his weapon drawn. "I still have to bring you in. Both of you. If for nothing else, then the killings back in Chicago. You're still wanted fugitives."

Balooga groaned. "Sebastian – we'd be dead if it wasn't for them."

But the agent's single-minded determination and dogmatic beliefs were not going to simply let them walk free.

It was the Native Alaskan who finally broke the agent's resolve. He stepped forwards to place his huge bloodied hands on the agent's shoulders.

"There has been enough bloodshed tonight. Too much. The loss of two more souls will not undo what has happened here. Nobody can pay for the blood that has been spilt. Not now. Not ever."

Fernandez stood silent for a moment. He lowered his weapon. Nevertheless, unable to simply turn a blind eye, he said, "You have a day's head start. Then I'm coming."

Anna understood his meaning.

***

Josh was about to tell the agent to go to hell, when he suddenly thought of the two victims that had been found dead, but seemingly unharmed. May be he could buy them more time.

"Those two women – the bank teller and the middle-aged one, look for needle-like punctures, tiny, maybe hidden in their hairline. Start there. Should keep you busy for the next day or two. Maybe give you something to fill your reports in with. Whatever."

Fernandez growled under his breath.

Josh just shrugged. "You wanted answers."

"And I'll get them. And you," Fernandez replied.

Josh didn't think so. Not the answers he was looking for. There was no simple test, trace evidence, clues, nor witness testimony that could categorically prove that both women had been of purest hearts, or righteous souls. That's why the beast had been unable to turn them. Infect them. And why, out of sheer spite, it had killed them anyway. Like it had tried with Josh himself.

As for the agent capturing him and Anna; then let the best man win. Josh knew, understood even, why the agent would not let them walk. Fernandez was driven with the same needs as the beast, only his determination was of moral goodness, and this rigid belief that what he was doing was honourable work and it would not allow him to simply stop. In some ways Josh admired this fact. The agent was only following his heart and obeying his inner beliefs. Josh looked about him for a moment, seeing the dead laid out around him. He sensed that the agent would not have succumbed like the infected had. Perhaps he too would have been taken with nothing but spite in mind.

Anna said, "Come on—Josh. We still have a day's head start."

Kavik Tonrar moved over to them. "Here, take the keys." He held out the keys to the state cruiser.

Josh hesitated momentarily before reaching out to take them. "Thank you."

Tonrar smiled gently, his eyes were still filled with the pain of his recent loss, but they'd also gained some strength in them too. He looked like these events had finally sobered him. How could they not.

Josh shook the Alaskan's hand. Glanced at Fernandez, grinned ruefully, before focusing on the Chicago detective.

"We good?"

"Yeah," Balooga replied, "We're good. I'm too goddamn tired to be chasing you two anyways."

Josh laughed. Then he turned his attention back to the agent. He tipped him a short salute, a respectful acknowledgment, and then said, "Until next time, Special Agent Fernandez."

The young man from Chicago turned away then. He paused at Anna's side. "You ready?"

Anna nodded.

They walked away from the three men, hands clasped tightly together. As they made their way towards the state cruiser, the sky in the east started to lighten, as the imminent arrival of the sun began to burn away the dark.

"We'd better hurry," Josh said.

Anna stopped him. "There is somewhere we need to go first."

"Where?"

"You made a promise."

Indeed he had. A promise that he intended keeping. He looked into Anna's eyes, and his heart swelled with affection. He loved this woman, from the very first moment that they had met. And he knew he always would do until his last dying breath.

His thoughts turned to the little girl they had rescued from Mexico—Isabelle. Life on the road would be harder with the responsibility of having a child, but it was a responsibility that he was willing to take. He was changing from day to day, leaving the boy that had escaped from Chicago behind, and now becoming the man he was today.

Anna gave him a hug, kissed him on his cheek. "Come on, let's go get her."

"Right," Josh agreed.

Anna reached the state cruiser first. The doors were still open. She paused at the hood. The rear wheels were buried in a mixture of mud and slush. She moved around to the rear, placing her hands on the trunk. Then, effortlessly, she pushed against the vehicle, slowly rolling the cruiser forwards until it cleared the obstruction.

Josh laughed. "Impressive—remind me never to get on the wrong side of you."

Anna grinned back. "I think you can handle me – don't

you?"

"Perhaps," he replied, moving around the vehicle to give her behind a playful slap.

Anna turned quickly to catch his wrist. Held him there for a moment, and then dragged him closer to place a kiss onto his lips.

Now this close, Josh could see that their encounter had scarred Anna with claw marks and bruises. A slight cut to her forehead. And a patch of blood had blossomed around her shoulder.

He looked her over carefully.

"What is it?" Anna asked.

He met her eyes. "Just making sure you're not about to go on the rampage, seeking out human flesh."

Silence prevailed for the briefest of time.

Then Anna burst into a fit of uncontrollable laughter.

"What did I say," Josh asked, his eyes quizzical, yet mouth bent into a grin.

"Josh— as if that would be something new, really."

Josh understood the stupidity of his anxieties. Anna was not about to turn into some lumbering undead dimwit. However, the time would come, and possibly soon, when yes, she would be forced to seek out comfort from the human condition.

But not tonight.

Josh took the keys from her hand and moved around to the opposite side of the cruiser. He was just about to climb in behind the steering wheel, when he abruptly stopped.

"Anna—I have one thing to ask," he said.

Facing him across the car, she said, "Shoot."

"After we leave Fairbanks, can we please keep things boring? At least for a little while."

Anna flashed him her most colourful smile. She opened her mouth ready to speak.

"I know—I know," Josh said, raising his hand to silence her. "We'll just have to wait and see what tomorrow brings…"

Other titles by Paul Cave

For Everything A Reason ISBN 9780956236-89-0

Joseph Ruebins is a natural-born fighter, a champion of his sport, yet no training could have prepared him for the events that were to follow at Madison Square Garden on the night of his ultimate fight. Ruebins had planned his retirement with precision and it wasn't supposed to be like this. Struck down by a sudden and debilitating stroke, Joseph finds himself in hospital; paralysed, fearful, and at the mercy of this cruel condition. When Joseph's roommate is murdered he becomes an unwitting witness and finds himself in mortal danger. Can this ex-champion of the world find a way, not only to survive, but also to protect his family - his life - his very existence..?

Something of the Night ISBN 9781908098-28-3

For years scientists had warned about the possibility of a global strike from outer space: a global killer. Mathematicians had calculated that once in approximately every sixty million years the Earth has been hit by a meteorite of such proportions it drastically changes our climate, plunging the world into a decade of nuclear winters. In a post-apocalyptic world in which the sun has been replaced by near-darkness, the few remaining survivors have been forced underground to protect themselves from the evil predators that roam the surface above. Something else is out there. Something that speaks intelligently, plans with cunning meticulousness and, just like its cousin, this new breed likes to hunt. Not the scrawny livestock and wild animals that cling to life on the barren land. No, this new breed hunts for something far more rewarding.

Cold Light of Day ISBN 9781908098-49-8

Josh Sawyer's passionate encounter with Anna, a beautiful and mysterious young woman, was one that would change his life forever. Josh must come to terms with Anna's deep, dark and terrifying secrets - that thrust him into a nightmare of violence and bloodlust. Suspected of grisly multiple murders, the couple are forced to flee Chicago, with the police and FBI hot on their heels. But a more deadly and evil threat is tracking them - an adversary from Anna's past.